EVERYTHING

THAT

MAKES

YOU

MORIAH McSTAY

KT KATHERINE TEGEN BOOKS
An Imprint of HarperCollins Publishers

Katherine Tegen Books is an imprint of HarperCollins Publishers.

Everything That Makes You

ISBN 978-0-06-229548-4

15 16 17 18 19   PC/RRDH   10 9 8 7 6 5 4 3 2 1
❖
First Edition

For Sam

There's no one thing that's true. It's all true.
—Ernest Hemingway

FEBRUARY 27

It was cold—too cold for the zoo. Still, the Doyles were here, looking at the cheetahs and deciding what to do next.

Ryan wanted popcorn.

Fiona wanted the pandas.

ELEVENTH GRADE

FEBRUARY

FIONA

Fiona scooted low in her chair. Damn Mr. Phillips and his English project. Why did he have to assign Trent McKinnon, of all people, as her partner?

Half the class reshuffled, and screeching chairs fractured the room's quiet. Books smacked onto reassigned tables. Trent started in her direction, and Fiona pulled her bangs as far forward as they'd go.

She'd loved this boy from afar since fourth grade, although they'd never said more than two words to each other at any one time. Now he was going to sit less than twelve inches away. God, and she woke up with an enormous red zit on the right side of her nose.

Lucy would be thrilled. Even now, her best friend was turning in her chair and mouthing *Oh. My. God.* behind Trent's back. Fiona ignored her. Still, she couldn't help notice how nicely he filled out his Union High School Lacrosse T-shirt.

He sat down on her right—damn it, she should have switched chairs, so he'd have to sit on her left. She slouched lower in her chair. From this angle, a pimple was the least of her problems.

"You do the reading?" Trent kicked his legs straight in front of him, ankles crossed. He gave a friendly, lazy kind of smile, like the earth wasn't shifting directly underneath them.

When she remembered how to breathe, Fiona craned her face too far around to answer. She probably looked like an owl. "Yeah."

Trent McKinnon's eyes made a brief sweep over her face, hairline to chin. It was so quick and subtle someone not looking for it wouldn't notice.

Fiona noticed.

She pinched her arm under the table. *Get over it, Doyle.*

"Good thing you're my partner," Trent continued, like he hadn't been caught ogling. "I need all the smart I can get."

Fiona stared at him a few seconds longer than socially acceptable. Trent McKinnon actually seemed happy to be her partner. And—*and*—he knew something about her. Just the "smart" bit, but hey, it was something.

So why on earth did she say, "How's the dumb jock thing working out?"

"So far, so good," he said, with a little laugh.

"Well, rein it in. I have goals." *What are you doing? Shut up, you idiot!*

This time, Trent glanced at her face—then gazed at her

steadily. His eyes weren't the pure blue she'd fantasized about for years, more a periwinkle with intermittent specks of green. A cowlick near his hairline made a subtle spiral pattern over his right temple.

She struggled not to faint.

Mr. Phillips handed out paper topics, interrupting the *most awkward moment ever*. Trent flipped through the packet before pushing it over. "You pick. Doesn't matter to me." He gave her another quick, heart-stopping look. "But I guess you knew that already."

She took the handout. At some point, they would need to set a time to meet—she'd need his phone number, his email—but she wouldn't mention it now. She didn't trust her mouth from going traitor.

It felt like she'd been snapping at people all day—Ryan for running late, her dad for his corny joke this morning. If *Trent McKinnon* couldn't restore her usual easygoing mood, the rest of the day was hopeless.

The bell rang, Trent gave a cool nod, and their paths diverged at the door.

Immediately after, Lucy grabbed Fiona's left arm and hissed, "What'd he say? What'd you talk about?"

"Nothing. The project." *I insulted him for no reason. He hates me.*

Fiona couldn't work up any enthusiasm for her usual, exhaustive analysis of All Things Trent McKinnon. Lucy, herself not a fan of boys in the romantic sense, usually tolerated these in-depth breakdowns for only a few minutes. Eventually, she'd cut Fiona off with something like, "Good Lord, enough already!"

Anyway, besides her awful behavior, the only part of the conversation that really stuck with her was that subtle—it was subtle, wasn't it?—sweep of his eyes over her face.

"Well, it's about time, I say," Lucy told her as they walked down the hall. "You have to talk to him, now."

"I don't *want* to talk to him."

"You're such a chicken."

Fiona rolled her eyes, but only her left eyebrow lifted from the gesture. The right never went anywhere.

Lucy rolled her eyes right back. "I know what you're thinking." She gestured vaguely to Fiona's right cheek. "But you make a bigger deal about those scars than anyone else."

"I do not." She blew it off most of the time—things like the new kid doing a double take in biology, or the coffee shop guy repeating her order loud and slow, like she was mentally challenged.

"What's keeping you from Trent McKinnon, then?" Lucy asked. "You're smarter, funnier, and prettier than nearly every other girl in this school."

"I'll be sure to share that theory with all the boys waiting to date me." Now at her locker, she looked over both shoulders. "Oh, wait. There *are* no boys waiting to date me."

"I'm not talking about your ridiculous hang-ups anymore today. Trent McKinnon. Specifics."

Fiona didn't want to play. Lucy didn't seem to care. She kept throwing out questions—"When are you going to meet?" and "Did your elbows touch?" Fiona was ready to snap, firmly not in the mood, when Lucy asked, "What's he smell like?"

"You did not just ask me what he smelled like," she snorted.

"I thought that mattered."

"Yeah, if he's unwashed. Otherwise, what am I supposed to say? He smells like cantaloupe?"

"Who smells like cantaloupe?" said another voice. Fiona's brother, Ryan, showed up, nudging her right shoulder. He was the only person she didn't mind standing on that side.

"Trent McKinnon," Lucy answered.

"He does *not* smell like cantaloupe," Fiona snapped. "I don't even think that's possible."

"My grandfather totally smells like cantaloupe," said Lucy.

"Is that the orange one or the green one?" Ryan asked.

"Orange," Fiona said.

"Oh, never mind. He smells like the green one. What's that called?"

"Honeydew," Fiona said. "Now that we've established the various melons, and the men they do and do not smell like, can we move on?"

"Why were you smelling Trent McKinnon?" Ryan asked.

"He's her new English-paper partner."

Ryan whistled, rocking back on his heels. "Maybe it's your lucky day, after all."

* * *

When Fiona and Ryan got home, their mother was standing at the kitchen counter, sliding flowers into a vase. "Did you two have a good day?" she asked.

As usual, she looked ready for an impromptu dinner party—shiny leather flats, sweater set, classic pearl earrings. Even the apron was ironed.

Ryan gave a generic grunt from inside the refrigerator. When he emerged, folded salami slices were hanging from his mouth. But it didn't matter. Their mother always focused on Fiona.

"Sweetheart, *please* make a haircut appointment," her mother said to her. "It looks terrible."

Anger, irritation, and—God, self-pity—surged through her like hot tar, filling up all her crevices. "Fits the rest of me then, right?" she snapped. Ryan stopped midchew, a limp piece of salami dangling from his fingers.

"Fiona," her mom said.

The stare-down went a few long seconds. Their golden-brown eyes would look identical, if it weren't for the thick ridge of scars bordering Fiona's right one. Maybe that's why her mother always won these little staring wars. She didn't have a ridge of inflexible flesh always tugging at her muscles.

Fiona stormed up the stairs and took her frustration out on her bedroom door. Luckily, the Doyles lived in an old house. Not only was her door solid enough to be slammed, it made a satisfying bang that would be heard downstairs.

"You've got to be freaking kidding me," she mumbled, staring at her bed.

A pile of preppy pink waited for her—the same designer-y stuff her mother always bought, even though Fiona lived in old T-shirts. Pushing it all to the floor, she flung herself onto the bed, face-first. She had the urge to cry, but she hated crying. Instead, she took off her shoes and hurled them across the room.

There was a knock. "What?" she snapped, her head buried under her pillow.

The door opened with a slow creak. She looked up to see the top of Ryan's head as he peeked in. With the same hair and eyes, they were constantly mistaken for twins. And both had fair, creamy skin, though Ryan had it all over his face, not just on the left side.

Ryan's eyes darted around the room, as if looking for objects that might be launched at him. "You okay?"

"Go away."

He came in anyway. "That's a lot of pink," he said, looking at the pile of clothes on the floor.

"Clearly, she understands me." She pointed to her navy Neko Case T-shirt and the black jeans she'd worn three days straight.

Ryan nudged her over on the bed, sliding next to her. They lay side by side, staring at the ceiling. "Bad day?" he asked.

"What tipped you off?" she snorted.

"The calendar."

"I'm not having my period, Ryan."

"Ew. Gross. That's not what I meant." He moved away—but then scooched back, so their shoulders touched. "You're always cranky today."

"What are you talking about?"

"February twenty-seventh."

"What's February twenty-seventh?"

"The day, you know. The zoo," he said. "Your accident."

It felt like a sandbag dropped on her chest. That couldn't be right, could it?

"How do you know that?" she asked.

"I saw it a few years ago," he said. "On Mom's calendar, with the birthdays."

The. Woman. Was. Obsessed. It might even be funny—if it weren't so infuriating.

"Why are you just now telling me?" she asked. Their heads shared the pillow, leaving only a few inches between their faces. The angle was awkward, and the muscles under her scars pulled.

"I thought you knew."

Uh, no. "That I'm cranky on the anniversary of an accident I hardly remember?"

"I remember it."

"You do?"

"I mean, not well. I was"—Ryan lifted his hands in the air, counting on his fingers—"what, six? But I remember going to that snack bar. It was empty, I think—just us. The guy at the popcorn cart, he looked like a grandfather, kept trying to pat our heads whenever we ran past him."

Fiona tried to picture it, but had no idea if the details coming to mind were memory or imagination.

"I remember the crash . . ." Ryan paused. His voice came out quieter when he spoke again. "Your scream. Mom trying to wipe the oil off with her scarf, and how your skin—" He cleared his throat. "Them tearing us out of there. How loud you yelled in the car. Nana buying me a milk shake in the hospital cafeteria." He turned to Fiona again, looking guilty. "I was really psyched about that milk shake. Sorry."

"You're forgiven." She even smiled.

He didn't smile back. "I feel bad. About all of it."

"It is what it is." Fiona hated talking about stuff like this, so she reached across Ryan and lifted her guitar from its place at the foot of her bed. Sitting cross-legged, she strummed some easy chords—the calming, predictable ones. C. E. G.

Was she really this pathetic every February 27? She hated drama, and here she was wallowing in it. You'd think the scars were suffering enough.

"That doesn't mean it doesn't suck," he said.

"I'm fine. It's just today, apparently. Which is ridiculous."

"Nah. This way, you get all the pissed-offedness out on one day."

She snapped her capo on the guitar's neck, at the fourth fret. "I don't have . . . that's not a word."

"I'd be pissed."

"Waste of energy. I can't change anything." She grabbed a Moleskine notebook off her bedside table. She'd been keeping these notebooks since seventh grade, around the same time her mom finally let her quit piano for guitar lessons. They weren't diaries or songbooks strictly. Most of the back pages were covered in rhymes. She'd pick a word, make syllable count columns, and see what matched with it. *Pride. Divide. Bona Fide. Jekyll and Hyde.*

She flipped pages until she found a blank spot, jotting down some more words to add to the rhymes and lyrics scrawled everywhere—not to mention her goofy hearts and Trent McKinnon's name.

"I can't change that I'm short," Ryan said. "It still annoys the hell out of me."

Fiona moved between guitar and notebook, playing through chords and writing them down next to the words. "You'll grow. Dad's six two."

"But I'm short now. Most girls want to be taller than their dates." Ryan leaned over, trying to get a look at her writing. "When are you going to let me hear one?"

Fiona's pen stilled against the paper. She stared at all the words she'd written—raw, aching phrases that explained her to herself, unfinished songs about unrequited love with Trent McKinnon. They told about her fears, which were many, and her hopes, which were unlikely. The words laid out her insecurities, her self-disgust, and, inexplicably, her pride.

Simply put, they were True. No way was she sharing them with anyone.

"Nothing to hear yet. Just scribbles, really." She changed the subject back to Ryan. "Dad said he didn't have his growth spurt until college. Freshman year he was five seven. By that summer, he'd grown five inches."

"I didn't come in here for you to solve my problems."

"Your problem has a solution."

"Yours might," he said quietly.

She swallowed down the lump in her throat. "There's nothing we can do," she said, mimicking so many of the other doctors she'd seen over the years.

"Things change. Science changes. That's what Dr. Connelly keeps saying."

"He's been saying that since I was five, Ryan."

"You never know."

She switched chord shape—A minor, C, E minor—wanting the notes off-center, like her. "Well, barring a miracle, this is who I am. Growth spurts and pink dresses won't fix me."

"You're not broken, Ona," he said, using the nickname only he used.

Tell that to Trent McKinnon, who will never love me.

He nudged her with his foot. "You're not broken," he repeated.

"I know. You're right," she said, knowing if she agreed, he'd let the subject drop.

She scratched out some lines and penciled yet another version on top of them:

I want love and skin.

I want to begin again.

FI

Fi was a sweaty mess. In the reflection from her phone, she saw a long, grass-colored streak stretching from her hairline to her chin, from where she'd wiped out. Her elbow would probably kill tomorrow—but she'd gotten the ball.

She was shoving her gear into her bag when she remembered Ryan was taking the car. He'd told her this, hadn't asked.

Cursing her brother, she scanned the field, but only freshmen remained. On the far side, she glimpsed Trent limping through the parking lot. He must have gotten hurt at practice. That or all his equipment weighed him down.

"McKinnon!"

He turned, scanned for the voice, and then waited in place as Fi jogged across the field. "I need a ride."

"Yeah, Ryan already told me," he said. "I was going to wait."

"You'd think he was my father," she muttered. "We're in

the same *grade,* for God's sakes."

"He was just making sure you had a ride."

"I'd have a ride if he didn't keep taking the car."

Trent shook his head. "The trials of Fi-Fi."

Everyone else, even her parents, called her the same thing Ryan always had, *"Fi."* But in middle school, Trent had decided to give her a nickname all his own.

"You're an only child," she said. "You don't understand."

They shoved their stuff in his trunk—sticks, backpacks, gym bags, all of Trent's pads. Trent had to push everything around a few times, before the lid would close. The car smelled like the sweet decay of fast food—and all the other afternoons of lacrosse-practice sweat.

Trent pulled out of the lot and began the well-traveled route to the Doyles. Fi sank into the familiar passenger seat, and they rode in comfortable silence a few miles.

"You really cracked that middie last week," she eventually said. "Did you break his stick?"

"First one of the season."

"That's so not fair. I'd get a red card if I played like you."

"Nothing like a girl who wants to crack skulls," he said, smiling.

"Which is all your fault." She'd never get over the injustice that girl's lacrosse didn't allow bodychecking. "Teaching me to play the men's game."

"I was *eleven.* How was I supposed to know y'all have those lame oh-no-don't-check-me-I-might-break-a-nail rules?"

Fi showed him her stubby, bitten cuticles as a rebuttal. "I'd take you out, if they let me."

"No doubt," he said, snorting. "But why am I always the bad guy? Weren't we in *your* backyard? And didn't you shoot on Ryan just as much as on me?"

"You hit harder."

"That's true." He pulled up to the curb in front of her house and turned sideways in the seat, his arm slung casually over the back of her seat. "Remember that time he pinned me on the ground? When I accidentally hit you in the face?"

"Accident. Sure." She was needling him, but he kept bringing up Ryan. Like she needed the reminder *they* were friends first.

"It *was* an accident." He ran a finger down her cheek, right where that long, grassy stain was. "I'd never mess up this perfect face."

She jerked away, smacking the back of her head on the window. Trent's hands remained suspended, touching skin no longer there, until Fi opened the door.

"Fi—" Trent started.

She left the car before he could finish. "I should get to my homework."

"Damn it, Fi. You can't keep running away."

"I'm not. I've just got loads—"

"It's been, like, two weeks. Shouldn't we talk about it?"

This was the third time he'd tried to "talk" since that post-game party—and the out-of-nowhere kiss that Fi was pretending never happened. Sure, it was a nice kiss. Like, surprisingly nice.

But you weren't supposed to kiss your best friend.

"I'll see you tomorrow, okay?" she said, already at the trunk.

Shaking his head, Trent popped it open. She grabbed her gear, arranging all three bags across her body for the walk up the driveway.

Usually, he'd yell "Later, Fi-Fi!" or honk "Dixie" as he drove away. Today, his tires squealed.

She pushed open the back door, dumped her stuff on the kitchen floor, and dug through the refrigerator. Her mom stood at the kitchen counter, arranging flowers.

"Where's your brother?"

Hello, Mother. Nice to see you, too. "Some study group. Trent dropped me off." Fi took a swig of orange juice straight from the container.

"What's he studying?" Her mom pulled a glass from the overhead cabinet and handed it over with a look.

"How am I supposed to know?" she snapped.

"Perhaps you should find out. A few more study groups wouldn't kill you."

"My grades are fine! I got an eighty-eight on my English test."

Her mom arched a perfectly tweezed eyebrow. "And last week's math test?"

"I've got a seventy-four percentage on draw," Fi said,

changing the subject. "That's the best in the state."

"What are you talking about?"

"The draw. In lacrosse." Fi spoke through a clenched jaw. "That sport I've played for seven years."

"How does that affect your math grade?"

"It'll get me into Northwestern," she said. "Are they recruiting Ryan?"

Her mother stiffened. "Go do your homework."

Fi palmed some grapes from the bowl on the counter, grabbed her bags, and stomped upstairs. A ridiculous pile of clothes waited on her bed—ruffled pink and green, a strapless dress, which was just so impractical. Fi picked up the lot, walked it into her parents' room, and dropped it on their bed. At dinner, she'd tell her mom none of it fit.

There'd be another pile next week, though. Because her mother wouldn't rest until Fi was someone else. Until she encapsulated some bizarre combination of straight As, strappy sandals, and Junior Cotillion.

Fi sprawled out on her bed, binders and folders in no real order but all within arm's reach. She plucked Panda from his little nook at the corner of her bed and cuddled around him.

She tackled English first, still annoyed about getting Lucy Daines as her project partner. Lucy had actually said, right after she switched to Fi's table, "We're doing this project my way, Doyle. And I'm not carrying you. I don't care about your season or whatever."

"I don't need to be carried," Fi had said back, *really* tempted to smack down Lucy's skeptically raised eyebrow. "I've got an A in this class."

"Let's keep it that way."

The way some of these people acted—Lucy, her mother—you'd think Fi was hopeless, when, in fact, she was THE BEST FEMALE HIGH SCHOOL LACROSSE PLAYER IN THE STATE. Why couldn't they just shut up and be impressed?

An hour later, Fi had finished everything but precalc, during which she spent the last twenty minutes glaring at a single problem. She considered calling Trent for help, but then remembered the cheek rubbing and didn't know what she'd say.

She hated that things were awkward now, that she had to even think before calling him. He'd been her best friend since fourth grade. He was the only person who didn't see her imperfections first.

Across the hall, light peeked out from under Ryan's door. Of course, *he'd* know how to do the math. She hated asking him, but this stupid problem wasn't going to solve itself.

She knocked and walked in. Ryan lay sprawled stomach-first on his bed, his legs bent at the knee with his ankles crossed in the air. Various binders and textbooks fanned out around him, an open math book closest to his head—just like she'd looked a moment ago, but in the opposite direction.

"Do you know how to do number sixteen?" she asked.

"You need to wash that thing," he said, pointing to Panda.

She tucked her bear behind her back. "He's perfectly sanitary."

Anyway, she couldn't wash him—he might not survive it. He was already lumpy in weird places, and his right ear was nearly furless, from when she'd rub it while sucking her thumb.

"Did you do sixteen?" she asked again.

"Yeah, just finished."

She sat on the edge of her brother's bed and scanned the problem. After reading it over twice, she shook her head. "I still don't get it."

Ryan walked her through it. "Why did you get the math genes?" she asked, looking back and forth between their papers as she wrote it out.

"We've got the same genes, Fi."

"Well, they're mixed up different. Math and I don't get along."

He pointed to the last line she copied. "X is seven."

"Clearly I got the penmanship," she muttered, erasing the nine.

"Maybe we could swap. You neaten up my work, I'll carry you in math."

"I don't need anyone to carry me!" she snapped.

"Are you all right?"

No. All you people are driving me crazy. "Why the hell do you keep taking the car?"

"You were coming home. It's on Trent's way."

"Maybe I don't *want* to drive with Trent."

"Why?" he asked, sitting up. "Did he do something?"

She waved him off, so not in the mood for the big brother thing. "It's my car, too."

"Fine. Sorry." He held up both hands, like a surrender, and nodded toward the math homework. "Do you need help with the rest?"

The next five problems might take her another hour. Or she could just get the answers from Ryan, who, of course, already figured them all out.

She clenched her jaw, said "Yeah," and just copied everything, not even pretending to understand.

"Don't worry about the math," Ryan said. "You've got other talents."

"Yeah? Like what?" It wasn't like her to fish for compliments, but it'd been that kind of day.

"Well, there's lacrosse," he said with that little laugh-snort he made.

She waited—seconds growing—wondering if he was going to list anything else.

Apparently not.

"Thanks for the help," she said, standing up. Back in her room, she collapsed on the bed with Panda, closed her eyes, and made her own damn list.

She was good at English. She was decently popular. She

was cute—not drop-dead gorgeous or anything, but she had her good days. She was funny.

Yes, she was good at lacrosse. She *lived* lacrosse.

But surely that wasn't everything.

MARCH

FIONA

Fiona didn't get why she needed the paper gown when all Dr. Connelly ever checked was her face. Her parents sat in the chairs across from her as the Scar Doctor poked and tugged and *hmmm*'d.

"When was your last physical?" he asked.

"December."

"It looks like you've been five foot six for a full twelve months. Does that sound right? You haven't grown any more?" Dr. Connelly asked, flipping through the open chart in front of him.

"No, that sounds right," Fiona said.

"Same with your weight?"

She'd worn the same pair of jeans for a year. She figured that counted. "It's stayed the same."

"And your menstrual cycle?"

"Uh, normal, I guess."

"How old were you when it started?"

She glanced at her dad, who looked unfazed by this embarrassing line of questioning. "Seventh grade. Thirteen."

Dr. Connelly went back to flipping through her chart. Then, pulling out a chair, he wheeled himself between Fiona and her parents.

"Now that Fiona's growth has leveled out, I think it's time we consider a broader range of solutions."

"You mean a skin graft?" her dad asked. His voice sounded thinner than normal. Grayer, if voice could have a color.

"Not the kind we've discussed before." Dr. Connelly handed her parents a pamphlet before giving Fiona one, too. The cover read *New Procedures in Full Thickness Skin Graft Transplants*.

She didn't open it. She'd seen enough over the past eleven years to know what was inside—horrid pictures, purple inflamed skin, stitches, and ooze. The words were impossible to understand, and none made real promises. It was always *43 percent better neovascularization* and *acceptably improved inosculation*.

"There's a new approach in allogeneic full thickness grafts. It's called a deep tissue graft, and it's showing reasonably exciting results on the cosmetic side. There's a specialist in town." Dr. Connelly wheeled back to his table, sorted through a few stacks, and handed a business card to her mom. "He's already performed a few. I think you should talk to him."

"Deep tissue?" her mom repeated, flipping through the brochure.

The Scar Doctor nodded. "It uses a significantly thicker segment of skin, giving the muscles a better opportunity to grow together. The aesthetic results are quite good."

"Thicker?" Fiona asked. She already knew the downside of the graft—they'd have to cut and scar one part of her body to fix another. What part was she supposed to sacrifice?

She opened her pamphlet cautiously and nearly vomited at a post-op picture of someone's angry, raw thigh.

"Yes," Dr. Connelly was saying. "After removing the entire damaged area, the surgeon will replace it with the healthy transplant."

My entire damaged area. "But . . . where will they take the new skin from?"

"A donor."

Fiona imagined Ryan having a chunk of flesh cut out of him. "Who's going to volunteer to do that?"

"No, Fiona," he said. "You'd receive it from an organ donor. We'd put your name in a registry and when a suitable match becomes available . . ."

Fiona's eyes widened. "Oh."

"Of course, the wait can be quite long." Dr. Connelly looked over at her mom and dad. "Especially since Fiona's not in a life-or-death situation."

"Who do we need to talk to?" asked her mom.

Fiona didn't pay much attention during the rest of the appointment, not that her input was ever requested. Her mom certainly didn't need it. Without even inspecting the brochure,

Fiona knew this deep tissue transplant was the answer to her mother's prayers. It offered the best promise—even if only a "reasonably exciting" one—of making Fiona presentable.

Like Fiona, her dad said little during the appointment. He asked his usual questions. "What are the real risk factors here, Stan?" and "What kind of recovery time are we looking at?" He focused on totally different details than her mom did.

On the drive home, none of them spoke for the first few miles. Fiona sat in the backseat and waited for the inevitable.

"So that was interesting, don't you think?" her mother said, starting the sales pitch.

Fiona shrugged.

"The things they can do now. It's a miracle."

"Well, I wouldn't go there yet," said her dad. "There's still a lot we don't know. We need to understand the risks."

"Of course. But there's no reason to think she wouldn't be a great candidate."

"There's no reason to think anything. We don't have any information."

The discussion—debate, argument, whatever—happened every year, and was always the same. Dr. Connelly would tell them about "the cure of the moment," her mom would get all excited, and her dad would try to squash each option dead.

Fiona normally agreed with her father, but for different reasons. While he cited terrifying statistics about general anesthesia and infection, she was just unimpressed by any of the options. Major surgery, pain, forced bed rest—and she'd still have the scars, just in a different place.

This time, though, Fiona was surprised to realize—*gasp*—she might agree with her mother.

When they pulled in the driveway, her parents were still doing their annual "Well, yes, of course, dear, but what about . . ." thing. Fiona left them to it and went to the back-yard, where she knew she'd find her brother.

"Watch this," he said when he saw her. She sat down on the back porch steps, and Ryan juggled the soccer ball between his feet, knees, and thighs. Several minutes later, he finally dropped it. "Shoot. How many was that?"

"Was I supposed to be counting?"

"Had to be eighty." He cradled the ball on his foot, tossed it up, and started again. "How'd it go with the doctor?"

Fiona shrugged. "We're meeting with a surgeon in a few weeks. New thing. Skin transplant. From a donor. It's kind of freaky."

"Will it be nasty?"

"Which part? When somebody dies and they cut him into chunks, or when they sew it into me?"

Fiona got a sick pleasure watching her brother squirm, knowing he couldn't tolerate anything the slightest bit gory. As he turned green, she said, "Sorry."

She stood up and stretched before coming down the steps to stand a few feet from him. "Pass it."

He studied her before he obliged. The two kicked the ball back and forth, though it was obvious Ryan was holding *way* back. Eventually he got lost in it, though, backing up a little after each pass. Fiona warmed to it, too, getting more comfortable with her footwork, tapping the ball between her feet a few times before sending it on.

"Good move!" Ryan said.

They scrimmaged for a few minutes, Ryan running past her with the ball, Fiona trying to steal it. She'd snatch it every once in a while, but Ryan was good—the star on the school team, a top player on the travel team. She knew he was taking it easy on her.

He always did.

She tired well before he did and plopped on the grass. "All right, I give. You win."

"Nice footwork. Too bad you can't play—the girls' team needs all the help it can get."

"Take it up with Mom and Dad."

Although what was the point now? When she was in elementary and middle school, Fiona pitched a fit every fall, begging her parents to drop the rule about no contact sports. But her parents and doctors would never give the all clear. "Fiona, what if you got hit in the face?" was the main argument.

Fiona's normal side, her left, was 80 percent of her mom, with some of her dad's distant Irish genes sprinkled in—fair skin, reddish-brown hair. But given the train wreck of her right side, it hardly mattered.

A ridge of scar tissue allowed only limited peripheral

vision in the right eye. Healthy muscles underneath pushed while the stiff skin on top pulled, so she winced constantly. Tight, shiny skin, forehead to cheekbone, pulled all the non-harmed bits of her—nose, mouth, eye—off-center.

As far as getting hit in the face went, she'd argued it couldn't get any worse.

"Oh yes it could," they'd answered.

"Everyone has that risk, not just me."

They'd shake their heads. "Everyone else has skin that can heal. You do not." Then, patting her back, they'd say, "What about golf?"

She'd say, "I'll find something else to do, thanks."

"They don't really have a choice," Ryan was saying now.

"Yeah, I know." She shrugged. "I'm not a jock, anyway."

"You would have been good, though." He pointed up at a cloud. "Chicken chasing a duck."

"I'd have *rocked*," she said. "Dinosaur on roller skates."

"More like a turkey." He was quiet a minute. "Do you ever wonder? If it never happened?"

Fiona could go days without even thinking about the scars—she avoided mirrors, so that helped. Yet, her scars never seemed far from Ryan's mind.

She'd catch him looking at her sometimes, his expression almost as stretched and pained as hers. When they were little, he ran a lot of unrequested interference, standing up for her in the cafeteria or playground if anyone tried to tease her. Everyone at school was used to her by now, but still he had this way of treating her—like she was breakable. She loved his attention. But hated the way she got it.

"I should get to my math," she said.

Once in her room, Fiona plopped down on her bed and picked up Dr. Connelly's shiny pamphlet of promises. She squinted her eyes so the photos morphed into colored blobs. She didn't understand most of it—what was "debridement" anyway? But the numbers seemed good. Seventy-eight percent. Eighty-six percent. Ninety-two percent. She was still clueless—but with better odds.

The odds look good / Though I got no clue.

Fiona picked up the closest Moleskine, scribbling the rest of the thought:

Would it make me / Enough for you?

Yet another set of lyrics—poems, whatever you called them—that she'd never share. Ryan, Lucy, not even Mr. Hernandez, her guitar teacher, had never heard a note written here.

Everything she played for others belonged to someone else. Someone else's songs, someone else's words, someone else's fears and hopes.

Her great irony: the pull to create her own music versus the push to hide it.

There was an "outside" part of her music she couldn't hide—her songs filled a dozen notebooks; guitar-string calluses covered her fingertips. But the "inside" part? It was like her music was stitched through her system, like tendons or blood cells. All of it—the rhymes, the chords—performed a vital function.

Revealing those very truest bits, opening herself up to others' opinions and criticisms, would be like going inside out. She might break apart completely.

She eyed the pamphlet's "Before" and "After" shots.

Split me down the middle / And I only come halfway.
But I could take your pieces / 'Cause everything's stolen anyway.

Without squinting, she read the material, trying to understand what the procedure could do—and what it couldn't.

It could give her new, smooth skin. It could fix her other Push-Pull—the battle of tight skin and frustrated muscles. It could erase the scars on her face, though the brochure made no promises about the scars on her confidence.

Even using all her dad's tricks for seeing the downside, she couldn't shake it. The upside still looked pretty good.

There was just one problem.

If she was going to be fixed, someone needed to die.

FI

At lunch, Trent smacked his tray on the table and sat across from Fi. "She'll be at the game today, right?"

Having just bitten into her tuna sandwich—and having at least *some* manners, though her mother might not believe it—Fi simply nodded.

"Think she'll check me out, too?" Trent asked. "While she's here?"

Fi swallowed, shaking her head. "She's the assistant coach from Northwestern's *women's* program. Are you planning on some life-altering surgeries?"

Trent snorted his Coke, nearly spewing it on Fi. "Think of all the time we could spend together."

She laughed. "I already get about as much of you as I can take."

Truthfully, Fi was relieved there was no way Trent would make it to Northwestern. First, for all the talk of grades, Trent made Fi look like a National Merit Scholar. Second, at heart he was just a good old southern boy; she couldn't picture him in cold, fast-paced Chicago. And lastly, if she couldn't manage the boundaries of their friendship here, what chance would she have if he was the *only* person she knew?

He rolled his eyes—then took another enormous bite of hamburger. "So what happens? After she watches you?"

"She falls madly in love with my transcendent style, runs onto the field after my last-second goal, and offers me a starting position and full ride." Trent snatched some apple slices from her lunch and she confessed, "I'm kind of nervous. What if I suck?"

He waved her off. "You don't have it in you."

She smacked his hand as he went for another slice, eating it herself. "Seriously. It's, like, huge that she's here."

"You've gone to their camps the past three years. The *head coach* has seen you before. The scout wouldn't be here if they weren't already going to make an offer."

"That Vanderbilt recruiter came last year for Mary Benton. Remember? She totally choked. No Maryland offer."

He paused to consider this before shaking his head. "Nope. It's utterly impossible. Even on your worst day, you're the best in this city."

"Yeah, well, this is *Memphis.* We're not exactly a lacrosse hotbed."

"Will you stop?" He scowled at her. "You'll psych yourself out."

"You're right. Deep breath." She sucked in a huge gulp of air. And another. And maybe four more, all really close together.

He reached across the table for her brown paper lunch bag, like she might need emergency hyperventilation assistance. "You all right?"

Once her nerves got under control, she nodded. "Little freaked out."

"That's even worse than how you get after kissing."

She glared across the table at Trent. "You don't have a gentlemanly bone in your body."

"Sure, I do," he said with a wink.

"Is this supposed to be helping?"

"I'm distracting you from your worries."

"By making me cringe?"

Trent balled up his hamburger wrapper, tossing it onto his tray. "Whatever."

He slumped into his chair, and the two studied each other over the table. Both had their eyes narrowed and arms crossed over their chests when Ryan walked past. He paused, looking from one to the other. "What are y'all bickering about now?"

"We're not bickering," Trent and Fi answered simultaneously, still staring each other down.

Ryan walked away, muttering, "Wonder what getting along looks like."

The day crawled and flew by all at once. Teachers snapped at her to pay attention, but Fi could only focus on the playbook in her head and the game tape of the other team that she watched at practice yesterday.

There were two girls who couldn't play with their left hands, no matter how pinned they got. One with true speed—she could move the ball fast, but her shot accuracy was unpredictable. There was a goalie who favored her right side. The defenders made messy stick checks—Fi could rack up some good foul calls from them.

By the time she got on the field, Fi felt calmer. Coach Dunn smacked her on the back, cast a knowing look toward the bleachers, and asked how she felt.

"Good," she said.

After warm-up drills, when she'd spied on the team a little, he asked again, and she answered, "Great."

"You're on draw," he said.

She grinned.

At the beginning of the season, Coach Dunn had told her, "I'm moving you to midfield, Fi."

"What?" she'd practically yelled at him. "I'm attack!"

"My center moved this summer. I need you there."

"But I'm the leading scorer!"

"So score," he'd said, "while playing center."

Annoyed *her* game was getting screwed up because some senior's dad got transferred, she had played the position begrudgingly at first. Once she reached her stride as middie, though, she never wanted to go back. She got the best of both worlds—defense and attack—and more space on the field to run, to muscle out plays, to go head-to-head. She got the draw, too—the two-girl standoff in the center circle that left one with the ball and the other chasing after it. Seventy-four percent of the time she was the one with the ball. She'd checked the stats.

The ref blew the whistle. Fi and the other team's center leaned into each other, stick head pressed against stick head, the small hard yellow ball sandwiched in the middle. Another whistle and both girls pressed out and up, flinging the ball skyward.

Fi netted it.

Blowing past the other team's midfielders, she tore up the field, switching to her left hand as a defender tried to check. Three defenders in front of her blocked all her options, so she passed to the attack behind the crease. The play went on a while—all the attacks and midfielders sliding in front of the goal, looking for a shot, while the attack behind the crease kept dodging her defenders. Fi saw an opening and pivoted around her distracted defender. Three steps to the goal, a pretty assisting pass by the attack behind the crease, and there it was—an easy fling into goal.

That would be One.

Another draw. Fi flipped it toward her left middie, and once again her team was on offense. But half were running one play while the other half ran another.

"Set up!" Fi was yelling, trying to pull them into some kind of pattern.

"Somebody set a pick," called the attack behind the crease, and a teammate cut to the goal.

"Midfields!" Coach Dunn was screaming from the sidelines. "Get up top!"

Even though Dunn was yelling at her to shift away, Fi knew the girl setting up was out of position. Sure enough, at the pass, the girl reached out her stick an inch short of making any difference.

The ball rolled as Fi and an opposing defender charged for it.

Their bodies collided less than a second after their sticks. There was a series of unpleasant snapping sounds, and for an instant, Fi felt a giddy pleasure—*I've finally broken someone's stick!* Both girls hit the ground. It wasn't until the ref blew the whistle that she processed the pain.

Grabbing her right ankle, Fi screamed obscenities she didn't realize she knew. Still, *she* had the ball.

The ref and Coach Dunn ran over. Despite the pain—it was like she'd been stabbed, from the inside out—she wondered why her hands felt sticky. When Dunn pried them from her ankle, they were covered in blood. She dragged her eyes away from her hands, looked toward her foot, and saw bone.

It hurt so, so bad.

Dunn carried her bodily off the field. Ryan and Trent ran over from where they stood on the sidelines, and in minutes, her dad was across the field, too, barking into his cell phone, then taking her from the coach's arms. Yelling at Ryan to open the damn back door already, he slid Fi across the backseat and wrapped an old gym towel under her foot to soak up the blood.

"Hold on, sweetie," he said, tearing out of the parking lot. "We'll be in the ER in ten minutes."

Fi felt like she was frothing at the mouth. In between groans, she cursed like a sailor. Her father didn't scold her even once, which made everything even more terrifying, because that meant he already knew what she was just now figuring out. They could *see* her bone. This was bad. This was very, very bad.

She'd been quiet thirty seconds, letting her head loll against the door and watching the trees whip by as her father sped to the hospital in rush hour traffic, when Ryan turned around from the front passenger seat. He looked gray. "Are you okay?"

"What the hell play were they running?" she barked back.

"Um—"

"They were out of position! Did you see that?" Fi knocked her head backward against the door, hoping a new pain would distract her from the red-hot, searing pain of ripped skin and snapped bone.

If only she'd listened to Dunn and shifted back.

If only she'd stopped a few steps before she hit the defender.

If only the defender hadn't made that weird pivot right.

Her dad hit a bump pulling into the parking lot, making Fi groan louder. "Sorry, baby," he said. "We're here."

He pulled in front of the ER doors and sprinted into the

building, while Fi lay moaning in the backseat. A few minutes later, he emerged from the sliding glass doors with the biggest man Fi had ever seen. He had to hunch over the wheelchair handlebars to reach them. He picked Fi up like she weighed nothing.

"Had a little accident, I hear," he said, a row of perfect white teeth sparkling against his dark skin.

"Well . . ." Fi trailed off, pointing to the blood-smeared backseat. The ginormous nurse peered into the car and frowned. "Hmm. We'll have to take care of that."

Despite the *blood everywhere,* it felt like forever before she was admitted. Finally, someone hoisted her onto a gurney, popped the metal side rails up, and wheeled her back. Her dad walked beside her, but he'd sent Ryan home with the car. Fi wasn't sure she needed all the things her father demanded that Ryan fetch. Maybe he was just getting rid of her brother before he passed out.

Trying to distract herself, Fi counted fluorescent lights as they proceeded down the hallway. She got wheeled into a room, and the nurses and doctors consulted with her dad, who seemed to lose a little more color with each conversation. Then a nurse came over to her, smiled, and said, "This'll just hurt a little."

After flicking the soft spot inside Fi's elbow a few times, the nurse pushed a tiny needle, strapped to a clear tube, into the vein.

After that, Fi lost track of everything.

FIONA

For years, Fiona had daydreamed about this—through circumstances beyond their control, she and Trent would be thrown together, forced to work side by side. Trent would be smart, clever, witty, and kind. Gradually, he would realize Fiona was the girl of his dreams. They would fall in love, for happily ever after.

Now, at this very moment, he sat directly across the library table from her, so no time like the present.

"Mr. Phillips said we could pick from all the books we've read so far this year. So I was thinking this one," Fiona said, sliding the packet between them and pointing to number four. *Please don't let him see my hands shake.*

Trent leaned closer, and Fiona pulled in a deep breath. Outside of spearmint gum, he had no noticeable smell. It was a little unfortunate—she was kind of hoping for a little cantaloupe.

"'In *The Sun Also Rises*, show how Hemingway used conflict to establish the identities of Brett and Jake,'" he read—then looked to her with a shrug. "I got no clue what that means."

"Well, you read it, right?"

"I'm a dumb jock, remember?"

Crap. "Sorry about that. Bad day."

"It's cool," he said, with just the prettiest smile ever.

"Well, we still have time."

She went through a quick outline—thesis statement, supporting quotations, historical relevance. Just in case, Fiona gave herself the meatier parts of the paper, like the section on the Lost Generation of World War I.

"Wow. You really thought this out," Trent said, flipping through her notes. "Wait, what's an expatriate?"

"Someone who doesn't live in his home country."

"Oh. I thought you meant, like, Randy Moss."

"Who?"

"He was a wide receiver, for New England. He's an ex-Patriot," he said, stressing different syllables.

"No." She decided not to overanalyze. "The main characters were mostly Americans living in Paris."

"I was wondering how the football thing fit in," he said. "Everyone living in Paris, huh? Doesn't sound so bad."

"It's a really sad story, actually."

"You're not a very good salesman."

"They're drunk a lot. It's kind of amusing."

"Awesome," he said in a lighthearted way.

She leafed through her book, finding the highlighted section that explained it better. "Here," she said, handing it over.

Trent took the book and read out loud. "'You're an expatriate. You've lost touch with the soil. You get precious. Fake European standards have ruined you.'" He looked up at her. "You've lost touch with the soil? What the heck does that mean?"

"The characters have all lived through World War I, and they're pretty battered by it. Morally lost, that's what Mr. Phillips said. They're struggling to find meaning."

"Good thing you're my partner," Trent said, dropping her book on the table. "I'd totally fail this on my own."

He wants *to be my partner!* "I need to keep up my GPA, too. Northwestern's my first choice."

"They have the best women's lacrosse team in the country." His blue eyes widened, showing off those flecks of green.

"Maybe I'll try out," she said, a little giddy from his gaze.

Trent laughed. "I don't think they take walk-ons."

Fiona snapped in a well-shucks kind of way. "They probably wouldn't like all my don't-throw-a-ball-near-my-face restrictions, anyway."

What insanity made me say that?

"Do you mind if I ask?" Trent said. "How it happened?"

Fiona shrugged. She was used to answering this question like it didn't bother her. "A disastrous run-in with a popcorn cart. I was five. We were at the zoo, in the snack bar. The machine got knocked over—I ran into it, I think. The oil flew out of it and landed on me." She shook her head. "It's pretty ridiculous."

"That sucks."

"It is what it is."

Even though that might not be true anymore.

Fiona still hadn't agreed to the surgery, though the lobbying was fierce. Her mom's main argument: "This will make your life better." Which was just code for *this will make* you *better.*

Her main fear: the horror of cutting out a sizable piece of herself, and—this was the kicker—*sewing in bits of someone else.* For the rest of her life, she'd be less than when she started. She felt like less than enough already, thankyouverymuch.

But God, the results did look good. Which was just as bad, really. Deep down, a little part of her agreed with her mom. She *should* throw this part of herself away.

Trent was watching her. "So why Northwestern?"

Fiona's heart fluttered. "They've got a great creative writing school. And music program."

"And that's what you want to do?"

Absolutely. "I think so."

"Like I said, good thing you're my partner, then."

The two spent the rest of lunch hour going through the book. Fiona pointed out passages Trent could use for his half. When the bell rang, they walked down the hallway. *Side by side. Together.*

"So, partner, when's our next date?" Trent asked, nudging her in the side.

Fiona bit down her giddy grin. She wrapped one free hand around her waist, where he'd nudged her. It was almost like touching him.

"Lunch tomorrow okay?" he asked. "After school's hard, with practice."

"Sure," she said.

"Don't lose touch with the soil, Doyle," he said with a wink. They parted ways, Trent going up one hall, and Fiona up another.

Lucy wasn't impressed by Fiona's lunch with Trent. *Or* the date comment. *Or* the plans for tomorrow. *Or* Trent's funny Hemingway quote. Instead, as they drove to the coffee shop, Lucy exercised her right to free speech about Fiona's spine-lessness. Fiona wondered what kind of fiery death awaited her if she kicked Lucy out of the car. It might be preferable to the current tirade.

Lucy had moved to Memphis from Brooklyn in fifth grade, and Fiona had always loved what her own dad called Lucy's "Yankee attitude." She had features drawn from practically every available genetic pool. Her hair was nearly four inches tall. She wore thrift-store clothes and spoke in hard-accented edges. She acted just like she looked—like she didn't give a crap what you thought.

And Lucy said exactly what she meant. Not like some

southerners, who thought they could say whatever cruel thing they wanted, just so long as they tacked "Isn't that sweet?" or "Bless his heart!" at the end.

Still, sometimes Fiona needed a break from Lucy's *Lucyness*. Apparently, that wouldn't be today.

At the coffee shop, Lucy plopped herself down on the couch right next to her and shoved a lime-green flyer under her nose. Coffee splashed across the tacky flyer—and the open pages of her Moleskine.

"Luce!" Fiona reached for the napkin dispenser and blotted away the jagged-edged stain. "Watch it."

"You dropped this," Lucy said, plucking the flyer from the floor and putting it in Fiona's lap.

Fiona gave the flyer a brief glance before turning her attention back to the notebook. "Open mic night. So what?"

"So you should do it."

"Yeah, right," Fiona snorted.

"That'd be awesome, Fiona," said David, a friend from school. "You could sing one of those."

Sitting across from her in a tattered recliner, David was pointing at her notebook. She'd been so absorbed in writing, she'd forgotten he was there.

She and David shared some classes, and they worked on the school paper together, but mostly, she knew him through Otherlands, the coffee shop David had "discovered." He was the first of their group of friends to push through the crowd of tattoos and piercings and order a latte. She respected him for that small bit of bravery.

The first time Fiona came here, she had loved the place immediately, with its battered concrete floor, mismatched furniture, and hand-painted quotes on the wall. Lucy had wondered out loud whether it was where garage sale chairs came to die.

Ever since, a random group from school would converge in the living-room-style back room—provided no college kids had claimed it first. Fiona and Lucy came a few times a week, often on Friday nights, since neither of them had much by way of a social life.

"I don't think I'm open mic night material," Fiona said now, dropping the flyer on the table.

"Because the competition's so fierce?" Lucy asked.

Lucy had a point. Like everything else about this place, the guidelines were loose. Just about anyone could perform in the every-other-Friday open mic night. People would read poems, sing, play the accordion, tell jokes, anything really.

"I don't have anything ready."

"You are single-handedly keeping those Moleskine people in business," Lucy said, pointing to the notebook in Fiona's lap. "You're telling me none of that scratching and humming has amounted to anything?"

Fiona glanced over her shoulder to the open mic "stage," a simple, harmless corner up front, framed by tall potted plants. She knew what it would look like at night, though—brighter than the rest of the coffee shop, a high black stool smack in the center so she'd be taller than everyone watching her, with her face all lit up. She cringed, not sure which freaked her out more—baring her soul or her face.

"Not really." Fiona pulled her bangs far, far forward.

"Fiona Doyle," Lucy said. "Two weeks ago somebody *mimed*."

David laughed. "She even got behind the microphone."

"A mime with a microphone," Lucy said, nodding with David. "That's who you're up against."

Fiona pulled her Moleskine closer in. "I don't have anything."

"You're such a chicken."

"Who's a chicken?" Ryan plopped down on the other side of Fiona, so her coffee splashed again.

"Your sister," Lucy answered. "She won't do open mic night."

"You really should, Fiona," David added. "It'd be cool to hear an original."

"Not gonna happen." Ryan looked over his shoulder at the coffee bar while he spoke. "She's *my sister*, and I haven't even heard any of them."

Attempting to change the subject, Fiona seized upon her brother's new weakness. "Who's that girl you keep looking at?"

"What girl?"

Fiona pointed toward the little pixie of a girl on the working side of the counter. Ryan blocked her shoulder with his, before she could turn fully. "Want to be a little more obvious?"

"So *this* is behind your sudden interest in my coffee shop?" Because of his soccer schedule, Ryan didn't come to the coffee shop often. He'd been here a lot over the past three weeks, though. "I thought we were bonding."

He rolled his eyes. "So what's her name?" Lucy asked.

Ryan took a sip of coffee. "Don't know yet."

"You Doyles," Lucy said, shaking her head. "The only way either of you will end up with anyone is if they knock you out with a brick and drag you away."

"Not taking advice from you, Luce," Ryan said.

"Why's that? Think I don't get how it works?"

"Oh, please. Don't make this a gay thing," he said. "You have no personal experience—boy or girl. I'm gonna stick with my own method."

"Which is what?"

"Smooth and subtle."

Lucy leaned back into the couch, propping her feet on the table. "You're so subtle, she's clueless you exist."

"I think sometimes it's best to take it slow," David said.

"See?" Ryan said, pointing at him. "David knows how to play it with the ladies."

"You guys might want to poll a few ladies," Lucy said. "It's the blind leading the blind."

"Again, you are so not a good source." Ryan plonked his mug on the table. Coffee spilled over the side, creating a little mug-shaped puddle.

"Because I'm not a lady?"

"Because you're worse than we are! You don't even *like* anybody." Ryan looked at Fiona. "Am I right?"

"Don't drag me into this," Fiona said, holding up her hands.

"David," Ryan said, "you like girls, right?"

All the blood in David's body suddenly appeared in his face. "Um, yeah."

"One in particular?"

"Oh. Uh. Yeah, I guess so."

David's entire head looked like it might explode from all that converging blood. Fiona felt sorry for him, but her brother didn't seem bothered. "Does she know?"

"I don't think so."

"And that's working for you, is it?" Lucy asked. "Pining for her in silence?"

"He's not pining," Ryan answered for him. "He's got a *plan*. There's *strategy*."

"Um, well, I hadn't really—"

Fiona nudged both Lucy and her brother. "Stop it." She looked at David. "Just ignore them. Lord knows I do."

"It's okay," he said with a smile. "I could use a little strategy. She's not going to fall in my lap."

"See?" Lucy said, gesturing to David.

"He was agreeing with *me*," Ryan countered.

Fiona shoved them both away from her. "Good Lord, give it up! Change of subject!"

Ryan and Lucy fell back against their sides of the couch.

A slow smile crept across Lucy's face as she focused on Fiona. "Well played, my friend."

"Hmm?" Fiona said.

"Changing the subject." Lucy faced Ryan. "Originally, we were discussing how your sister's a chicken. *Somehow* we got off track."

"You used me, Fiona," Ryan said, his hand over his heart. "I'm hurt."

The speed with which Ryan and Lucy switched from enemies to allies always amazed Fiona. She tried to look innocent. "I'm not chicken. I just don't have anything."

"You're such a liar," Lucy said. "And a chicken. *And* the only person in the world who could probably make a song out of 'liar' and 'chicken.'" She then proceeded to sing—off-key— *"You're a chicken who makes your friends sicken."*

"That's terrible," Fiona groaned.

Ryan latched on to Lucy's truly awful tune. "And a liar who will . . ." He faded away, incapable of finishing such dazzling poetry.

"Catch on fire?" David offered.

"Trip on a wire?" Lucy said.

"Make it stop!" Fiona said, clapping her hands over her ears.

"Join a choir?"

"Break the pliers?"

"People!" Fiona yelled over the insanity of lyrics. "Leave the rhyming to the experts!"

All three looked at her, eyes raised. After an exasperated sigh, she said, "You can call me a liar. A chicken. A denier. Say it's singing I desire. I'll just wait till you tire."

They all smirked, because the truth was, Fiona's brain was made for this. Her body—spirit, whatever—was not.

"Yeah, I guess that's better," Ryan said, taking a lazy sip of coffee.

"So you're going to sing then?" David asked. "At open mic night?"

Fiona snorted. "I don't think the chicken song's ready yet."

Lucy looked at Fiona, with one eyebrow drawn down. This was the have-I-got-a-deal-for-you look. Not one good thing had ever come from it. "How about we kill two birds with one stone?" she said.

"I don't want to kill any birds," Fiona said, feeling like a cornered animal herself.

"Too bad. We're making a bet." Lucy looked between Fiona, Ryan, and the coffee shop girl. "If Ryan talks to that girl, you play at open mic night."

"You can't make a bet between two *other* people!" Ryan said.

"I'm perfectly satisfied with my situation. I've got no stakes," she said. "You don't want Fiona to sing?"

"Of course I do."

"I'm right here, y'all," Fiona said. "How about *I* decide what's good for me?"

And Fiona had already decided. First, she felt no desire to

force a girlfriend on her brother. Second, performing live—in front of an *audience*—was not going to happen.

"Because you *aren't* deciding," Lucy said. "We're going Tough Love."

Fiona was relieved that Ryan didn't look as convinced as her best friend. Wait—did he think she'd be awful?

Fiona looked toward the girl her brother couldn't stop staring at. She was average height, with a pixie-size body and a cute little turned-up nose. A wide blue streak cut through the front of her short blond hair, and she had several earrings in both ears. Fiona wouldn't have pegged her for Ryan's type.

The girl was laughing with a tall guy behind the counter with her. He looked older, at least in college. Tattoos covered his arms. He couldn't look more opposite then her shortish, preppy jock of a brother.

"He has to ask her out," Fiona said, crossing her fingers. "And she has to say yes."

Lucy clapped her hands and leaned back against the couch, laughing. Ryan's eyes narrowed, like *What the heck just happened?*

Then to her infinite horror, he grabbed his mug off the table, took a big swig, stood up, and said, "Guess I'm gonna catch myself a blue-haired girl."

Fiona's heart stopped beating. What had she done? *What had she done?*

Fiona and Lucy shifted around to watch. "Y'all can't stare," David said. "It'll never work then."

"Okay. Narrate it to us," Lucy said. She turned back, pulling Fiona with her.

David kept his eyes fixed behind them. "He's up there, leaning over the counter. She's refilling his cup. It looks like he's saying somethi . . . Oh, she just laughed. Okay, now he's got his mug back. There are a few other people up there, but it looks like she's ignoring them." David slowly shook his head. "Y'all, she's actually talking to him."

At this point, Fiona couldn't stand it. Her future teetered in the balance of these next few moments. Her brother might get a girlfriend—she'd not spent much time thinking about this, and she didn't like the idea of it at all. But much, much worse—she might have to play and sing *her* songs in front of people.

She turned around to look. Ryan leaned across the counter. The girl smiled at him, leaning in, too, with her fists tucked under her chin. Every few seconds she'd laugh.

"Well, that's impressive," Lucy said.

Fiona didn't reply. Ryan was heading back, looking smug. He had *swagger*.

He sat beside her, freshly filled mug in his hand, and kicked his feet up on the table. Swinging his arm over her shoulder, he gave Fiona a squeeze. "Time to prepare your song list, little sister."

FI

It had been two weeks since the Game. Yesterday, Fi and her parents had met with the orthopedic surgeon to discuss her "future."

"This is you when you came in," he'd said, tapping on the light board. Fi's X-rayed leg was grossly crooked—and then there was that disconnected piece. "Just look at that bad boy."

"It does look pretty bad," she'd agreed, while her dad had just looked at the film and shaken his head.

"Worst I've seen in a while." The doctor had pointed to the second film, this one dotted with solid, metallic objects. "Eight screws are holding you together."

"Forever?"

"They'll be in there forever, yes," he'd said. "You'll be stronger than before."

"When can I get this off?" she'd asked, knocking on the tacky, bright-pink cast that covered her whole foot and ended just below her knee.

"Let's worry about getting you healed first," her dad had said.

And now she was at home, with Panda keeping her company in her temporary prison—aka the couch. The doctor's instructions: two more weeks "taking it easy." No school; she wasn't even allowed to walk farther than the bathroom. When she finally got cleared to leave the house, she'd need people to carry her books for her at school. She'd have to wear skirts, since no normal pair of pants could fit over the monstrosity on her leg.

In six more weeks—after *two full months* of taking awkward baths with one leg hanging over the tub—the cast would come off. She'd still have months of physical therapy.

She swore that if she survived this forced relaxation, she'd never sit on this living room couch again. Ever.

Through the kitchen doorway, Fi watched as her dad hung up the phone, took a deep breath, and came into the living room. He sat down in the armchair across from Fi, her mom perched beside him on the chair's arm. "That was Coach Dunn," he said. "He wants to know what to tell the NU assistant coach. The one who came to the game."

"Why's he have to tell her anything?"

Her dad pointed to her encased right leg.

"I'll just send them the tapes from the end of this season," she said. "Those should be better anyway."

He raised his eyebrows. Her mother sighed and shook her head.

"Fi," he said, "you won't be playing any more this season. The doctor explained that yesterday."

"I'm sure he was just being conservative," she said, waving him off. "Anyway, it would only be the last few games. Like five, at most."

He closed his eyes and rubbed his temple. "Just because the cast is off doesn't mean you're healed. You'll still have *months* of physical therapy."

"I can do the therapy, too." She pinched the soft spot on her waist. "I'll have grown into a whole second person by then. More work the better."

"Fi, this season is over for you," her father said, speaking in his *serious conversation* voice. It was the only time he ever lost his fourth-generation-southern-man drawl. His words lost all their soft edges. "*If* you follow all the doctor's instructions then *maybe* you'll be able to play next season."

Fi waited for the qualifier, like *Of course we'll argue you're ready* or *Since it's so important to you, I'm sure we can work something out.* But the seconds ticked by, and her father kept staring at her.

"Dad, but, that's . . . ," she finally spluttered. "The scouts make all the decisions in your junior year. . . . How can I get an offer? I've got to play!"

"It's nonnegotiable," he said.

"I'll never get a spot! By next spring, all the decisions will be made."

"The past few years at summer camps will make a difference." Her father's voice went lower. And slower. It was like he was speaking to a toddler. "Scouts saw you."

That wouldn't be enough. They needed the stats from this season—which so far only amounted to two games, the second of which landed Fi in this stupid cast.

"You could walk on," he said casually, like her entire future wasn't on the line.

"You can't *walk on* Northwestern. It's the top program in the country."

"Fi," her mom said, "why don't you look at this as an opportunity?"

"What?"

"You can focus on other things now. Like your grades."

"Really?" Fi challenged. "You want to get into that now?"

"You have a 3.0 for a school that wants a 3.6. Since you brought up Northwestern, it seems an appropriate thing to discuss."

"Stats, people! That's why the stats matter," Fi yelled, throwing her arms in the air. "I lead the city in goals. I'm ranked one in the state."

"You play women's lacrosse, Fi," her father said, leaning forward. "You can't make a career out of it."

"Dad, I'm sixteen."

"Lots of kids know what they want to do when they're

sixteen," said her mom.

"I want to play lacrosse!"

"Well, *I* want to be independently wealthy and summer in France," her dad said. "However, that's unlikely to happen, so I better revise my expectations."

Fi glowered at her parents. How could they not feel even the slightest bit bad for her? "You want me to give up?"

"Not necessarily," said her mom. "But maybe this injury will let you explore some other possibilities."

Fi slumped back on the couch. For the past four years, she'd had one, singular goal: play lacrosse for Northwestern. All the work she'd done in middle school and varsity—training, camps, summer leagues, competitive teams—had been with that one goal in mind.

It had only taken five minutes to lose the thing she loved more than anything.

Fi pulled Panda in and spoke into his patchy head. "This sucks."

Her mom grimaced. "Language."

"This is so not fair."

"Life's not fair, Fi," her father said.

"Can't you, like, feel sorry for me for two seconds? I've got a compound break in my ankle, which hurts and itches and just"—she looked directly at her mother—"*sucks*. I'm stuck on this couch when I could be on the field. I've got SATs and ACTs coming up, on top of all the stuff the teachers are loading on me . . ."

Her father closed his eyes. "Let's try to keep it in perspective, shall we? We're talking about a broken ankle. If this is the worst thing that ever happens to you, count yourself blessed."

Ryan walked in, looking beyond sweaty. He leaned on the doorframe and wiped his face with his jersey. "What's going on?"

"Just learning how blessed I am." Her eyes narrowed at her parents as she pointed at her able-bodied brother. "What about him? Does he get the same lecture?"

Ryan's expression said *Dear Lord, help me.* Her dad replied, "He's not the one whining, Fi."

"Because he doesn't have *a broken ankle.*"

"He also has a 3.5 and volunteers with the church youth group," her mom said.

"And plays second-string to a freshman," she shot back.

Ryan flinched, and she regretted it immediately. Brother-sister issues notwithstanding, it wasn't fair to drag him into this.

It was true, though. She was better at lacrosse than he was.

"Enough!" her father barked, standing up. "You will not finish the season. You will do all the physical therapy prescribed. You will make whatever grades you need to get into Northwestern—or whatever school offers an acceptable alternative. And you will *stop feeling sorry for yourself.*"

He stormed from the room, followed by her mother. Ryan stayed in the doorway.

She *should* apologize. After all, he couldn't help that he

was the smallest guy on the team—and men's lacrosse made hockey look civilized. She wondered if he regretted switching from soccer to lacrosse. With his speed and moves, he'd have been an incredible soccer player, even at five six.

Still, she wouldn't—*couldn't*—apologize for doing this one thing better than he did. "I didn't mean to bring you into it," she said instead.

Shaking his head, Ryan turned and walked away. She was alone with her misery—until her phone buzzed.

"What?" she snapped, recognizing Trent's number.

"Whoa. Easy."

"Sorry," she mumbled. "Unless you're calling to make me feel bad or guilty or whatever, in which case I'm hanging up."

"Guilty about what?"

"Not being grateful my freaking ankle's broken."

There was a pause on Trent's side. "I'm assuming I've missed some key points."

Despite herself, Fi laughed—because Trent was the only person who *got* her most of the time. Who knew the right thing to say and how to say it—when he wasn't insulting her, that is.

"It does suck, though," he said. "When can you get off the couch?"

"Another week—maybe two." She glared into the kitchen. "Probably two."

"But the cast will be off before States, right?"

Fi groaned. She'd totally forgotten about States. They'd

won last year for the first time ever. They were going to defend their title. Shaking her head, Fi told Trent the news before she could tell her teammates—no more lacrosse for her this year.

She heard him suck in a breath. "Man. That bites."

"Finally. Someone who understands the total suckiness of this situation."

"I'm sure Ryan gets it."

She didn't fill Trent in on how bitchy she'd been to her brother, just moments before.

"We worked on a cool play today," he said. "You should see it."

"You'll have to find some other girl to beat up. Nothing I can do with it."

"But you could still *see* it. It's pretty awesome."

She stared at a hairline crack in the plaster wall across from her. It looked bigger than yesterday; she should probably tell her mother. "Hmm, sitting on a chair and watching someone else drill," she said. "Think I'll pass."

"It's a double slide you can run from either crash or near-man."

"Are you *listening* to me⸮" she snapped. "I'm out for the season! Can we talk about something else⸮"

"What, you're just going to pretend lacrosse doesn't exist⸮"

"Because I don't want to watch you run a stupid play⸮"

"You wouldn't have said it was stupid yesterday."

"Yesterday, I still thought I could play."

"Just because you can't play doesn't mean it's not there."

For years, lacrosse and her dream of Northwestern had been as much of her as her bones and skin. One freak second—one bad play—and it was gone. How pathetic that even her best friend didn't understand. "Can you just stop shoving my face in it?"

"I'm not—"

"Forget it. I gotta go." She hung up, flung the phone to the floor, and glared at the crack in the wall. Who knew how long she'd have to exist on this god-awful couch and in this vile cast—while lacrosse went right on without her.

APRIL

FIONA

Fiona was sitting in Otherlands, biting her fingernails to shreds and staring at the stool. It sat right underneath the spotlight. Some girl sang Radiohead a cappella—off-key, but hey, she was *up there*. She had those holes in her ears, and the lights shone through them. It was impossible not to stare right at them.

"Only one more to go," said Lucy, pointing to the blackboard list on the wall.

Fiona chewed on her thumb.

I don't want the glaring lights / Blazing down on me.

"*Where* is Ryan?" Fiona said.

"With Gwen." Lucy nodded toward the bar. "He walked in about ten minutes ago."

Fiona looked over her shoulder. Ryan and Gwen the Blue-Haired Coffee Shop Girl leaned across the counter toward each other. Gwen glanced in Fiona's direction and smiled.

Fiona didn't smile back. The blue-haired girl was stealing her brother when she needed him most.

Finally, Ryan left Gwen and walked over to Fiona and Lucy's table.

"Glad you could join us," Fiona said, when he sat down beside her.

Ryan held up his hands in surrender. "Calm down. I was just saying hey."

Lighting up my fears and frights / For all the world
to see.

"Whatever."

He leaned forward, nearly knocking his forehead against hers, and spoke quietly. "You'll be fine. No one's even paying attention."

"So they won't notice if I don't go."

"Ona, you can do this."

Give me the cold and dark / A little cave for me.

She felt like she was drowning. Well, if she was going under, she was going to drag her brother down with her. "I can't believe you're making me do this, Ryan."

He gave her the same, pitying expression she'd get from everyone else tonight. Like she was some poor, ravaged, special needs girl. And her lyrics, why did she have to make them all so *personal*? She may as well go up there naked.

The girl onstage said, "Thank you very much," and clunked away in battered clogs. Lucy gave a bored clap, looking past Fiona toward the door. Her eyes got huge. Ryan followed her gaze, and then his eyes got huge, too.

"What?" she asked, craning to see why they were gaping.

Lucy gripped Fiona's chin, so she couldn't turn to look. "Nothing. Just somebody . . . dropped coffee."

"So, Fiona, what are you thinking about playing?" Ryan asked. Loudly. He scooted his chair closer.

"Why are y'all acting so weird?" Fiona pushed Lucy's hand away and looked across the coffee shop. Trent McKinnon waved.

Lit up by the single spark / That your smile sets free.

Fiona waved back numbly. "No way. No. Freaking. Way."

"What's he doing here?" Lucy asked, just as dumbstruck.

Fiona pulled her hair in front of her face. "I can't sing in front of him. Half the songs are *about* him."

"They're about *him*?" Ryan said.

Lucy scowled at Ryan and grabbed Fiona's hand. "He'll have no clue. He won't know."

"I can't do it."

The three argued back and forth, two against one. Lucy and Ryan threatened, pleaded, encouraged, but Fiona held firm.

Ever since this stupid bet, Fiona had waffled back and forth about playing tonight. There was something to be said for *finally doing it*. Maybe her anxious panic would disappear if she just sucked it up and played. Now, she'd never know. Trent McKinnon may as well have had the words *Don't Play, Fiona* tattooed all over his glorious body.

The coffee shop guy took the microphone, looked at the blackboard, and said, "And now, the musical stylings of Fiona Doyle."

Fiona shook her head. Lucy tried to shove her up, but Fiona grabbed her seat with both hands.

"Laryngitis. Can't do it tonight," Ryan called out. The coffee shop guy shrugged and called the next name on the list.

With a lump in her throat, Fiona watched a guy and girl with flutes take the stage. Self-disgust and relief coursed through her, to a soundtrack of fluted bluegrass.

Five performers later, the coffee shop guy called for one more round of applause, thanked everyone, reminded the crowd there'd be another open mic night in two weeks, and told the person with the white Honda Accord they were about to be towed.

"There's always two weeks from now," Lucy said.

Fiona folded her napkin into increasingly smaller squares.

"You lost your voice?"

It was Trent. Fiona's eyes widened in panic. She nodded.

"That's so weird. You sounded fine earlier today."

She fiddled with her bangs and shrugged.

Trent said "hey" to Lucy and turned to Ryan. "Great game last week, man. Wicked goal in the second half."

"Thanks," Ryan said. He gave a quick nod toward Fiona. "You came to hear her sing?"

"Yeah, sure." Then he smirked and pointed his thumb at

the counter behind him. "And to ask out that girl. I've been scoping her out for weeks."

For a moment, Fiona lost the power to breathe. When she finally sucked in a meager bubble of air, it felt like her lung had been punctured by an old, dirty nail. Her air simply seeped out, rustier than when it came in.

Ryan stood up, his full puffed-up height nearly five inches less than Trent's. Was this him being the "protective brother"—or was he just jealous about Gwen? "Already beat you to it, dude," he said to Trent.

Trent raised his eyebrows and took a step back. "So you're the reason she told me no. No harm trying, right?" He gave Ryan a cautious look before speaking past him to Fiona. "Hope you feel better. And don't lose touch with the soil, Doyle," he added, with a thumbs-up.

He walked away, gathered up the lacrosse players who'd come in with him, and left the coffee shop.

"What the heck did that mean?" Ryan asked, looking down at her.

"Hemingway," Fiona said, waving away the explanation.

"Well," Ryan said, mad again, "he's an asshole."

"No, he's not," Fiona answered. "You're just pissed he wanted to ask out your girlfriend."

"*That* is not why I'm pissed," he said, shaking his head. Then he headed over to Gwen.

As Fiona watched him go, David came over and sat in Ryan's abandoned chair. "You have laryngitis?" he asked her.

Fiona nodded yes. Maybe she could pretend to have it the rest of her life.

"She just froze." Lucy snorted and got up. "Be back in a sec. I need coffee to wash down all this drama."

Fiona fiddled with her mug, trying to breathe past her leaking, rusty lungs and broken heart. David drummed his fingers on the table. "Sorry," he said. "About tonight."

She shrugged. If she opened her mouth, she might vomit.

She'd been an idiot to think her pathetic self could wind up with Trent McKinnon. *And* she was a coward. Her fear of everyone's judgment, of their pity, mattered more to her than her music.

All those notebooks and calluses, those hours spent playing and writing—what the hell was she doing it for? In the cruel space of three minutes, she'd lost Trent McKinnon and music. And really, what else did she have?

Scars, damn it. She still had the scars.

"I mean, I know it's not my fault or anything," David was saying, still drumming his fingers. "It's just too bad, that you panicked or whatever." He scooted his chair closer and cleared his throat. "But it worked out for me."

"How's that?" she asked quietly.

"Well, you'd probably have been swamped with adoring fans, and I wouldn't get the chance to talk to you alone. It's a rare opportunity."

"We were editing the paper all yesterday afternoon."

"Mr. Phillips was there. That's not alone."

She shrugged at the logic. She was too emotionally drained to debate the point.

David leaned closer, looking a little nervous. "So, now I've gotten past step one in my strategy—"

"What strategy?"

"I've taken Ryan's advice to heart, come up with a plan to get the girl to notice me."

"David, what are you talking about?"

"Like I was saying, step one was to get her alone. So that's checked off. Now I just have to ask her out."

"Ask who out?"

"Wow, and you're not helping. Like, at all." David took a deep breath and straightened up. "Would you like to go out with me sometime? A movie or something?"

Fiona stared at him. "Me? You want to go out with *me*?"

"Would that be okay?"

She forced herself to look at David, to see past *the friend*. And the *averageness*. It was the least she could do.

He'd looked past all the below average of her.

He wasn't uncute. He was fair-skinned, like her, but freckled and dirty blond. He had the lean frame of a cross–country runner. His eyes were a pretty, light brown. They reminded her of an amber pendant her mom sometimes wore.

What would a date with him be like? Probably like everything else she did with him, but with popcorn. After the movie, they'd drink coffee and talk about the school paper.

Which wouldn't be terrible. She liked talking to him. He

was smart and funny. Nice.

She had once told Lucy that if Trent McKinnon was ice cream, he'd be rocky road covered in sprinkles. David might be more vanilla, but nothing was *wrong* with vanilla. She always took some when offered.

Vanilla could never break anyone's heart.

"Um, yeah," she said. "Sure."

David smiled. It was a nice smile. He had very straight teeth. "Awesome. What about tomorrow?"

She laughed and shrugged. "My calendar just happens to be free."

"Great. I'll pick you up at seven."

The chair on the other side of her made a screech as Lucy pulled it back. "Where are we going at seven?"

Fiona glanced from David, who looked stricken, to Lucy, who looked clueless. "Not you. David and me."

"David and you what?"

"Are going to a movie. Tomorrow."

A slow smile spread across her best friend's face, and Fiona gave her an anticipatory kick under the table. Lucy grimaced and leaned forward to rub her shin. "Sounds delightful."

"Okay. Well. See you tomorrow," David said. "Sorry, again. About tonight."

She shrugged, rediscovering her laryngitis.

"Are you *kidding* me?" Lucy shoved her in the shoulder. "You're going out with David?"

"What's wrong with David?"

"Nothing, I guess." Lucy's eyes glazed over a moment as she considered. "He's nice. And . . . I don't know what else. I never thought to notice. Since he's not *Trent McKinnon*."

Fiona felt the tears brewing. She hated to cry, and now she was going to do it in the coffee shop.

"Hey," said Lucy in a rare, gentle voice. "It's okay."

"You're right. I couldn't play. I *am* a chicken."

"Are you really that scared you'll suck?"

She shook her head, sniffling. "I'm kinda good, actually."

"Then what's the problem?"

"If I get up there, no one's even going to listen. They'll see the scars. That's all I'll be."

"If you *don't* get up there, the scars are all you'll be."

"The songs are so personal." Just thinking about it, her hands were shaking. "To just throw them out there, for anyone to dissect, it's terrifying."

"So are you worried about the songs or your face?"

"Everybody will just overanalyze everything."

"Wonder what that would be like," Lucy muttered. "But what's this got to do with David and Trent McKinnon?"

"I think it's time I gave up on Trent McKinnon."

He would never love her. Admitting it felt like having her insides forced out.

"So he wanted to ask out the blue-haired girl?" Lucy said. "No biggie. He just doesn't know you well enough, yet."

"We've spent hours together in the library!"

"Yes, because nothing says seduction more than a high school library."

"The blue-haired girl could have seduced him in the library."

Lucy opened her mouth and then closed it. "Ryan's right. He's an asshole."

"Why? Because he's not attracted to the geeky smart girl with half a face? That'd mean ninety-nine percent of the male population are assholes." She felt numb, tapped out. She'd used a year's supply of angst in one hour.

"I think you underestimate the male population."

"It's got to be bad when the lesbian tries to bolster my faith in men," Fiona said.

"Can we please stop referring to me as *the* lesbian? It can't be just me, right?"

"Uh, I have no idea."

"It's what I get for coming out in high school. Could be *years* before these other girls catch up." She slumped in her chair and spoke to the ceiling. "I mean seriously, there's got to be at least one."

"We're pathetic," Fiona said with a huge sigh. "Crossing our fingers that we get *one*."

FI

Fi was sitting on the couch—the *damned couch*—when Ryan came home from school, dropped a stack of homework in her lap, and sat down across from her.

She wanted to lash out at him, sitting there in his uniform, all sweaty and dirt-smeared, but she held back. Instead, she picked up the bulk of homework, weighing it in her hands. "Please tell me this is for the whole week."

"Just today," he said.

Fi scanned the pages from English, along with the unfamiliar writing in the margins. "She's already picked the topic. And given me an *assignment*."

"Who?"

"Lucy Daines, worst partner ever."

"On the English paper? What book are y'all doing?"

"Faulkner, apparently," Fi said, still reading through Lucy's highlights, notes, and *instructions*. "The two short stories."

"Trina Simmons and I are doing *The Red Badge of Courage*," Ryan said. "We started today at lunch. It's a big part of the grade."

She gave her unsympathetic brother a look before tossing the stack of homework onto the coffee table. "I. Am. Going. Insane." She let her head flop backward onto the armrest. "If I'd just moved back in position. If I hadn't gone for that ball none of this would have happened. Life would be *normal*."

"Yeah," Ryan said after a moment, "but you can't change it. Might as well look on the bright side."

"Which would be?"

"You only have to deal with Lucy Daines on paper," he said, nodding to Fi's stack of homework. "No face-to-face."

"True."

"You get to watch *Cupcake Wars* nonstop."

"I'm *sick* of *Cupcake Wars*. Like, totally sick of it." She pointed to the wall directly across from her. "Do you know there's a crack in the plaster over there that looks like the east coast of Florida?"

"Wow, you *are* bad off." He studied her. "When's the last time you, like, moved?"

"This morning. Bath."

"Okay, time for an intervention," Ryan said with a laugh. "Come out with me tonight."

"Right." She couldn't remember the last time they'd done something alone, without their parents or friends. She pointed to her cast. "Slight mobility problem."

"I'll help you," said Ryan. "Anyway, I'm not doing anything major—just open mic night at Otherlands."

There was a coffee shop about five minutes' drive away, but she'd never gone in. "That grungy place?" It looked run-down, with an old, hand-painted sign out front.

"It's got character. This open mic thing's supposed to be, uh, *unique* is how I heard it."

Fi vaguely remembered Trent mentioning going there, although he never said anything about an open mic night. "Who told you that?"

"Girl who works there."

Her eyes narrowed on her brother. "What girl?"

"A girl," he said, rolling his eyes. "Do you want to come or not?"

Fi looked in the direction of the kitchen. "Where is everybody?"

"Mom went to the grocery store, I think. Dad's still at work."

Fi figured she wasn't the coffee-shop type, what with her lack of tribal scarves and ironic T-shirts. Anyway, she never had the luxury to just *hang out.* School and lacrosse took up all her time.

But she didn't think she was an *anti*-coffee shop kind of person, either. Plus, no parents meant no one to stop her.

She pushed herself upright. "Go shower, then help me get to the bathroom when you're done."

When they got to Otherlands, Fi clutched Ryan's arm and

hobbled up the ramp to the back door. It was weird needing his help so obviously and publicly.

The crowd moved aside at the sight of her Day-Glo cast. "People are staring," she muttered.

"It's just your imagination."

Mismatched tables and chairs crammed nearly every inch of the place. A beaded curtain behind the bar barely disguised a bunch of boxes, crates, and dirty mugs. Lines of poetry were painted across the walls and on the concrete floor.

"Everybody in here is pierced and tattooed," she whispered, scanning the crowd. "Or has those giant holes in their ears."

"Not everybody." At the counter, Ryan leaned toward a tiny girl with short, light blond hair streaked in blue. She smiled when she saw him, then she moved to the side so the other guy back there—a tall guy with tattoo vines covering his arms—could take orders. Ryan gestured between the two girls. "Gwen, this is my sister, Fi."

Wiping her hands on a towel, Gwen reached a thin arm across the counter. "Hey, Fi. Nice to meet you."

Fi shook the waif's hand, worried she might break it.

"Can I get y'all something?" Gwen asked. Looking at Ryan, she asked, "Decaf?"

He nodded and looked to Fi. She read the menu overhead but had no clue what to order. "Something not too coffee-ish?"

Gwen laughed. "Sure."

A few minutes later, Gwen handed over a large mug

filled with milky foam. Fi pointed to her cast. "I need to sit somewhere."

Ryan nodded, and they both surveyed the shop. Every table was full.

Fi began to panic slightly. This little bit of activity made her foot ache. She was dizzy and out of breath. If she felt like this after three weeks, what would her game be like after a year?

Ryan gestured to the full tables. "There's nowhere."

"Seriously," she whispered, leaning in. "I need to sit."

He pulled back to study her before scanning the café again. Finally, he clutched her arm and walked her to a table for four, where two guys around their age sat. They had dark, wavy hair and looked about the same height.

"Y'all mind if she sits?" Ryan asked, pointing to the two empty chairs and then at Fi's cast.

One of them had nice, olive skin, the other was fair like Fi and Ryan. The fair one stood, pulling out the chair just in front of her and gesturing to it. "Not at all."

At the same time, Tan Guy reached over to Fair Guy's chair and pulled it toward *him*, closing the distance between the two boys.

Fi considered pointing out that broken ankles weren't contagious. Instead, she looked to the nice one, who still stood near, offering help. "Thanks," she said.

Ryan pulled the remaining empty chair toward her and pointed to her cast. "You should keep it elevated."

"Where will you sit?" she asked.

Her brother gestured behind him, back toward the blue-haired girl. "I can hang out there."

So much for brother-sister time. "Is this the mysterious study group?"

Giving a half smile, he said, "Be back in a bit," and left her with the two strangers.

Fi wasn't sure what to do. Should she check her texts or look otherwise busy? The place was packed with people talking loudly, even shouting across the room, yet the two boys at her little table silently looked into space. Quite deliberately not at her.

She was studying the little tabletop menu when Fair Guy pointed to the corner, where a microphone was sandwiched between two brown plants. "Here for open mic night?" he asked her.

"Oh. Uh, yeah—I guess so."

Fi and Fair Guy stared at the personless microphone for several long, painful, silent moments. The boy shifted his gaze, looking to where his fingers toyed with the edges of an old book in front of him. Then he smiled and reached a hand across. "I'm Marcus." He looked over his shoulder to Tan Guy. "And my antisocial brother's name is Jackson."

"Fi," she replied, taking Marcus's hand. Jackson narrowed his eyes when they touched, like she was diseased.

"*Fee?*" Marcus asked.

"F-I. Short for Fiona." She pointed toward Ryan, now bent

so far over the counter he risked falling onto the other side. He was saying something to the girl—what was her name? Gail? Gwen? "*My* antisocial brother nicknamed me when I was little. It just stuck."

Marcus glanced over at Ryan before nodding toward Jackson. "We're twins, too."

Fi looked between the two boys, who, outside of the wavy black hair, looked nothing alike. Marcus was creamy-skinned and slight. He had light brown eyes to Jackson's green. They seemed roughly the same height—close to six feet, she'd guess—but Jackson had football player shoulders. Tall, dark, and handsome, her mother would say. Too bad he was such a jerk.

Fi shook her head. "We're not twins. Well, Irish twins, but that doesn't count."

"What's an Irish twin?" Marcus asked, his head tilted cutely to the side.

"We're ten months apart."

"Ah." He laughed. Jackson sighed noticeably.

Marcus shoulder-nudged his brother, but kept his eyes on Fi. "Y'all go to West?"

"No, Union. You?"

"Homeschool."

She'd never known anyone who was homeschooled. "That's cool," she lied.

Another awkward silence threatened as Fi noticed that, in addition to being nice, Marcus was a creep-up-on-you-slowly kind of cute. Soft hazel-brown eyes and smooth, fair skin, offset by that jet-black hair. She stopped caring what Jackson was doing. "So, what happens at open mic night?" she asked.

It only took half a minute to explain, but it was the perfect opening for everything else. He asked about her cast, which led to a surprisingly heartache-free discussion of lacrosse. He didn't know much about it, a refreshing break from Trent.

"It was created by Native Americans," she said. "They used it to train their men as warriors."

"I just finished a book about that. Kind of," he said, giving a quick summary about how different tribes reacted to early settlers.

His hazel eyes lit up when he spoke, and his whole face smiled. She'd never been so captivated by the struggle of native peoples.

She talked about getting her grades up in time for college applications. She told him about Northwestern.

"Hey! Jackson's applying there, too." He poked his brother in the ribs.

Jackson acknowledged this with a brief nod. Fi nodded, too—then turned back to Marcus.

"What's the book?" she asked, pointing to the dog-eared paperback on the table.

"*Selected Essays of Jean-Paul Sartre*." He held it up, showing her the cover. "If no one went onstage, I was going to read from it."

"You're kidding," she said.

"Seriously. Look." Flopping it open, he read, *"One is still what one is going to cease to be and already what one is going to become. One lives one's death, one dies one's life."* He laughed and put the book back on the table. "It was a spur-of-the-moment decision. Probably better for everyone I didn't follow through."

"You like to read?"

"Love it." He'd just reread the Lord of the Rings trilogy and told her some jokes she didn't get. Even though he was home-schooled, they followed the local school curriculum, so they talked about some of the books they'd read for English this year—the Faulkner short stories, *The Sun Also Rises, The Grapes of Wrath.*

An hour later, ten people had taken the microphone and left it, but neither of them noticed. Fi had no idea whether Jackson had paid attention—she'd tuned him out.

She turned when Ryan nudged her shoulder. "Mom just called. She's freaking that you're out."

Crap. "It was your idea," she said.

"We gotta go. Let me say bye to Gwen." Then he walked away, completely forgetting she couldn't walk on her own.

Fi pushed herself up. "Sorry." She gestured to her leg. "Usually he's a little nicer, but could you, uh . . ."

"Sure." Marcus got up, offering his arm.

Jackson stood up so suddenly that the table and mugs shook. He came to her other side, his arm similarly outstretched. "Here, take mine," he said.

The boys shared a look before Marcus sighed and stepped

away. Having no other choice, Fi took Jackson's arm. With Marcus a step behind, the three walked across the coffee shop.

When Fi got to her brother, she grabbed him and muttered an awkward thanks to Jackson. He shrugged and walked back to their table.

Marcus watched as he walked away. "My brother's usually a little nicer, too."

Ryan was still with the blue-haired girl, so Fi wasn't sure what to do next. In a matter of seconds, Ryan would remember their mother and drag Fi home. But she liked this boy, with his brainy book references and offbeat sense of humor. "Well, it was nice meeting you."

"Wait," Marcus said. "Can I have your number?"

She rattled off her number so quickly, she hoped she didn't look desperate. He typed it in his phone and pushed *send*. Her phone buzzed in her pocket.

"So you'll have mine, too," he said, smiling everywhere.

Ryan finally noticed his crippled sister and the boy with her phone number. "Thanks for bringing her over, man."

"My pleasure," Marcus said.

"Right," Ryan said, brow furrowed. "We need to go."

Fi pointed to her arm linked around his. "I've been waiting."

She said good-bye to Marcus, who told her he'd call, and she didn't even mind that Ryan grunted under the awkward bulk of her weight as they walked outside. All the way down the ramp, to the car, and on the drive home, she barely noticed the cast or the pain or her brother's curious glances.

His name—*Marcus. Marcus King*—swirled through her brain on endless repeat.

As she cradled the hand Marcus had shaken, Fi asked Ryan, "Do we have Lord of the Rings?"

"In the attic, I think."

"How long is it?"

"Three books, like, four hundred pages each. Why?"

"I've got all this time now," she said. "I think I'll read it."

She hoped she wouldn't finish it before he called.

TWELFTH GRADE

JANUARY

FIONA

When Fiona got home from school, her dad was sitting at the kitchen table. He held up a thick envelope.

"Is that—" she asked.

His grin was huge. "From Northwestern. Mailman just dropped it off."

She took the envelope like it might explode, turning it back and forth in her hand.

"Open it," he said. "I'm dying here."

She slid a finger under the seal and pulled out the five or so papers folded tightly inside. Her dad read over her shoulder. Two seconds later, he whooped, spun her around, and hugged her like she was little again.

"You got in!" He called upstairs. "Caroline! She got in!"

Fiona sank in the chair and reread the letter twice. Early decision. Classes available in both the creative writing program and the music school. Requirements to maintain the scholarship.

She held up the letter. "I got a partial scholarship."

Her father whooped even louder. "Caroline, get the hell down here!"

Her mother came down the stairs, dripping wet in her robe, her hair wrapped in a towel. At the same time, Ryan walked through the back door, his soccer uniform clinging to every part of his body it touched. Grass, sweat, and dirt smeared the rest.

"What's going on?" they asked in unison.

When her dad told them, Fiona was swamped in hugs of varying degrees of moisture. Her mom started to cry. Her dad commanded Ryan to shower and made reservations at Folk's Folly. Fiona sat back and reread her letter five more times.

"Can Lucy come to dinner?" she asked.

"Of course. David, too?"

Oops. "Yeah. David, too."

What was with her, lately? What kind of person *forgets her boyfriend*? A few weeks ago, she'd gotten sidetracked by a song she was working on and forgotten all about their date. She kept zoning out during his exhaustive Monday morning football analytics. She even might have blanked out on his birthday, if her calendar alert hadn't saved her.

A few hours later, the Doyles, along with Lucy, David, and Gwen—Fiona had forgotten about her, too—sat around a table loaded with steaks, enormous baked potatoes, and spinach so drenched in cheese and butter Mrs. Doyle said it couldn't possibly have any nutritional value.

After five toasts, her dad looked across the table at Lucy. "Heard from anywhere yet, Luce?"

Lucy shook her head. "Keeping my fingers crossed for NYU. Boston College as a backup."

"We never could get the Yankee out of you."

"Not that you didn't try."

"Not that we didn't try." Her dad turned to David. "What about you?"

"Oh, I'm from here," he said.

"No, son. Schools."

Ryan choked down his steak, and David's whole face bloomed pink. "Um, Dad's pushing Ole Miss, but I think I like UT Knoxville better."

"Those are both a long way from Chicago," Gwen said, looking between Fiona and David. "What are y'all going to do?"

David's eyes darted over to her dad before giving Fiona a smile. "We'll work it out."

Fiona smiled back—then refocused on her steak. It wasn't like a line of boys would be waiting for her at Northwestern, anyway. To her mother's—and, inexplicably, Ryan's—growing frustration, she still hadn't committed to the surgery. Yes, getting fixed excited her, but wearing someone else's skin freaked her out more.

So she stayed off "the list," even though Dr. Connelly kept reminding her that "the list" didn't guarantee a match. She could end up on it for years—which seemed almost as awful as staying scarred. Imagine finally deciding to cut away this piece of herself—to admit that *the real* Fiona wasn't acceptable—and then have nothing come of it? She'd live the rest of her life feeling even worse than she did now.

"That's why Ryan and I applied to schools near each other," Gwen was saying. "No matter what, we won't be more than four hours apart."

"Clemson. Totally Clemson," said Ryan, over a mouthful of food. "That coach loves me."

"Don't talk with your mouth full," their mom said. "And we still haven't agreed about that. If you play Division One, you won't have time for anything else."

"I can handle it."

Ryan had grown six inches over the past year, morphing from a thinnish, five-foot-six *guy* into a six-foot *man*. It was like all his bones stretched outward, pulling skin and muscle with them. He looked really big and really skinny all at once. He was fast as ever but harder to knock down. The scouts loved him.

"I just think you shouldn't take a good Division Two team off the table," their mom said. "That one we saw in Virginia looked perfect for you. It had a great business program and a good class size."

"Wrong state," Ryan said, shaking his head.

Their mom dismissed this with a wave. "It's not that much farther."

"Gwen and I already decided."

"Sometimes you have to be flexible, Ryan," she said. "Life doesn't get handed to you in exactly the package you want. Right, Fiona?"

Everyone at the table looked at Fiona, who fought the urge to roll her eyes.

You mean, not the package you *want, Mom.*

"So . . . ," Lucy said, breaking the awkward pause. "Which schools are you looking at, Gwen?"

"Well, Art Institute of Charleston would be great. It's about three and a half hours from Clemson. Furman has a great painting professor, and it's only thirty miles."

"Wow. You really thought this out," Lucy said, a little wide-eyed.

Fiona bit back the sarcastic comments. She knew she wasn't fair to Gwen, who was nice and smart and funny and adored her brother. She was edgy enough to hang with Lucy, sweet enough to get along with David. If Fiona had met her any other way, they'd have become friends.

But Ryan met her first. And ever since, he belonged more and more to Gwen and less and less to Fiona, which was simply unacceptable—and totally out of her control.

Fiona couldn't remember the last time he came into her room to talk. She missed him. Even though she saw him every day, she missed him.

"Fiona? The scholarship?"

Fiona blinked herself out of her fog and focused on the

table staring at her. "I'm sorry, what?"

"The scholarship," David repeated. "Are there requirements or anything?"

"Oh. Um, I've got to keep a 3.5. And take at least one music and creative writing class each quarter. Publish something in the literary magazine." Fiona looked at the ceiling, trying to remember. "That's it, I think."

"That shouldn't be hard," her dad said. "Those classes are why you're going."

"The grades," she pointed out.

He waved her off. "Piece of cake."

"Publishing."

Lucy snorted. "Just take something from the Moleskines. It's not like you don't have the material."

Good Lord. "Yeah, well, we'll see."

Her mom announced it was probably time to get going, and her dad paid the check. Ryan took Gwen home. Lucy ruffled her hair and said she'd see her tomorrow. Fiona walked with David to his car, to say good-bye.

"I can't drive you home?" he asked.

"You live the other way. I might as well go with my parents."

"I'm pretty sure your dad thinks I'm an idiot," David said, looking across the parking lot, where her parents were waiting by their car. "And he terrifies me."

"What? Why?"

"Our first date, he was *cleaning his shotgun* in the living room."

"That's nothing," she said. "For the guy before you, he was washing fake blood off the golf clubs."

He laughed, pulling her in for a quick kiss. "So there *have* been other guys."

"Oh, so many. Couldn't list them."

"Speaking of which . . . we should have that conversation. Like Gwen was saying."

One of the great things about David was how laid-back he was. They could talk for hours about nothing terribly important. And there wasn't a point to this conversation, anyway.

"I don't think I can keep up with the mileage calculations," she said.

He frowned. "Fiona, we need to get going," her dad called.

David dropped his hands from her waist.

"Who's the chicken now?" she teased. After a light poke in the ribs, she kissed his cheek. "Thanks for coming."

"Of course," he said, smiling. "You got into *Northwestern*."

She smiled back. "I got into Northwestern."

On the drive home, her father griped that the dry cleaners kept shrinking his waistbands. Her mother laughed but didn't complain herself, since she probably hadn't gained a pound since she was eighteen. Even after two children, Caroline Doyle looked infuriatingly good.

"I can't believe my baby's going to college," her dad said,

looking at her through the rear-view mirror.

"Both your babies," Fiona said.

"Too many changes," he said. "Now that I think about it, everyone should stay home."

"Too late," she replied. "Early decision. It's a done deal."

Her mom turned to face her. "Speaking of changes."

All the air went out of her—and took her good mood with it. "God, Mom—"

"I just think that now's the time to make this decision."

Fiona gestured at the dark night sky out her window. "Now?"

"I want you to be happy," her mom replied. "And I think you'd be happier—"

"It's late, Caroline," her dad said as they pulled into the driveway.

"Bruce," her mom said, looking at her dad now. "We have to decide on this."

"Well, it's not going to be tonight," Fiona said, getting out of the car before either of them could stop her.

In her room, she walked right up to the mirror over her dresser, putting her fingers on the scars and leaning in close. Turning her head, she studied all the angles. She inspected her flaws just like she imagined her mother did.

The woman had no idea what it was like to be imperfect. If Fiona went through with this surgery, would it matter? Would it fix her—her skin-deep problems, at least—enough that her mom would finally back off? That alone might make it all worth it.

But did she really have to get part of her cut away? Go through months of pain? Someone had to *die* before Fiona could finally—*finally*—get a portion of her mother's approval?

What a terrible trade-off.

Even worse for the dead, skinned person.

FI

When she got to the school gym, Fi found a sweaty Trent grunting under the Smith machine. He got up, wiped the bench off, and pointed Fi toward it. "Where have you been?"

She sat. "Coach Dunn intercepted me."

"What'd he want?"

"To harass me."

Trent squinted at that last piece of information but didn't pursue it, thank God. She was sick of everyone's opinion on the subject. So what if she was looking at Milton? *Looking, not committing, people!* Wasn't this what her parents had wanted, for her to widen her sights a little?

Anyway, Milton was a good school, not too big, not too small. It was in Memphis. True, the lacrosse team was club—that part pretty much sucked—but you couldn't have everything.

Trent slid four fifty-pound metal disks *off* the bar, leaving just fifteen on each side. "Do two reps of twelve," he said. Sitting on the bench across from her, he bossed her around, saying things like "Bring it lower" and "Don't push up so fast."

She would have fought back, but it took too much effort.

Three weeks ago, the doctor had given the all clear for these extra, after-school workouts—which, okay, she needed. The season started in a month, and she was sadly out of shape. The sooner she sucked it up and got started, the better.

Still, overcoming ten solid months of couch potato wasn't easy. It had been push versus pull. *Train hard! Get back to the sport you love!* vs. *Ah, what's the hurry?*

So far, couch potato had won.

"I'm upping your weight," Trent said, sliding another ten-pound disk on the bar.

"You upped it last week."

"That's what personal trainers are for."

"You. Are. Not. A. Personal. Trainer," she managed to grunt out.

"Three times a week, I am. Doctor approved, too. So shut up and do fifteen curls."

Trent was in his glory, watching her suffer. These workouts had been *his* idea. Frustrated with "Lazy Fi-Fi," he'd actually *lobbied her parents* to get the orthopedist's okay.

They moved between weight machines, hit the treadmills for a fast mile, and looped back through for another circuit. Trent was healthy and six foot two, but still didn't alter his workout for a girl, five foot six, with an injury. They'd talk a little, but Fi was out of shape. She tried not to waste breath.

After *two minutes* in plank, she finally collapsed face-first to the ground. "You're going to kill me."

"Well, we're done." He snapped her with his towel. "Anyway, Milton's *club team* is killer. Wouldn't want you to get cut."

"We're not getting into this again."

"Just never thought you'd give up lacrosse for a guy."

"I'm not *giving up*," she snapped. "And it's not like I *want* club."

"So why do it?"

"I'm doing the best I can with my choices," she said, grabbing her bag.

No, her dream college experience didn't include Milton. But priorities change—and you can't have everything.

"Anyway, what if he gets hit by a bus?" Trent said. "You could end up with no lacrosse *and* no Marcus."

"Don't be ridiculous."

Trent shrugged. "Need a ride?"

"No, I've got the car." *Remarkably.* "I'm going to Marcus's house."

"Like that?" Trent said, pointing at her sweaty clothes.

"I'm going to *shower* first." She could just imagine what Marcus's parents—or, God, Jackson—would say if she showed up like this, dirty and covered in germs.

"You should just move in," he said. "You're over there enough."

"Can we not do this?"

"I'm not doing anything," he said, pulling on a sweatshirt. "Run tomorrow. At least two miles."

"*Two?*"

He held up two fingers. "Later, Fi-Fi. Have fun with the boyfriend."

Fi grabbed a quick shower and drove to Marcus's house. She'd managed to get the car today, but it was rare. Trent dropped her off most of the time. Generally, he had been pretty decent about Marcus. He seemed *much* angrier about lacrosse and Milton.

She'd called Trent the night she and Marcus had met— right after she sent Ryan to the attic, to find the Lord of the Rings books she never finished.

"I met someone," she'd told him, probably grinning like an idiot.

When he didn't respond, she'd remembered their unresolved kissing issues. "I'm sorry . . . I just, well, he was really great. And you were the first person I wanted to tell."

"Why?"

"You're my best friend."

She'd heard him sigh deeply. "Okay," he'd said eventually. "Tell me."

For the next few weeks, Trent had teased her some—that mean kind of teasing that really didn't suit him.

Fi-Fi, you've got bigger biceps than he does. You sure you didn't get a concussion along with that broken ankle? You really think that pale, skinny guy can handle a jock for a girlfriend?

"If I'm so unappealing," Fi finally snapped, "why would *you* want to date me?"

"Good question. You're probably not my type, anyway."

"So go *find* your type and stop picking on Marcus!"

"I'm not picking on him. I'm being honest!"

"No, you're being a spoiled brat! You didn't get me so now no one can."

"Don't flatter yourself, Fi. I'm not heartbroken."

"Then stop acting like an ass."

"Well, *you* stop being all sappy. You've got the most amazing boyfriend in the whole world! We know!"

"I don't do that."

"Oh my God, if I hear one more *Marcus says* I'm going to punch someone in the face."

It was their worst fight ever. They stood there, staring each other down and breathing hard, until Fi just deflated.

"I hate this," she said. "I hate fighting with you."

"We always fight," he said, but he was slumping a little, too. "Ask Ryan."

"Not like this. I want to go back to normal."

"Yeah, me too."

They hugged until Trent had noogied her.

After that, a new girl—and another and then another— grabbed Trent's attention. "I'm trying to find out my type," Trent told her. "Like you said."

She was pulling up to Marcus's house when her phone buzzed.

A text from Trent: *2 miles. Finish in no more than 15 mins.*

And right after, from her brother: *I need the car in an hour.*

She rolled her eyes and rang the bell.

Jackson opened the door, frowning. "I didn't know you were coming today."

"Sorry I didn't clear it with you. Is Marcus home?"

A rhetorical question—of course he was home. His overprotective family hardly ever let him out of the house.

"He's not feeling well," Jackson said.

"You say that every time I come over."

"It's true every time you come over."

"Look, I haven't eaten peanuts. I didn't roll in flour. Let me in."

He kept his place in the doorway. "Does he know you're coming?"

"I can just text him, Jackson." She held up her phone.

Finally, he stepped aside. "He's upstairs."

Despite the weirdness of the King house, the Girlfriend in the Bedroom policy was a big perk. The whopping five times Marcus's parents let him come to her house, *her* parents didn't let him up the first step.

Jackson followed her as far as the kitchen, where Marcus's mother stood elbow-deep in some mysterious concoction. She wore latex gloves and a *hairnet.* "Well, hello, Fi," she said, like it was a surprise to see her there.

"Hi," Fi said, pointing toward the stairs. "He's in his room?"

Mrs. King nodded. "Might be sleeping, though." With her

hands immersed in the mystery pot, she nodded toward the pill divider on the kitchen table. "Could you bring up his four o'clocks?"

"Sure."

"Don't forget—" Jackson said.

"I know," she said, trying to keep her tone pleasant in front of Mrs. King. "Wash my hands and count to fifty. I only did it wrong one time."

"It only takes one time," he said.

Good Lord, he is PARANOID. Fi soaped her hands while singing—in her head, twice—the alphabet song. She used three paper towels to thoroughly dry. Then she filled a glass with water and picked his three pills from the "evening" box in the twenty-eight-slotted pill case and went upstairs.

"Hey," Marcus said thickly, turning to his side and opening his eyes.

"Little late for a nap, isn't it?" She sat on the bed, holding her pill hand out.

He scooped them from her palm, swallowing them down with a quick drink of water. Wrapping his hands around her waist, he pulled her down beside him. After a long kiss, he said, "You're a great way to wake up."

He looked pale. "You don't look that great," she said.

"You're so good for my ego," he said, rubbing a thumb along her jaw.

"Seriously. Are you not feeling well? Should you call your doctor?"

"Just how it is," he said, giving an easy shrug.

She hated how Marcus was never fully *well*—hated it more than he did. She remembered that fight with her parents, when her dad told her to stop whining about her broken ankle. He was right—things could have been so much worse.

She'd never forget the first time he vomited in front of her—well, on the other side of the door. Marcus tore into the bathroom, and she listened to him hurl. It was a gut-wrenching sound.

He came out a few minutes later, pale and embarrassed. "You okay?" he asked, keeping a distance like she might spook.

"*You're* asking *me?*"

"I'll understand if you want to leave."

She felt like *she* might vomit. "Do you want me to leave?"

"No. Not at all."

Then he hugged her. He smelled like mint toothpaste.

Now, Marcus picked up her hand and put it on his head. She ran her fingers through his hair, and he bent into it, closing his eyes like a cat. "Don't worry, I'm fine," he said.

"I hate how you're stuck in the house. You've been in bed all day, haven't you?"

He pulled her closer. "Well, *I'm* not complaining about the bed."

They spent the next few hours as they always did—a loose pattern of making out, talking about their day, doing homework, and making out. At six, her brother texted *where's the car!* just as Jackson pounded on the other side of the door. He had a unique, side-of-the-fist, angry kind of pound that she'd never heard anyone replicate.

Marcus gave her a quick peck on the forehead, before sitting up. "Yeah?"

"Dinner," Jackson called through the door.

"'Kay. Be down in a sec."

Fi stowed her books in her backpack. Marcus made like he'd help her out, but she shook him off. She didn't like how he looked, now that she was a few feet away and had a better perspective. He looked paler than when she got there. "Are you sure you're all right?"

He wagged his eyebrows as he dragged his fingers through her hair, combing it out. "Just dandy."

She eyed him a minute before deciding to believe him. At the front door she gave him a quick peck on the mouth. "I'll call you later," he said.

I NEED THE CAR!!! Ryan texted.

She would have complained about her rude brother, but she glimpsed an irritated Jackson watching them from the hallway and knew it could be worse.

FEBRUARY

FIONA

Fiona was in no mood for Lucy's rant, but David had gotten sucked right in.

"Why not dump weed killer right into the Mississippi, then?" Lucy asked, squaring off with him. He sat beside Fiona on the coffee shop's battered futon.

"That's not what I meant," he said. "But you can't expect all the big farms around here to go organic. It's just not practical."

"Fiona, does your boyfriend know it's that kind of thinking that's destroyed our ozone layer?"

David had yet to develop the skills to avoid Lucy's Injustice-Du-Jour debates. On any other day, Fiona would have been a nice girlfriend and helped him out. But today was February 27, the day she was always bitchy—as Ryan had been kind enough to point out last year. Today, it was every man for himself.

Fiona stood up, taking both her Moleskine and mug. "I'm getting a refill."

When she got to the counter, Gwen held out her hand, taking the mug and refilling it without instruction. "Are you coming with Ryan tonight?"

"Um—"

Gwen handed the mug back. "My art show?"

"Oh, right. Your show."

"I've got three paintings. My teacher thinks a few local art dealers might even come."

Gwen went to a high school for performing and fine arts. All seniors participated in a show—which Fiona found equally intriguing and horrifying. "Let me double-check with Ryan."

Gwen nodded. "I'm heading out in a minute, to get ready. It's at six."

"Right, I know," which she didn't. Nor did she want to go.

Just then, Ryan walked in and planted a quick kiss on Gwen. He turned to Fiona, his smile fading. "How you doing?"

"I'm fine. Why?"

Ryan reached over to pick up the mug of decaf Gwen had already poured. He pointed toward an empty table in the corner. "Come sit with me."

She wasn't sure which was worse—this annual February 27 heart-to-heart with her brother or Lucy's sermon in the nook. At least she'd get him to herself.

As she walked behind him, her eyes came level with his shoulder blades, rather than the back of his head. He looked so much older than her now.

At the table, he studied her over the rim of his mug. "I want to talk about the surgery."

Fiona's breath came out in an audible *ooof*. "God, why?"

"Because you've gotta make a decision."

"Maybe not making a decision is the decision."

"Is it?"

She used her index finger to circle random patterns across the wood. "Why do you want me to decide now? Why can't it be next year? Or ten years from now?"

"If you don't do it soon, you *will* have to wait. The recovery time is four months, at least. It's not like you can schedule it whenever you want it. If the donation is there, you've gotta be ready for it."

"I know."

"Once you get up to Chicago, you won't have that chunk of time again for four years. You've already got all the credits you need to graduate, you're already set with college. It's the perfect time."

"Did Mom pay you or something? What's with the sales pitch?"

"You're suspicious, because I want what's best for you?"

"How do you know this is best for me?"

"You want to wallow every February twenty-seventh from now till you die?"

"It's one day! Every other day I'm fine."

"You're burned every day, Fiona."

"Yet you make a bigger deal about it than I do," she snapped. "*You* didn't get burned, Ryan. I did."

Ryan looked at the table. "I know."

"So you can't be all high-and-mighty about what I should do."

"I'm not. I just want to help. I want to make it better."

Make me better, you mean. "Is it that hard to look at me?"

It was a hateful thing to say. She was equally pleased and horrified as all expression melted off his face.

She stood, picking up her Moleskine. "Tell Lucy and David I went home."

"I'll drive you."

"I want to walk."

"No, let me—"

She held up her hand and walked out without a glance or a word to anyone else.

It wasn't a long walk home—maybe a mile—but it was cold and gray in that way that only Memphis in the winter can be. Not cold enough to justify buying a two hundred dollar puffy down coat, but never warm enough for the bulky sweatshirts everyone made do with instead. And the *gray.* She hadn't seen actual sunlight in a month and a half. Maybe vitamin D withdrawal was the real reason she was so foul by the end of February.

Tossing her hood over her head and pulling the drawstring

tight, Fiona bundled against herself and began the trudge home. Gradually the walk warmed her. Cold, clean air filled up her lungs and scrubbed them clean. She unfolded slowly, each vertebra notching itself upright when good and ready. Twenty minutes later, her hood was down, her back straight, her good cheek flushed.

At some point, Fiona found herself simply *standing.* A low wall edged the lawn just beside her. She was only a few blocks from home, but she walked over to sit on it. Not moving forward or backward, but sideways.

She breathed, in and out. She felt the cold, hard stone poke into the cold, hard of her tailbone. She stared ahead at nothing in particular.

Ryan was right, of course. Everything was horrible on February 27. She was horrible.

On February 27, she was *scarred.* Every bit of her—face, heart, soul, brain—was mauled and mutilated. She was nothing but damage.

She hated it all. Her scars, her self-pity, herself.

She wanted to be whole.

She pulled her Moleskine and pen from her pocket and began to write:

Accidents and incidents / Freak twists in coincidence

Build me up, like bones and skin

I want love and sin

Let me lure you in

Let me begin again

But this fate and skin / They trap me in.

Well, she didn't write it all at once. There were stops and starts, scratched-out lines, rearranged words. Countless breaths came in and out while the sun dipped away, and the night crept up. She only vaguely noticed the lost light and cold fingers, but this was a perfect kind of trance.

She looked up when the car honked.

Ryan screeched to a jerky stop at the curb in front of her and hopped out. "Where the hell have you been?!"

"Here," she said, looking at him with a groggy, afternoon-nap feeling.

"It's been two hours."

Fiona looked at the—even grayer, like burnt charcoal—sky. "Wow. I didn't realize—"

"What are you *doing*?" he said, in a furious panic.

She folded the Moleskine, resting it on her knees. "I was walking. And then writing."

"It's a thirty minute walk home—tops—from the coffee shop, Ona. It's"—he looked at his watch—"six thirty."

"Wait, doesn't Gwen have a thing?"

"Yes, she does. You'll notice I'm not there."

It was bad, she knew, to feel a little triumphant about this. "What, you thought I was abducted or something?" She pointed to the long row of large, turn-of-the-century houses lining the street. "We're not exactly in a high-crime area."

He sat beside her and pulled at the weeds growing through

the cracks in the wall. "Anything could have happened. I didn't know."

Ryan looked tense and edgy, not yet recovered from his ridiculous—but sweet—panic. Fiona's heart broke a little for him. For the moment, she forgot her problems and stepped out of her mood. She nudged his shoulder with her own. "You're a mess. Talk to me."

He rested his hands in his lap and looked straight ahead, toward the house across the street. "I just get lost in your story sometimes."

"Lost in my story?"

He nodded. "Like . . . there's this place you're supposed to be, and it's my job to get you there."

"Where am I supposed to be?"

He shrugged. "If I knew, I wouldn't keep screwing it up."

"How are you screwing it up?" she asked, thoroughly confused. It was like someone had sliced the pivotal chapters out of the "story" before she even got a chance to read it.

Ryan's eyes rested on the house across the street. "How am I *not* screwing it up? I push you to talk about things you don't want to. I push David to ask out the girl of his dreams. I push you to do open mic night. I push you into a surgery you don't want. I just push."

Fiona had never thought of it like this. Not at all. "I like that you're in my story."

He shook his head and kept staring across the street. "I think about it a lot—if the accident never happened. Do you?"

"Sure sometimes, but it's pointless. I'm not a poor-me kind of girl." He looked at her then, one eyebrow raised. "Well, not usually," she said, nudging his shoulder again and acting breezier about the whole thing than she felt. He looked so burdened. "I was little, Ryan. There's no way to know what I'm missing, or who I'd be otherwise. Stuff happens every day that sets us in one direction or another."

"Like what?"

"I don't know. Stupid stuff." She considered a minute then said, "You have this killer caffeine headache but somebody else gets the last Coke so you do awful on a final. Your class rank gets screwed. You don't go to the right college, where Mr. Yeah Probably is waiting. So you meet Mr. Well Maybe, instead. He talks you into switching majors so you get a job that doesn't really do it for you but it takes you out of the country all the time and you—"

He cut her off. "Your comparing caffeine withdrawal to a face covered in scars?"

"Half-covered." She followed Ryan's gaze back to the house across the street. Light blazed from all the bottom floor windows. Flickering blues of a television created the only light on top. "Anyway, plenty of everyday things can make just as much impact. Remember how you tried lacrosse in fourth grade? What if you'd stuck with that? You could potentially be someone else completely."

Ryan shrugged.

"If we tried to analyze how every little thing changes us," Fiona continued, "nobody would get anything done."

Ryan tipped his head toward her and smiled. It was a small smile—a saddish one—but a smile all the same. "I feel like it's my job to fix it."

Now it was Fiona's turn with the sad smile. "I thought you said I wasn't broken."

He shook his head. "Not fix *you*. Fix it."

"What's the difference?"

He took a deep breath. "Three hundred sixty-four days of the year—I don't know, you're *Fiona*. Fun and sarcastic and just you. This day, not so much. That makes the problem an *it*, not a *you*."

"So according to this logic, we fix the scars, and my problems are solved?"

"You don't think?"

It was a nice idea, one she probably clung to herself more than she'd like to admit. "There's some safety in it, this way," she said. "Like, I can always blame something for all the parts of me I hate. What if I'm just as pathetic with a full face?"

"You are the least pathetic person I know."

Fiona didn't agree with this at all, but that was a different argument. "It's a scary idea, carrying around someone else. I'll be benefiting from *someone dying*."

"You can't take responsibility for that. That person chose to donate for his own reasons. It has nothing to do with you."

"But he—she—chose it for *bigger* reasons probably. Something more heroic. Not so some girl could be pretty. Or regular."

"Who's to say that's not heroic? Who says it needs to be? Whoever it is might just have checked the box with a *Sure, why not?*" Ryan nudged her shoulder. She wasn't looking at him, but she knew he was smiling. "Not everyone agonizes over every little decision, Ona."

She was pretty sure organ donation didn't fit in the every-little-decision category, but she didn't press the point. This back-and-forth with her brother felt too nice, even if the topic was morbid.

A second television flicked on across the street, in the room just next to the other TV. The lights flickered in unison, like both were tuned to the same channel. "So you think I should have the surgery?"

A few quiet moments passed before Ryan answered. "I do."

"Why?"

"I don't know. Because you can?"

What a simple reason—no grand philosophy behind it, no gut-wrenching self-evaluation required. It was easy and obvious and lovely.

She decided to follow her brother's lead.

She rested her head on his shoulder and said, "Okay, I'll do it."

FI

When Fi first started dating Marcus, she'd talked to a girl on her lacrosse team who was allergic to everything—peanuts, soy, wheat. Even though her friend joked about her hermetically sealed lunches, she'd told Fi, no, she didn't count to fifty while washing her hands.

"So what's *really* wrong with you?" Fi asked Marcus, one night later on.

"It's just a weird food thing," he said. He launched into an exhaustive scientific explanation about allergy vs. intolerance vs. sensitivity that made her eyes glaze over.

While she still didn't understand it, she was getting better at rolling with it. For example, a few days ago, Marcus had gotten some weird bug, and Mrs. King had imposed a strict quarantine. Since Sunday, they had only talked by phone. She missed his smell and his arms around her and the feel of late afternoon stubble against her cheek, but she didn't really mind the occasional break. She liked staying up late, curled into her covers and snuggling with Panda, talking quietly about everything and nothing.

"What's on your bucket list?" Marcus had asked last night, over the phone.

"Um, I don't know. I've never really thought about it. Go to Paris?"

"I want to ride a camel to the pyramids in Giza."

"A cruise would be good."

"Swim in the Dead Sea."

"Skydive, maybe?" she said.

"Have dinner with the president. A photo tour of the Arctic."

"Yours are better than mine."

He laughed. "I lie in bed a lot. I have more time to think about it."

"I want a dog," she added. "When I have my own place. Mom's allergic."

"We used to have a cat. Tanya," he said. "Dad gave her away when I started reacting to the dander."

"Oh. Never mind then. I don't need a dog."

He was quiet a minute. "I'm sorry."

"For what?"

"Being sick. Screwing up your life."

"Because I can't have a dog?"

"It's not fair to you. We've never even been to a movie."

"We've seen plenty at your house. Or started to, at least," she joked. He didn't laugh.

"Okay, sure," she said. "It sucks we can't go to the movies or hang out with my friends. But it sucks more that you have to drink those awful shakes your mother makes. That you're always tired. That you can't eat anything. That's what I really hate."

She knew that he didn't believe her, but it was true. She loved being Marcus King's girlfriend. He made her better. Sometimes she couldn't believe he'd picked her.

It was enough, even if it was only covert late-night phone calls.

All this morning and through school, she felt badly about the conversation. She worried that Marcus worried about her. So this current phone call—which came while she was digging through the fridge—surprised her.

"Whatcha doin'?" he asked playfully.

"Just got home," she said, folding salami slices into her mouth. "You sound better."

"Much better, actually. I'm sprung for the afternoon."

"What do you mean, *sprung*?"

"Want to go somewhere?"

She froze. *This* was the kind of list she'd spent hours on, not some far-flung bucket list. Even so, her mind went blank.

"I was thinking the coffee shop," Marcus said.

"Um . . ." Not her first choice. Not her eighth choice, even.

"My favorite place ever," he said. "Since I met you."

"Well, when you put it like that," she said. "You talked me into it."

"Jackson wants to come, too. Maybe you could bring Ryan? I think they'd get along."

Their first time out, and his brother was coming? She would not be snide. She would not be snide. "See you in twenty minutes."

She went to the backyard, where Trent and Ryan were playing lacrosse one-on-one. "Marcus wants to go to the coffee shop."

Both boys lowered their sticks. "*Marcus* wants to go?" Ryan asked.

"Got a reprieve. Jackson's gracing us with his presence, so you're both coming. I need a buffer."

"This should be interesting," said Trent.

Now here they all were—Ryan and Gwen sharing a beat-up recliner, Fi and Marcus tucked together in the middle of the ratty futon, Trent on her side and Jackson on his. Their first ever group outing.

Bringing along backup was a good idea. The Doyle side outnumbered the King side, and Jackson was acting—*gasp*—the slightest bit friendly. Like he'd gotten caught up in this "big night out" as much as she had.

Curling up even closer to Marcus, getting all snuggly under his arm, Fi looked up at him. Always fair, Marcus looked healthy nonetheless, with a little flush in his cheeks, a crisp look in his eyes. For possibly the eleventh time that night, she said, "You look so good."

He kissed her forehead. "I feel good."

"Dude, you have crazy allergies," Trent said. "There's this girl on the lacrosse team who's allergic to everything, but she still comes to school."

"It's different," Fi said, shooting him a *shut up* glare.

"I tried her gluten-free potato snack sticks once," Trent continued. "Tasted like salted cardboard."

Fi wanted no allergy—intolerance, sensitivity, whatever—talk tonight. "So why the sudden freedom?" she asked, nuzzling more deeply into her cute, cute boyfriend.

"Maybe they just wanted us out of the house," Marcus said, laughing.

Jackson made a gagging noise and put his mug on the table. "Ugh. Gross." Gwen's eyes darted between his mug and him. "Not the coffee," he said. "My parents' sex life."

Marcus did a spit take into his green tea.

"I walked in on my parents when I was ten," Trent said. "Dad said they were wrestling. It scarred me for life."

"I can top it," Gwen said. "Hippie neighbors, in their sixties. Two a.m. naked time in the backyard hot tub every Tuesday."

"Please. Mine's worse," Trent said.

"There are four of them."

And so it went, each person telling a story that had the slightest thing in common with the other's and on and on and on so that no one really knew how they ended up on Marcus's story about the guy who went to Europe with four hundred dollars and still managed to backpack six whole months.

"Another thing for the bucket list," he said, nudging Fi and Jackson at the same time.

Jackson shook his head, his eyes focused on the ceiling.

Fi was about to smack him when Gwen said, "I want to do junior year abroad in Italy. Florence. See Botticelli's *Birth of Venus*. Michelangelo's *David*. Paint there."

Ryan pivoted, brows drawn. "Since when?"

"All my life," she said. "I've told you that."

"Uh, no."

"Uh, yes. It's on the spreadsheet."

"What spreadsheet?" Trent asked.

"All the schools we're applying to." Gwen ticked off her fingers with each item she listed. "We've got columns for art programs, athletic division, scholarship potential, ranking of the business school. Stuff like that."

Ryan's girlfriend must be the only spreadsheet-making painter in existence. Weren't the creative types supposed to be clueless and flighty, always losing their phones and forgetting to put gas in their car?

"It's sorted by distance," Gwen said. "Since we're probably not going to the same place." She nudged Ryan with a small smile. "Not many business-painting-lacrosse schools."

"How does *Italy* affect the distance tabulations?" Ryan asked her.

"It's probably a wash against all the pre- and postseason

training," she said, with a look. "Not to mention the travel games."

"O-kay," Fi said. No public displays of issues tonight. "Who wants something?"

"My break's over, anyway," Gwen said. "I'll get the refills. You two stay here," she added, smiling warmly at Fi and Marcus.

Fi curled back into Marcus. "Looks like my family's not the only one that's crazy," he whispered.

"They really excel at it, though," she said. "Like, maybe the top ten."

He laughed and kissed her on the head.

"Ugh, stop kissing my sister," Ryan grumbled.

Grabbing Marcus's jaw, Fiona brought her boyfriend's face to hers for an inappropriately long and public kiss—that she never got to finish. Jackson groaned, "Good Lord," while Ryan and Trent threw pillows at them.

They pulled away from each other, and Marcus shifted down, propping his feet on the table. He winked at his brother. Fi stuck her tongue out at hers.

"That was a disturbing display of germ-swapping," Trent said.

"You use your sleeve as a Kleenex," Fi said, but regretted it immediately, as Jackson started eyeing Trent's shirt suspiciously.

"So, Jackson," she said, quickly changing the subject. "Have you heard from Northwestern?"

She knew the answer. Marcus told her he'd gotten the letter a few weeks ago.

"I have," he said, like a normal person might. "But I'm deferring a year."

"Why?"

Jackson took a long sip of coffee. "It's just not a great time."

"I thought we talked about this," Marcus said, looking straight ahead, not at his brother.

"I heard your opinion," Jackson said. "I just have a different one."

"It's as good a time as any, Jackson," Marcus answered.

"So then later will work, too."

Fi had been *thrilled* when Marcus said Jackson was going off to school. Even so, she understood Jackson's position. Or what she *guessed* was his position, since he sure as hell wasn't going to tell her about it.

He didn't want to leave Marcus.

Neither did she.

"You can do that?" she asked. "They don't mind?"

Jackson studied her with an expression she couldn't read. "I don't know if they *mind.* But yes, you can do that."

Marcus nudged her. "You can also transfer in—either in the second semester or sophomore year."

"You can only transfer in if they accept you," she said.

"Yes, but they can't accept you when you never apply."

Fi curled in on herself when Marcus said that last bit, making a point of not looking at Ryan or Trent.

"What?" both yelled at the same time.

"You never applied?" Ryan barked.

"Freaking unbelievable," Trent said.

"I'm sorry," said Marcus. "I thought they knew."

"They do now," she muttered against his chest.

For the next five minutes, Trent and Ryan alternated the rant. *Was she crazy? She'd wanted to play for Northwestern since she was fourteen! She took the SATs three times to get the right score. What was all the rehab for? What was all the work for? That coach wanted her, which was a stroke of luck right there. Girls from Virginia and Maryland and New England got those spots, not girls from Memphis. Did she have any idea what kind of opportunity that was? It was the best program in the country!*

"Okay, y'all," Marcus finally said. "I think she got the point."

"You could have interrupted them earlier," she said.

Trent stormed off dramatically. Ryan shook his head in disappointment and followed. "I'm going to get some food," Jackson said, and left as well.

"You okay?" Marcus asked.

She shook her head, not able to talk past the golf-ball-sized lump in her throat. Crying in Otherlands—with Trent and *her* obnoxious brother and *his* obnoxious brother all nearby—was unacceptable.

"I'm sorry," he said again.

She wanted to yell at him, but that would ruin their one night out. "You shouldn't have said anything," she said.

"They're not wrong," he said. "I saw that email. The coach wants you."

"It's too late now. The team's set."

"Maybe not. Maybe whoever else she had in mind for your spot said no. Or got a better offer. You could at least check."

"Are you trying to get rid of me?" Good Lord, now she really was going to cry.

"You sound like Jackson," he said. "And I'll tell you the same thing I've told him. I feel horrible that you're changing your life for me."

"Maybe I'm the girl with the better offer."

"It's not a one-or-the-other, babe." He pointed to the table where they first met. "The first time I saw you, you had an awful pink cast over a horrid compound break, and you still couldn't shut up about lacrosse. And Northwestern. You said it was your *dream*, Fi. How can you not go after it?"

"Because my dream changed."

It wasn't like choosing between the two things she loved more than anything had been easy. The night she'd finally tossed all her NU brochures into the trash, she'd clutched Panda for dear life, like she was a little kid. She'd never cried so hard.

"But you can have both," he said.

She'd spent eight months trying to figure out how to do just that. It was impossible. "It's too late. I missed the deadline, and I already said yes to Milton."

"Just email her and check. One more time." He touched her

cheek. "Let me live vicariously through you."

Fi's heart broke a little when he said that. "Would you apply, too?"

He paused a moment before nodding. "Sure."

She figured he was humoring her. But still, he looked sad when he should be happy. "Okay," she said. "I'll email the coach."

Marcus bloomed into one of his full-face smiles. And without the brothers and best friends to mock them, they got to finish that kiss.

APRIL

FIONA

"Oh, that looks nice. I think it's my favorite so far."

Fiona twisted side to side to get the full angle of this, the fifth dress she'd tried, and looked at her mother through the mirror. Her mom pointed to the dress's hemline and waist. "It shows off your figure."

The dress hit mid-thigh, showing more leg than made her comfortable. But her mother was right about the waist, how it cinched in then flared out. She looked curvier than she really was.

Fiona felt down toward the hem. "You don't think it's too short?"

"Not at all. Might as well show off what you can."

And there it is. Fiona's eyes flicked away from the legs she always covered to the face she never could.

She reached behind her to find the zipper. The dress dropped to the ground, puddling around her ankles. She hopped back into her worn, comfortable jeans and pulled on her hoodie. "I'm not going."

"Why not?" her mother asked with a sigh. The fluorescent lights overhead cast her in an unattractive, orange light.

Fiona shrugged and laced up her Chucks. She couldn't believe David wanted to go to prom. *Prom.*

"I'm not a prom kind of girl," she'd told him. Many times.

"If you go to prom," he'd replied, "you'll be a prom kind of girl."

They'd gone round and round about it for weeks. She felt sort of bad—he hardly ever pushed for anything. But then he should have picked his battle more carefully.

Checking the mirror, she pulled her hair as far forward as possible before walking out of the dressing room. Her mother plucked the dress off the floor.

"I'm buying it," she said, passing the dress to the cashier. "You need to go."

The cashier handed her mom the receipt and the bag, and, with a saccharine smile, turned to Fiona. "That sure is a pretty dress. I bet it looks real nice on you." She spoke slow and clear, like Fiona might have a mental disability.

"It does," her mom said, clueless to the condescension. "She looks lovely in it."

Fiona rolled her eyes and walked through the door. Her mother caught up with her in the parking lot.

"Give me a reason," her mother said. In the natural light,

she looked her usual, beautiful self. "A good reason why you won't go."

"I don't want to."

"Not good enough."

Fiona collapsed into the car, pulling her legs up against her chest. She fiddled with the radio, which her mom promptly turned down.

"What about David?" her mother asked, pulling out of the parking lot.

"David will be fine."

"It's his prom, too, Fiona."

Curse her, she was right. David should get prom if he wanted it—it was just that she *didn't* want it more.

"I'm putting my foot down on this. It's your senior prom."

Fiona slumped further into her seat, hoping this latest attempt to "improve her" would fizzle away if she ignored it long enough.

"So you're going. No discussion."

"What?" Fiona nearly yelled. "You're going to *make* me go to prom?"

"Yes." Her mom pulled into their driveway, turned the car off, and looked at her daughter. "Consider it a favor—I've taken the decision out of your hands, so you might as well go and enjoy yourself."

Too furious with her meddling mother to respond, Fiona slammed the car door and stormed inside, passing Ryan in the upstairs hallway.

"What's wrong with you?"

Fiona flung herself on her bed. "Mom."

He followed her. "She's not that bad."

Fiona had long given up trying to explain her mother's evil powers to Ryan. Testosterone probably blocked his ability to detect it. She'd just wait until he got married—his wife could fill him in. "She's making me go to prom."

Ryan closed the door behind him. Nudging Fiona over, he stretched out beside her on the bed. Lately he'd resumed this little tradition. "Why don't you want to go? Should be fun."

"Ugh. Wearing high heels and acting all couple-y?" The dancing. The pictures. The other girls closely inspecting each other's dresses and hair. "It sounds awful."

Ryan turned sideways. It put Fiona in that too-close, wincing position, so he pulled back a little. "You have to come. Gwen doesn't know a lot of people."

Fiona sighed, cursing the private pledge she'd made to be nicer about Gwen. Then again, she had a suspicion that Fiona-being-nicer-to-Gwen had some correlation with Ryan-being-nicer-to-Fiona, so she kept at it.

"Besides," her brother continued, "you've got to take the chance to get out now, while you still can. Once we get the call, you're out of commission for months."

Once we get the call everything changes. She dragged a pillow over her head and groaned. She wasn't sure when she'd made the transition from, "I'm on an *organ transplant list!*" to "When the hell is it going to be my turn already?"

"We're never going to get that call," she said.

"Sure we will."

She tossed the pillow at him, which he easily deflected. It plopped to the floor, a single feather lighter. The little white wisp of down took its time floating into Ryan's hair.

She reached over and plucked it out. "I'm cosmetic. I'll never be at the top of the list."

He shrugged, unconcerned. "How many people could possibly need *skin*?"

In the end, Fiona was not strong enough to fight all the battles. Her parents, Ryan, Gwen, even Lucy—whose opinion, Fiona argued, shouldn't count since she wasn't going to prom herself—bugged her so much that she caved. "*Fine*. I'll go," she said. "But I'm not going to have fun."

David was not brought into the debate.

Since Fiona didn't have the slightest idea how to make herself cute, Ryan was banished to the first floor while she and Gwen got ready together. Lucy came over for moral support—and to mock them.

"Can I do your hair?" Gwen asked. "Mine's too short for anything fun."

"When did you dye it pink?"

"Last night. With all the work I put into resewing that dress, I figured my hair should match it." The dress she'd bought thrifting hung on Fiona's closet door. With its asymmetrical hemline and off-the-shoulder sleeves, it looked nothing like the boring, poufy thing she'd shown them at the coffee shop a few weeks ago.

"That's the coolest dress ever," Lucy said.

Gwen curtsied and pointed Fiona to a chair. "What about like this?" she asked, pulling Fiona's long wavy hair all the way back.

"Uh, I like the bangs down. On the right."

"Oh. Yeah, sorry." Gwen dropped the hair, and it fell over Fiona's face like a curtain. "I always forget."

"Forget?"

"About the scars."

"Don't even bother," Lucy said, rolling her eyes. She sat at Fiona's feet, opening a bottle of sparkly blue nail polish. "She won't believe you."

"Well, it's true," Gwen said, pulling and twisting all the while. "They just go away, once you get used to them."

They just go away, do they?

"Hey! Easy," Lucy said, poking Fiona's hand where it now clenched the armrest.

Lucy caught Fiona's eye and held it. Through her stare, Fiona communicated the injustice of Gwen's thoughtless comment. Lucy just gave a slow, warning shake of her head. "You mess up my first and only manicure," she told Fiona, "and I'll kill you."

"Um," Gwen said, looking back and forth between Fiona and Lucy. "What I meant was, I don't see them, you know? I just see Fiona."

"I totally agree," Lucy said.

"I can do something like this instead," Gwen said. She held Fiona's hair in messy sections, so the side bangs covered all the bits they were meant to.

Fiona took in a breath and released her death grip on the chair. A fight with Gwen would mean a fight with Ryan, which she didn't want. "Sure, whatever."

Gwen improved her by curling iron, while Lucy painted her nails—fingers *and* toes. It was like a montage from a bad movie—*here's where the ugly girl bonds with her friends and learns that everyone has beauty in them somewhere.*

An hour later, she was *finally* ready. Somehow Gwen managed to get most of her hair back, while long, loose curls hung in front of her scars. She looked polished, sure, but she didn't want to give the impression she'd really *tried.*

The doorbell rang before she could mess it all up.

"David's here." Her mother came in, all smiles.

Here's where the mother gets teary-eyed and says "Oh, you've grown into such a young lady!"

"You both look lovely," her mom said, looking from Gwen to Fiona.

Fiona muttered thanks. "Isn't her hair pretty?" Gwen said, gesturing to Fiona.

Her mom nodded. "It is."

Her eyes are glistening.

"Let's get this over with," Fiona said, clomping down the stairs in as unladylike a manner as possible.

It felt silly, how Ryan, David, and her father beamed up at her and Gwen as they came downstairs. Mr. Doyle kissed her head, his eyes glistening, too.

"You look really pretty," David said.

Fiona picked at her dress. "You don't have to say—Ow!"

Lucy stood beside her, pinching her arm. "Just say thank you," she hissed.

"Thank you," Fiona mumbled.

Five painful minutes later, Fiona, David, Ryan, and Gwen left the house, blinking from the camera flashes. Fiona and David slid in the backseat, Ryan and Gwen up front. Her brother couldn't keep his eyes off Gwen—or wipe that stupid grin off his face.

"I like your dress," David said.

Fiona frowned down at herself. "It's not too much?"

He wrapped his hand in hers. "No. It's nice."

Prom was at The Peabody, a fancy old hotel downtown—grand piano, enormous lobby fountain, gilded ceiling, the works. In the ballroom, Fiona and David caught up with friends, and she couldn't help herself from taking part in the ritual she had dreaded. *Yes, I love your dress. Your hair looks great like that. Your earrings are awesome.* When David wanted to get pictures, she didn't argue, just let him drag her around. When she wanted to dance, he did the same.

Halfway in, when David pleaded for a break, they wandered to the refreshment table. David got her a drink and excused himself for the bathroom. Fiona waited for him, and someone tapped her on the shoulder.

"Looking good, partner."

Oh, how easily the traitorous flutters returned. Trying to keep her cool, she gestured to Trent's tux. "You too. Who knew a gentleman was hiding under that lacrosse uniform?"

Trent laughed. "Don't tell anybody."

"Secret's safe with me," she said. Where had she kept this easygoing banter hidden all these years? It could have come in handy.

He took a sip of punch. "Heard you're going to Northwestern."

His eyes should be illegal. She nodded. "You?"

"Ole Miss. Not the greatest lacrosse team, but they gave me money, and it's only an hour away."

And full of girls who will admire you from afar. "That's cool," she said.

"I should get back. Just wanted to say hey."

"Hey." She put forth her best smile.

"Hey," he repeated, smiling back. "By the way, your hair looks good like that."

Okay, Gwen is forgiven. David walked up, and Trent gave him a friendly nod. "Don't lose touch with the soil, Doyle," he said and walked away.

"What did he want?" David asked.

"To say hey," Fiona answered. She cast a last look in Trent's direction before finishing her drink and dragging

David—*your boyfriend,* she reminded herself—back onto the dance floor.

Juniors and seniors crammed the dance floor until the band left the stage. By the end of the night, nearly every one of them was a sweaty mess.

When it was time to go, Ryan smirked at her. "Well, look who had fun."

She shoved him. "It wasn't terrible."

David's arm snaked around her waist, pulling her back against his chest. "What wasn't terrible?"

"I'll get Gwen," Ryan said. "Meet you at the car in ten minutes."

"What wasn't terrible?" David repeated, spinning her around to face him.

"Nothing. Brother-sister thing."

David eyed her for a moment before leaning in to kiss her.

Fiona wasn't an advocate of public kissing—unlike Ryan and Gwen—but she'd already thrown all her other rules out the window. So she wrapped her arms around David's neck and kissed him back.

FI

Ryan eyed his watch. "Fi, I gotta get Gwen."

Fi clenched her jaw and glared at the clock on the mantel. They'd planned this *for a month*. Prom would be huge and public, and it took Marcus weeks to convince his parents. After all that, he just *forgot*? "Where the hell *is* he?" she said.

"Language, Fi." Her mom sat beside her, realigning the pleats on her dress. "Are you sure he knew the right time?"

Fi held up her phone, showing her mother the string of Prom Planning texts.

From two days ago:

Fi: Be here at six and the three of us will get Gwen.

Marcus: K

Fi: I plan on looking awesome.

Marcus: I too shall look awesome.

From yesterday:

Marcus: Mom says I'm supposed to know the color of your dress?

Fi: Pink, but not pink-pink, more like melon.

Marcus: Cantaloupe¿

Fi: Is that the pink kind¿

Marcus: And the delicious kind.

Fi: You can eat cantaloupe¿

Marcus: Can and do. See you tomorrow at six.

From today:

Fi: I was right. I look awesome.

Fi: Forgot to tell you—there's a party after. Think you can go¿

Fi: This isn't like a wedding. We're allowed to talk.

Fi: Where are you¿

In addition to the texts, she'd called him five times. She never got an answer.

Shaking his head, Ryan grabbed the keys from the table. "Sorry, Fi—I need to go."

"Go on. Have fun," their dad said.

Fi got up and paced the length of the living room, saying "Where *is* he¿" over and over.

"It's certainly not like him," said her mom. "I'm sure there's a reasonable explanation."

Fi was about to say *someone better have died* when her phone rang. Glimpsing Marcus's name on caller ID, she lunged for it. "Where are you¿"

"It's Jackson."

"Jackson," she snapped, furious. "This is my *prom*. Do you have to mess with it¿"

"Marcus asked me to call. He's in the hospital." He named

the hospital and room number. "Visiting hours end in forty-five minutes, so if you want to see him, you better get down here."

He hung up. She stared blankly at her phone before relaying Jackson's message to her parents. They assaulted her with questions—*Why? What happened? Is he okay?*

Fi had no answers, so the three of them drove to the hospital to get some.

Once at the hospital, her mom took over, and Fi said a rare prayer of thanks for her mother's bossy streak. After getting directions to the room and leading the way, she paused in front of Marcus's door and pointed to a seating area down the hall. "We'll be down there," her mom said. "Take your time."

Numbly, Fi pushed open the heavy wooden door, behind which a paler than normal Marcus lay on the bed. Tubes snaked between him and the three beeping machines at his side. He smiled sadly. "So that's what a cantaloupe dress looks like."

She looked down at herself. She totally forgot she was dressed for prom.

"I'm so sorry I messed up tonight." He gestured for her to come closer. "You look beautiful."

A stupid dance was the least of her worries. "What's going on? Why are you in here?"

"It's not a big deal. They just want to run some tests. I'd hoped to push it off. I mean, it's your *senior prom*." He groaned this last bit, talking more to the ceiling than her. Then he frowned at his tubes. "I was overruled."

"Did you eat something you're not supposed to?"

"Uh, not exactly," he muttered.

Okay, somewhere, she'd missed a critical piece of information. "Why do you need tests?"

Just then, the door swung open, and Jackson walked in. He gave the briefest of nods in her direction before turning to Marcus. "Results won't come till Monday. You have to stay."

Marcus groaned. "That's two nights. Seriously?"

"Well, maybe it wouldn't be two nights," Jackson barked, "if you mentioned *feeling like crap* a little earlier."

Marcus held up a hand to interrupt him, then winced.

Fi jumped. "Are you okay?"

Marcus held out both hands, slowly, as if to say *Stay calm.* "I'm fine. It's just the IV. It tugged on my skin."

Fi tracked the line of the tube dangling from his skin to the clear plastic bag suspended over his head. "Why do you have an IV?"

"Standard procedure, I think."

It was like she'd walked out of a movie and come back ten minutes after the good guy figured out who the bad guy was. "Standard procedure *for what?*"

"For heart failure," Jackson answered.

She shrieked "What?" as Marcus snapped, "Leave it alone, Jackson."

Jackson ignored his brother and spoke directly to Fi. "There's this *little thing* Marcus hasn't told you. He's dying."

Fi fell back in her chair, looking at Marcus. "You're—"

"Jackson's just being dramatic. As usual," he sighed. "I'm not dying."

Jackson flopped into the chair on the other side of the bed. Casually, he propped his feet on the bed frame and tipped himself backward. "Whatever gets you through the night, brother."

If Jackson would just leave, Marcus could explain everything. Trying to ignore him, she asked Marcus, "Please tell me what's going on."

Marcus reached for her hand. She leaned closer and gave it to him. "I should have told you. I'm sorry. I just—I didn't want to worry you and there's nothing we can do until—well, until we can do something. So I, uh, left it out of our conversations."

"You left it out?" she whispered back.

He gave the same apologetic shrug he used when he ate the last piece of vegan, gluten-free pizza without asking, like these two things were similar. "About four years ago, I got an infection. It was a fluke thing, probably from food."

"Like food you weren't supposed to eat?"

"No, like food poisoning. I didn't have the food stuff till after I got sick. The infection kind of wrecked my immune system."

"Food poisoning gave you allergies?"

"They aren't allergies. It's intolerance."

Fi waved away the distinction, since it just didn't matter anymore. "What's this got to do with your heart?"

"Well, the infection didn't just wreck my immune system. It weakened my heart, too. The muscle. It's called cardiomyopathy."

"But—you're eighteen."

"It happens," he said, shrugging. "And it makes me short of breath. Tired. Not very hungry. The food intolerance just seemed like an easier way to explain it." He said this last bit with guilty, puppy-dog eyes.

"Easier?" Fi asked.

"Yeah," Jackson said. "*I have a heart condition* is really tricky."

Fi glanced to Jackson, too stunned to glare. She shook her head slowly back and forth. "I had no idea."

"Not very observant, are you?"

"Shut up, Jackson," Marcus said. He looked at Fi. "Don't listen to him. It's my fault. I should have told you."

"Why didn't you?" she asked, quietly this time, regretting bringing Jackson into the conversation.

Marcus took a deep breath, his eyes on their hands. "When I got sick—I mean, when it progressed to my heart and the doctors figured it out—my parents flipped out. When the doctors said this all might have started from food, Mom became Queen of All Things Organic. When they said my immune system was weak, Mom and Dad pulled me out of school to reduce exposure. You've seen how everyone reacts about hands and germs."

He pointed to Jackson, who maintained his cool expression during Marcus's speech. "Even Jackson dropped out of school, so he wouldn't rub up against any sick people."

"I didn't *drop out*," Jackson replied.

"Fine. He *joined me in homeschool*," he said.

"It wasn't just because of exposure."

Marcus took another long breath before looking back to Fi. His smile looked falsely reassuring. "The past four years—before I met you—my life was about avoiding. Avoiding certain foods. Avoiding overexertion. Avoiding anything that could get me sick."

"But—" Fi paused, thinking through the information. "You don't avoid me. And I go everywhere."

"Yes, you do," Jackson answered.

"Can't you find somewhere else to be?" Marcus growled.

"Mom told me to wait here."

Fi noticed the IV tugging at Marcus's skin as he rubbed his temples, so she gently pulled his hands back down. "It's fine. Just talk to me."

He smiled weakly, his thumb circling around the back of Fi's hand. "That day at the coffee shop—I wasn't even supposed to be there. Mom sure as hell was against it, but Jackson had been to their open mic night, and it sounded fun. I'd been feeling good for a few weeks, so I just left with Jackson before she could really get into arguing. And, well, you know the rest."

Fi pointed at the bed. "Clearly I don't."

"I'm sorry. I know I should have told you, but it was so, I don't know, *refreshing* being around people who just knew me as Marcus King, Fi's boyfriend, rather than Marcus King, sick kid. It was like having a different life." Looking straight at Jackson, he snarled, "It gets exhausting, being surrounded by people who constantly remind me how freaking fragile I am."

"Fragile's better than dead," Jackson said. He turned hard eyes on Fi. "All that time he spent with you and your family. Do you have any idea how dangerous that was?"

Fi blanched. "I didn't know. He never told me."

"I'm right here, y'all," Marcus said.

Fi looked back at him and, knowing she probably sounded like an idiot, asked, "So, what's heart failure exactly? What's that mean?"

"It means his doesn't work anymore," Jackson answered. "He needs somebody else's."

"And then he'll be better?"

Jackson let his chair fall back forward. The wood legs made a crack against the tile floor. He leaned over, his forehead in his elbows, and spoke facing the ground. All the sarcasm left him. "That's the theory."

"Again, right here," Marcus said.

"Yes," Fi snapped, suddenly furious at her *perfect boyfriend*. "But you don't tell me anything!"

Jackson looked up at her. His green eyes were bloodshot and shadowed. For once, he looked more exhausted than annoyed.

He was right, she'd been clueless. All the signs! How Marcus couldn't walk far without getting out of breath, how thin he was—and getting thinner, she hadn't failed to notice. How much he slept.

Someone grunted from the other side of the heavy door, which jerked forward once then fell back closed. On the other side, Mrs. King snapped, "Jackson, help me!"

Jackson opened the door, and Mrs. King walked in, her arms full of books and magazines. Nudging most of these into Jackson's arms, she turned to the bed. Once she noticed Fi, a slow, creeping smile appeared from sheer will. It was like an approximation of happiness.

Mrs. King's eyes darted toward Fi's and Marcus's hands entwined together across Marcus's chest, and the smile faltered. Fi wondered if, over the years, Mrs. King had learned how to see harmful microbes with the naked eye.

"Fi, good to see you," she said. Sad eyes traveled down Fi ever so briefly. "Your dress is lovely. We're so sorry about your prom."

Fi looked down at the bright, melon-colored dress. She felt ridiculous. "It's fine."

The door swung open yet again, this time pushed by Marcus's father. At the sight of Fi, he stopped short, as his wife had. "Well, Fi, you look beautiful."

Jackson looked just like his father—tall, dark, and broad-shouldered. Marcus was so *thin* compared to them.

Suddenly, Fi's hands started shaking, and her voice left her.

He was *sick*. But surely . . . was he really *dying*? Her entire body shaking now, she sank into the chair.

"Um." Marcus gave her a worried look before looking at his family. "Secret's out."

"We wanted him to tell you, sweetheart," Mrs. King said. "But he didn't want to—"

"Can I just go home now?" Marcus asked as Fi wiped tears from her cheeks.

"No, you cannot," snapped his mother. "You have to wait until Dr. Frank releases you, which he will not do until the results come back on Monday."

"I already told him that," Jackson said.

"If you would have mentioned something last week," Mr. King added. "When you started feeling off—"

"I told him that, too."

"Shush," Mrs. King said, smacking Jackson on the shoulder. Then she gave Fi a worried look—and another forced smile. "Fi, I passed your parents in the hall just now, and didn't so much as nod. Let Mr. King, Jackson, and I go say hello."

She threw her purse back over her shoulder, grabbed her husband with one hand and Jackson with another, and left the room.

Fi stared at the closed door. She'd always assumed Marcus's family was just over-the-top crazy. Turned out they were normal, and she was under-a-rock clueless.

"I'm sorry," Marcus said.

The anger snuck up on her. "For what?" she snapped. "Being bedridden? Or lying to me?"

He clenched his jaw. "I'm not an invalid."

She pointed at the tubes surrounding him. "That's debatable."

"This is exactly why I didn't tell you," he said. "I eat some bad chicken when I'm fourteen, and everything goes into lockdown. All these rules and precautions—what I can eat, where I can go, how to *wash*. I'm being slowly strangled by good intentions."

He dropped her hand and cast an angry look out the window. "I just want to be normal. I want to be eighteen. And then nineteen and twenty-five and forty and eighty, just like everybody else."

"But you're not." Fi knew it wasn't what she *should* say, but she said it anyway.

"I was until you found out."

"Lying to me doesn't make it go away!"

"I don't need you to point that out, Fi," he snapped. "I *know* I can't go up a flight of stairs without getting light-headed. That I can't go four hours without a nap. I'm not trying to hide from it. I just want to live outside of it sometimes."

"Everything was fake then. *We're* not even real."

"Yes we are!" he shouted, sitting up quickly. The machines began a furious round of pinging.

"Marcus, stop! Lay back down!"

He collapsed back, breathing heavy. Her hands still shook, but she grabbed his. They were frighteningly cold.

"I don't want you to die," she said, crying.

"I'm not going to die," he said.

"Do you promise?"

With a small smile, he nodded.

"What has to happen?" she asked.

"Well, we're still trying to figure that out. I'm on medication now. But a new heart would help."

"Is that hard to get? A heart?"

"I'm O negative, which makes it a little harder. But I'm on the list."

They stared at each other a little bit after that, Fi perched on the edge of her chair; Marcus reclined on the semi-upright bed. Their hands stayed clenched together in Marcus's lap.

"I'm so mad at you," she said.

"I know," he said. "I'll make it up to you. I promise."

"Don't die. That'll make it up to me."

"I'm not going to die," he said again.

"So what do we do now?"

"Wait, pretty much."

"Well, how long can you, you know, wait?"

His fingers still tracing lazy patterns against the back of her hand, he said, "Don't worry. It'll be fine."

But that wasn't really an answer.

MAY

FIONA

Mrs. Doyle peeked her head into Fiona's room. "Almost packed?"

Pretending like this wasn't the biggest, scariest thing she'd ever done, Fiona calmly gestured to the clothes on the bed—sweatpants and some button-down shirts she stole from Ryan. "I think so. I won't need much, right?"

Her mother looked at the piles on the bed. "You'll be in a hospital gown most of the time. Underwear. Socks. The button-downs are a good idea." She looked at Fiona's desk. "Do you have anything to read?"

Fiona tossed a few books and a Moleskine into the bag, folding the clothes on top. She looked over at her guitar resting in the corner. She felt like a mother abandoning a child. "Yeah, but I probably won't get the chance. It sounds like the bandage will be pretty big."

Perching on the end of the bed, her mom patted the space

beside her. Fiona eyed her warily but sat. "We don't have much time, Mom. They want me there in an hour."

"I know. I just wanted to talk a minute."

Fiona stiffened. "Okay. What about?"

After a long, slow exhale, her mother spoke to the wall across the room. "You don't have to do this, you know. You can change your mind."

Fiona looked at her mother. "What? I thought you wanted—"

"What I want doesn't matter. What do *you* want?"

"I want this."

"It's a major procedure, Fiona. It could be great, but there's always a risk."

"I know that."

Her mom nodded slowly. "You have great instincts, you know. Not many kids your age have that." She laughed a little. "Not many adults have that."

Fiona stared hard at her mother, looking for signs of illness, head trauma, alien abduction. "Are you okay?"

"I'm just worried. My little girl is going into surgery."

Fiona shook her head, confused. "It's the miracle cure you've always wanted. I'm getting fixed."

Her mom gave her a weird, sideways look. "When did you get so brave?"

Brave? The girl who sat mute in the coffee shop? "Mom, we don't have a lot of time."

Being a scarred girl with a beautiful mother pretty much

sucked. It happened all the time—teachers, other kids at school, even her mom's own friends would tell Fiona things like "She couldn't be old enough to be your mother," or "Your mom's so *pretty*." And then the complimenter would look suddenly mortified, like *Oh no, I've called attention to this poor girl's unfortunate condition.*

So Fiona dressed like a boy and wore her hair in her face, like she couldn't have cared less about the "beauty" thing. Even though deep, deep down, she *did* care. She carried around her vanity like a secret, shameful addiction.

Now some twisted form of fate offered a new option—with conditions.

One: acknowledge her secret vanity. Two: sacrifice part of herself.

And she said yes.

Then she spent months of waiting for—she was horrible—someone to just go ahead and die already.

Now, hours before she was going to do this thing that took twelve years to happen, her mother was, once again, making the fight impossible to win.

"I still want to do it," Fiona said.

"All right." Her mother kissed her forehead and stood up. "The timing really couldn't be better, could it? Two days after graduation, with the whole summer to heal?"

"Yeah." *Very thoughtful of this person to die so conveniently.*

"Don't forget your toothbrush," her mom said. "Meet you downstairs in five minutes."

The next three hours, Fiona sat in no less than seven deceptively hard upholstered chairs and answered the same questions over and over again—*Nothing to eat since breakfast. No prescription drugs. No other history of illness.* Her hand ached from signing all the forms. She nodded as doctors went through the organ transplant rules again and again. She got her blood pressure taken at least three times and smiled falsely at all the nurses who smiled genuinely at her.

She was trapped in a cycle of administrative hell when all she wanted was to move forward already.

Finally, doctor number three gave Fiona the all clear to go back for prep. An enormous male nurse, hunched slightly to reach the handlebars of the wheelchair in front of him, told Fiona to "Saddle up and bring your posse with you."

Looking gray, her father picked up her bags while her mother gathered all the forms together into neat piles. Ryan stood statue-still, a deer in the headlights.

Craning her neck up to the ginormous smiling nurse behind her, Fiona asked, "What do they do back in prep?"

"You'll get changed, we'll sterilize the area, start fluids in the IV for anesthesia—"

Fiona looked at Ryan. "You can wait in the room. It's okay."

Ryan tried—and failed—to look calm. "Don't be stupid. Of course I'm coming."

"Ryan—"

He held up a hand. "I should be there. I need to be there."

"Why? To watch me get poked with needles?"

Ryan wobbled and leaned against the wall. The enormous nurse took a few steps toward him, hands held up like he might need to catch Ryan at any moment.

Fiona shook her head. "Lord, you're pathetic. You don't have to come."

"No. It's okay, I'll come."

Their mom took over, loading all the bags—Fiona's suitcase, a tote bag of magazines and books, her own overnight bag—into Ryan's arms. "The point is moot, Ryan. I need you to handle all these. Take everything to Fiona's room and stay there until we come."

"But—"

Mrs. Doyle snapped, "I can't manage everything, Ryan. Just do it, please."

With loaded arms, Ryan walked over to Fiona and kissed the top of her head. "See you soon. Good luck."

Then the giant nurse took charge, pushing Fiona from the room and leaving the pack-muled Ryan behind. Her parents followed, the lot of them heading down a cold, white hallway. Buzzing overhead fluorescent lights provided background music for the world's smallest, most stressed-out parade.

She looked over her shoulder to her mother. "Thanks for sparing Ryan."

Mrs. Doyle winked her right eye. Fiona wondered if a few weeks from now, she'd be able to do that, too.

Prep took a long time. Fiona answered the same questions,

this time in a hospital gown and from a bed. Nurses swabbed her face at least four times. She watched, fascinated and repulsed, as the skinny needle poked through the surface of her flesh and sank in—her first, and hopefully last, IV. She fiddled with the bed controls, when they finally left her alone. The bed grinded and whirred as it followed her fickle commands—up, down, back, forward, high, low—until her mother groaned at her to stop.

The surgeon and anesthesiologist were the next crew to ask the exact same questions as the nurses already had. The anesthesiologist went through her shpiel—risks of side effects and death, et cetera, et cetera. Her dad turned an as-yet-undiscovered shade of gray.

What the hell am I doing?

Numbly, Fiona nodded that she understood, and the anesthesiologist calmly clicked another bag onto the IV stand over her head. "This should make you feel a little spacey," she said, injecting something directly into the IV line.

"It's so smooth," Fiona said. The world swirled around itself, and reality went two-dimensional—the last moment she'd recall of her scarred life.

Blinking her one free eye against the—really, did it have to be that bright?—overhead glare, Fiona thought her parents' faces might split apart from the grins.

From somewhere out of her line of vision, Ryan said, "Jesus, she looks terrible."

"Ryan, shush," snapped their mom. "She just got out of surgery. What did you think she'd look like?"

"Not like a freaking mummy," he muttered back.

Fiona tried to lift a hand to feel the bandages, but her father's hand gently pressed it back down. "Don't touch, sweetie."

Fiona wanted to snap back that she wasn't five, but the drugs wouldn't let her voice out of her throat.

The next twenty-four hours passed in an unpredictable in-and-out, with the *in* not much more than thwarted attempts to scratch at bandages and grunts for more pain medication. It wasn't until solidly into day two that a reasonably clearheaded Fiona opened her single available eye to a bright new day streaming through the window. Ryan sat in front of it, doing a bored flip through their mother's *Southern Living*.

"Hey," Fiona muttered.

"Hey, stoner." Ryan smiled back.

"Was I bad?"

"Nah. Lots of babbling. And whining. *Oh, the pain, the pain.* You're such a wimp." His smirk faded to a look of concern. "Does it really hurt?"

Fiona pushed herself up slightly, wincing. "It's not too bad."

Ryan didn't look like he believed her.

"How's it look?" Fiona asked.

He frowned and shrugged. "Couldn't say. You're still covered with bandages. The doctors have come in and changed them, but I, uh—"

"*I'm* the wimp? You left, didn't you?"

"Well, they say it'll take a few weeks for the graft to take anyway. It doesn't look good right now."

"It doesn't?" she asked, a little panicked.

"No, that's not what I meant. The doctor says it went great. He says you'll be better than new."

"Oh." *Better than new.* What the heck did that mean?

"Yeah. Great, right? Worth a few months of bandages."

Fiona didn't bother to bring up the excruciating pain, the itch of stitches, or the freakiness of wearing someone else's skin. "You're awfully confident for someone who hasn't actually seen it."

"It's just, well, I mean, it doesn't look like regular skin, yet. It's too, uh, fresh."

A rolling table rested at the end of her bed, suspended just over her feet. Fiona wondered if she should offer Ryan the pea-green vomit bucket sitting on top of it. "Are there lesions?" she goaded. "Any discharge?"

"Please, stop." Ryan looked like he might faint.

Fiona pointed to the mirror on the table. Ryan handed it to her, watching as she studied herself.

Bandages covered the right side of her face, neck to hairline, including her right eye and entire nose. Her hair sat in a greasy mat on her head, and what little skin did show looked slightly jaundiced. "I look *terrible*."

"Oh, please, nobody cares," Ryan said, rolling his eyes.

"Stop being such a prima donna."

Fiona glared at him with one eye. "Pus. Ooze."

Ryan smacked his hands over his ears as the surgeon came through the door. Her parents followed right behind.

When the surgeon started peeling back the bandage, Ryan asked, "Anybody want anything?" and walked out of the room before Fiona or her parents had a chance to answer. The hospital room door didn't make a sound as it slowly closed.

Everything hurt—peeling off the tape, lifting the bandage, gently testing the sutures, and inspecting the graft. The surgeon asked her a few questions along the lines of *Can you feel this? What about this?* Fiona was used to a dull, awkward throb in her cheek, but this was *pain*—white-hot and searing along the border of what was hers and what was borrowed.

Putting on a new dressing, the doctor said he was pleased with it so far. Everything looked great; the match couldn't have been better; she was healing nicely. He wanted her to stay a few days more, but after that she could recover at home.

"She's due at Northwestern in mid-September," her mother said. "Should we defer it a semester?"

The doctor shook his head. "Shouldn't be a problem. That's a solid sixteen weeks. The stitches will be long gone. She'll have a scar around the edge, which should fade with time but might never fully go away. She'll still be experiencing numbness in the area." He looked at Fiona. "We talked about that, how you might not ever get total feeling in the graft. Do you remember?"

Fiona nodded—then winced. Her hand automatically went to her face, but the doctor caught it and brought it back down.

"Don't touch it." He looked back to her mother. "She's handling it great, though. I won't give the all clear for a few more weeks, but I don't see any reason to keep Fiona from her life any longer than we need to."

FI

It had been five days.

The world had been Marcusless for five days.

Fi hesitated at the back of the church. Standing on her right side, her mother leaned and whispered, "Where do you want to sit?"

Nowhere. I want to go home. "I don't care," she answered.

Her mother pointed the lot of them to a pew in the back. Just as they began to shuffle in, a boy Fi had never met before tugged on her arm. "Are you Fi Doyle?"

She nodded.

He smiled. "I'm Will, his cousin. Aunt Ellen told me to find you. They want you up front."

"Oh." Fi gestured to her family—and to Gwen and Trent, who she guessed counted as family, too. "My parents? And—"

"Yeah. Y'all come on."

They followed Will the Cousin up front. So many people

were crammed into this small, sacred space. Hundreds of people she didn't know were saying good-bye to the boy she knew best.

Fi sat between her mother and Trent. Her mom pulled her close, until Fi's chin rested on her shoulder. Tucking into her mother reminded her of Marcus. But then, everything reminded her of Marcus.

Trent sat on the other side of her, solid and breathing. She hated him just a little for it.

The organ started playing, and what was left of the King family—mother, father, Jackson—processed up. The people she didn't know came to the pulpit, one after another, telling wonderful stories about Marcus. She thought about her own stories: Marcus telling her jokes over the phone; Marcus beating her at Scrabble—and then throwing the game; Marcus protecting her from *Cujo,* as she hid her face against his chest during the first, and only, horror movie they watched; Marcus kissing her; Marcus lying beside her, dragging his hands through her hair.

She wished her final memory of him was different—something funny or kind or adorable—not of a bony, nearly colorless boy, mumbling under a haze of drugs and unable to get out of bed.

She stared at the metal urn on the altar. Now he was only memories and the contents of a jar.

Back when Fi naively believed Marcus's bucket list conversations were purely philosophical—not because he really needed to *think this thing out*—he'd said he wanted to be "picked clean and burned up." At the time, she was horrified. Now she understood what he meant. He wanted to give whatever useful bits he had left to someone else. He'd spent the last part of his life waiting for the same favor.

She didn't realize she'd been crying until the service ended. Her mother gently nudged her upright, and Fi saw the dark wet of her mother's silk shoulder. "Sorry."

Her mom waved her off. "Come on. We have to go to the reception."

"We do?" Fi eyed the church of strangers, not sure if anyone here knew who she was.

"We do."

They piled into the Doyles' minivan, and her dad followed a line of cars to the Kings' house.

In all the hours Fi had spent in this house, she'd never seen anyone here besides Mr. and Mrs. King, Jackson, and Marcus. Marcus had mentioned he had cousins, aunts, and uncles in town, but she'd only seen them in pictures.

His family's antisocial tendencies always felt strange to her. Her own parents knew *everybody*. The Doyles couldn't go to dinner, the grocery store, the gym without running into someone they knew from work or growing up here or just because he was somebody else's sister's husband's cousin or something.

The Kings, however, were a little insulated family island, and as far as she knew, she was the only visitor. So when her family trailed her into the Kings' house for the reception, everything felt wrong. There was no odd smell from Mrs. King's homemade herbal remedies. All the lights were on. The place was packed with people.

Marcus would have loved it.

She burst into tears. Ryan grabbed a chair and helped her into it, while Trent knelt by her with a tissue. She hated making a scene, but she couldn't keep it in.

"You need anything?"

With a hiccup, Fi swallowed the latest round of sobs and looked up at Jackson. He stood in front of her, looking annoyed, flustered, and exhausted all at once. She stood, too, wiping her cheeks with her palms. She would not have Jackson looking down on her. She would not be weak with him.

"I'll be fine," she said. They were still by the door—Fi hadn't even made it four steps inside before breaking down.

He pointed over his shoulder to the back of the house. "There's food and stuff back there."

Food. This place never had normal food just sitting out, where Marcus might accidentally inhale dairy. "Okay."

The two stared at each other, and Fi wasn't sure what to do. Her mother broke the tension. "Jackson, I am so sorry for your loss," she said, placing her hand on his arm.

Jackson looked at Mrs. Doyle's hand on his arm and then at Mrs. Doyle. "Thanks."

"Marcus was . . . well, he was wonderful, wasn't he?"

Jackson stepped backward. "I should check in with my parents."

Mrs. Doyle brought her hand away from Jackson, resting it on Fi's back instead. "Of course," her mom said.

"Still a charmer, isn't he?" Trent muttered as Jackson walked away.

"Shush." Gwen poked him in the side. "His brother just died."

Trent shrugged, and Fi sank back into her chair. She wasn't there long before Will the Cousin came looking for her. "Aunt Ellen and Uncle Peter wanted you to come back to the family room. Meet some of the family—if you're up to it."

"Of course," she said, faking her mother's calm.

The group of them walked through the house, Will fielding some pats on the shoulder as they went. In the family room, Fi stalled in front of the photos.

She'd always loved this room, how all four walls were covered in pictures—big ones, little ones, black-and-white, color—all hung with no particular pattern, just a chaos of family memories. Nearly all were from at least four years ago, when Marcus was still let out of the house.

"He was such a cute baby," Mrs. King said, standing beside her.

Fi pointed to one of Marcus and Jackson together. Their arms were looped around each other's shoulders, like they might choke each other with brotherly affection. "How old are they?"

"Six? Maybe that's the zoo?" She tapped the frame, her finger lingering on the space over Marcus's shoulder. "That looks like a cage, doesn't it?" Shaking her head, she scanned the wall of photos. "There are so many here. It's hard to remember each one."

"They were adorable."

Mrs. King nodded, smiling. "Couldn't keep them apart."

Fi looked over her shoulder to Jackson, who stood in a corner, his hand wrapped around the back of his neck as he stared out the window. "Will he be all right?"

Mrs. King followed Fi's gaze and sighed. "I hope so."

Fi felt the tears burning in her eyes, her throat. Even though meeting Marcus's family would be the polite, proper thing—what her mother would do—Fi pointed to the sliding glass doors against the rear wall. "I might go get some air."

"Take your time," said Mrs. King. "Do you want to take some food out with you?"

Fi looked at the dining room table, loaded with hams and casseroles and brownies. "It's so weird seeing all that out."

"Believe me, it's taking all my restraint not to throw it out the window and bleach the table."

Despite everything, Fi laughed. Mrs. King did, too. It was only a second, though, before both petered out, like they simultaneously remembered there was nothing funny left, ever.

Fi pointed toward the sliding doors again. "I think I'll just, you know, sit."

Fi pushed and pulled at the door handle, trying to force the panels open. Jackson came over, finally, reached past her hand and flicked the lock. She nearly fell into him as the glass door suddenly slid open.

Blushing, Fi wiped her hands on her skirt and mumbled, "Thanks."

He nodded and went back to his vigil at the window.

Even though it was hot, Fi was glad for the fresh air, for the white noise of traffic rather than the droning sadness inside. There were a few chairs and a wrought-iron table in the center of the deck, but Fi walked to the steps and sat down. She and Marcus had never spent much time in the backyard. His mother was paranoid that a vicious strain of attack pollen would do him in.

He'd even said that exact thing a few months ago, when the trees had started to bloom and Fi was itching to get out of his stuffy house. She'd laughed at the joke.

Joke was on her.

It was a good backyard, too, with a huge magnolia right in the center—the best kind of climbing tree. Fi wished she didn't have a skirt on, that there weren't all these people here. She'd climb it right now and maybe never come down.

She heard the door slide open. Jackson crossed the deck and sat down on the steps like her. He sat a good foot away, his elbow resting on his knees, and stared at the yard like she'd been doing. "I fell out of that tree in second grade," he said. "Broke my arm."

Fi looked back to the tree. "I was just thinking it looked like a good climbing tree."

"Mom got spooked after that," he said. "Freaked out when I went up too far. Marcus and I would play under it a lot, though."

She smiled. "Play what?"

"I don't know, kid stuff."

They sat quietly after that, in each other's presence but not really. More like two bodies sharing the same space through a fragile truce.

She wasn't sure when this truce started, really. Ever since prom, when Fi was let in on *the secret*, Jackson had backed off. Maybe it was because she'd become as paranoid as he was— no need to remind her about hand washing, anymore.

Or maybe, it was because Marcus looked *so horrible,* Jackson didn't have the energy to care about Fi one way or the other.

Marcus was a big fat liar. He didn't get better. He didn't even make it out of the hospital. Well, she supposed he did, at the end. But hospice didn't count.

After those first tests on Marcus's white blood cells came back, everyone, including Marcus, notched up their tension level. There were additional bags clipped to his IV pole, more tests run. Each one came back worse and worse. The IV pole got an extendable arm to handle the growing medications. Marcus got hooked up to even more machines.

Instead of filling him up, all those IV bags just sucked him dry. He disappeared, piece by piece, before her eyes. Her sweet, skinny Marcus got skinnier and skinnier, paler and paler, sleepier and sleepier. His room started looking more like an apartment than a hospital room. There were plants in the windowsill, cards, and a few crayon drawings from some younger cousins taped to the wall. An additional table was brought in so the Kings could eat dinner together.

She came over after school, spent as much of the weekend as was allowed. Five days after Hospital Prom, she'd gotten a reply from that email she'd sent to the Northwestern coach, the one meant to humor Marcus. Truly, she hadn't thought anything would come from it.

She'd been sitting by his bed, flipping through the emails on her phone, when she saw the NU address. She showed it to Marcus right after she read it—*So glad to hear from you Fi, yes, we actually might have a spot, last-minute injury from another recruit, why don't you come to the camp this summer, we'll discuss it then*. It was the first time he'd smiled—really, *really* smiled—in days.

She slid the phone back in her purse. "How much do you think she'll hate me when I cancel on her again?"

"Why would you cancel on her?"

Fi looked at him like the crazy person he was. "Marcus, don't be ridiculous. I'm not going away when you're like this."

He clenched his jaw, like he always did when he got annoyed. But now the bones in his face were so prominent, he looked almost skeletal.

In the end, she made a deal with him she'd have been happy to keep. She'd go to camp if he got better.

She didn't study for exams. She walked through graduation like a zombie. Her parents took Ryan, Fi, Gwen, and Trent out to a depressing dinner where no one talked about Marcus, but everyone was thinking about it.

The Kings had a little cake—gluten-, egg-, and dairy-free—for her at the hospital. No one ate much of it. It was pretty awful.

Her graduation day was the same day the doctors brought up hospice.

Fi wasn't sure what it meant at first—she figured it was yet another experimental treatment. Even after she heard the doctors say to the Kings, "We want to make sure he's comfortable" and to Marcus, "Have you given any thoughts to what arrangements you'd like?" she still didn't get it.

"How much time does he have? Really?" Jackson asked.

Mrs. King grimaced at the question—but leaned forward to hear the answer all the same.

One of the doctors cleared his throat. Putting a hand on Marcus's skinny, skinny shoulder, he spoke right to him. "It's hard to say, of course. It depends on what you decide to do about medication. But the end could come soon—within the week."

All the air left the room. Fi's heart shriveled in the vacuum.

Marcus had left the hospital the day after the discussion, insisting he wanted to die in his own home. His parents moved a bed downstairs, into the same dining room now covered in inappropriate meats, breads, and casseroles. Two days later, he died in his sleep.

Fi had been with him the evening before it happened. She talked to him, looking into his eyes—but she couldn't be sure that he heard or saw her. By then, he was in so much pain—and on so many drugs—that it was hard to know if he registered her voice or her fingers intertwined with his. If he felt her tears drop onto his cheeks. She told him she needed him, she loved him, she didn't know what to do without him. He kept mumbling something that sounded like "soft with rot" over and over.

Now, Fi inhaled the scent of magnolia blossoms and grass, and the cedar of this hard deck. Her butt was sore, the pollen made her sniffle, little beads of sweat trickled down her back. Still, this self-imposed exile was better than the air-conditioned pleasantries of the reception. Even if she had to share it with Jackson.

More to herself than anyone, Fi spoke out loud. "I don't know what to do now."

Jackson looked toward her, the top of his head dangling between his arms, his chin resting on his shoulder.

"I mean," she hesitated, not sure how to explain it. Not sure why she felt compelled to tell Jackson of all people. "I don't know who I *am* now."

He just nodded.

"Before I met him, all I cared about was lacrosse. Then, I don't know, all I cared about was *him*." She glanced at the date square on her watch. "There's a camp at Northwestern in a few weeks—Marcus wanted me to go, but I just can't. It's like, none of it matters at all."

She'd emailed the coach the day after Marcus died. In a long, rambling message, she explained about the broken ankle–coffee shop coincidence that brought her and Marcus together, how wonderful a human being he was, so full of big ideas and dreams that would never get to come true, how he had just died and left her alone, and how could anything really matter after that, she was sorry she wasted the coach's time but she wouldn't be coming to the camp.

Fi got a reply the next day—a concise two lines to Fi's fifty.

Fi, I am so sorry for your loss. He sounds like a wonderful person. I wish you the best in whatever you choose to do. Candace Starnes.

Jackson kept looking loosely at Fi—kind of at her, kind of not really. Eventually, he said, "It's like Picasso. Cubism."

Fi wrinkled her brow at this subject change but nodded at him to go on.

"That's what it feels like. Someone took reality, pulled it in all directions, cut the stretched out bits into pieces, and then glued everything back together in all the wrong places."

Fi had never heard so many normal, nonvenomous words come out of Jackson's mouth. "Why do you hate me?" she asked.

"You took my brother," he answered simply. He sounded numb.

Fi recognized the tone—it's how she sounded, too. "He was with you more than me."

"He was dying." Jackson looked away from Fi, to the tree he didn't climb. "I didn't want to share."

That she understood in the deepest part of her soul.

Fi studied him in profile. The past month hadn't been kind to Jackson. He was a thinner, paler version of himself. He looked a little more like Marcus this way. "Why are you talking to me now, then?"

"No reason not to. Marcus isn't here to fight over." He looked back at her, resting his head against his upper arm, as he'd done before. "And you're the only one who misses him almost as much as I do."

COLLEGE—
FRESHMAN YEAR

SEPTEMBER

FIONA

"You look great. Don't worry." Her dad placed his hands on her shoulders, equal weight on each, and turned her away from the mirror she'd been obsessing in front of. "It's remarkable, the difference."

She gave her best *I'm fixed now* smile, though moving into the dorm today, and officially becoming College Fiona, brought back some of the old nerves.

Fiona's right hand went to the bottom edge of the single fine scar line, the boundary between what was hers and what was borrowed. It was strange, how the pain had faded—from the old scar, from the surgery. No feeling at all replaced it.

Only when following doctor's orders did she let her fingers creep over the line into "foreign territory." He'd told her to apply some creams and to test for the return of sensation. Fiona wanted to correct him on this last bit. Sensation would never *return*—not unless the original owner came back from the dead and took this missing piece back.

She didn't like to touch it, but she had no trouble staring. All her life, she'd ducked past mirrors. Now she sought them out. In just four months—all her doctors commented on the speed of her recovery—her face had transitioned from an unsettling raw look to the deceptively clear skin she had now. The faint oval outline that would likely stay with her forever—the New Fiona/Old Fiona border—had become less purple, less "angry." The surgeon said in a few years it would barely be noticeable, especially around the hairline.

The scar didn't bother her, anyway. Ryan said it added character. "Tell people you used to be a pirate," Lucy had offered.

Her dad was still looking at her, shaking his watery-eyed head.

She patted his shoulder. "Okay. Deep breath. We need to go."

"This isn't natural," he said, picking up her bags. "Having two children start college in the same year."

Fiona snorted. "That's what happens when you have kids ten months apart."

He winked at her. "Caroline, I'm checking out," he called toward the closed bathroom door. "Come down when you're ready."

Fiona leaned over to pick up a bag. "Nothing over ten pounds," he snapped.

"I know," she groaned. Only two weeks left of Healing

Period Restrictions. She'd take the drugs forever, but she would be glad to be done with the weight limits and the creams.

She was ready to *start*.

Plus, she hated feeling useless. When they moved Ryan into his dorm six weeks ago, all she could do was sit on his unmade dorm bed and text updates to Gwen. *He & his room-mate are picking desks and beds. He's putting shirts in the dresser. Mom's teaching him the right way to fold.*

She slid her laptop bag over her shoulder—three-point-one pounds, she'd weighed it—and her mom emerged from the bathroom. "Fiona, it's cold outside," her mom said, looking her usual, perfect self. "Put something else on."

Weather appropriate gear—her mother's new obses-sion. Yesterday she'd ransacked Michigan Avenue, bringing back bags full of gloves, scarves, coats, and pullovers. Pick-ing through it—how had her mother managed to find *frilly* fleece?—Fiona had said she'd packed Ryan's old coat.

"You can't walk around campus in that old thing," her mom had said. "How would that look?"

As Fiona had learned since the surgery, this brand-new, high-end cheek had *not* lessened her mom's quest to make her suitable—i.e., better.

"I'm fine, Mom," she said now.

In the elevator, Mrs. Doyle looked at Fiona through the mirror. "How lucky you healed so quickly. No one would ever know."

We'll keep it our dirty little secret, Mom.

"Are you okay? Nervous?" her mom asked. "It's a long way from home."

"I'll be back in three months," she said, desperately hoping to avoid a heart-to-heart in the Holiday Inn Express elevator.

"You've never been gone so long before."

Fiona had never been gone at all. The longest time away had been the nights she slept over at Lucy's.

Who was she kidding, that she could do this? Start a new life, as New Fiona? Make new friends? Compete with some of the smartest kids in the country?

The elevator doors opened to the lobby. "Mom," Fiona said, faking calm and gesturing for her mother to go first. "What could possibly happen in three months?"

It turned out she had nothing to be nervous about. Fiona loved college.

Loved it.

Even though she'd lucked into a single, she shared a suite and bathroom with six other girls, whom she liked. The first night, Lexie From Des Moines commanded they all bond over popcorn and pictures. The girls cooed over Ryan. Lexie called David her HTH—*hometown honey.* No one asked about the scars, because Fiona had passed around pictures she *wasn't* in.

When she talked in class, when she met new people, when she walked around campus, there were no double takes, no furtive second glances. Well, that wasn't exactly true. There were a few. But they were the good kind.

The first time it happened, she and the other girls in her suite had gone to a party. A cute hipster guy scanned their group as they walked in. When his eyes caught Fiona's, she bristled, expecting the recoil. Instead, he gave a flirty smile.

She gaped at him, not thinking to smile back—so he moved on to Bethany From New York, who was more skilled at flirting.

Not that she was looking to meet boys. The few other times the eye-lock thing happened, she stumbled away, clueless about what to do next. Anyway, she and David never had gotten around to the awkward "What exactly are we doing?" conversation. Dating other people hadn't been strictly *forbidden*—but she was pretty sure it wasn't *encouraged*.

Notwithstanding the unclear dating guidelines and her inability to flirt anyway, Fiona embraced her growing social life by following one simple rule: say yes.

Zoey From Chicago: Want to go to *Much Ado About Nothing*? The theater department's putting it on.

Fiona: I'll be there.

Miriam From St. Louis: There's a weird lecture on German philosophers in the student union. Come with me?

Fiona: Sure, sounds fun.

Bethany From New York: Battle of the Bands on Greek Row!

Fiona: Let's go!

Lexie From Des Moines: You've never had kimchi? We must go eat Korean food RIGHT NOW!

Fiona: Hang on, I'll get my wallet.

Yes, I'll go to that party. Yes, I'll come to dinner. Yes, I'll hang out.

Yes. Yes. Yes.

She rarely second-guessed the "Yes" philosophy. Maybe when Miriam talked her into spending Evanston's last warm Saturday in a dark theater watching an art film about doors—wide doors, glass doors, sliding doors, revolving doors. By the end, she just wanted to walk through the closest one.

And maybe these Tuesday and Thursday mornings spent in the "Musical Theory Circle" were nearly as weird as that movie.

She was required to take a music course for her scholarship, and this was the only class with openings. A *lot* of openings. According to the syllabus, the class would expose her "musical expressions to the echoes and undertones of all the discarded creations preceding it."

There were ten of them in Circle, and, like Fiona, most had guitars, though a few had violins. A boy in her geology course—which pretty much everyone called "Rocks for Jocks"—lugged an enormous double bass to every class.

Professor Edward Fleming, aka "Flem," bowed to the girl with the clarinet and said, "Ah, the mighty reed."

He said this every time.

Flem had thinning brown hair, which hung in a sad pony-tail. In addition to his *endless* supply of neck scarves, he also sported a goatee and pipe.

That's right, pipe.

"My fellow explorers!" said Flem. "We continue our quest! Let us push past our boundaries and reveal the hidden worlds of music seeking to be traveled!"

According to Flem, this was to be accomplished by dissecting 1980s power ballads.

After a particularly sad—or hilarious, she couldn't decide which—class, Fiona called Lucy as she walked home. "I am supposed to, *ahem,* 'reinterpret "Is This Love," 1987, Whitesnake'—that's one of my dad's eighties hair bands, by the way—'in such a way as to reinform its relevance in modern day culture.'"

There was a pause on Lucy's end of the line. "I'm panicking. I have no witty retort."

Fiona laughed. "Wait, there's more." Mimicking Flem's tone, she read from her assignment sheet. "'Surgically remove any four-count phrase of your choosing, reinterpret it and, after introducing it back to its once familiar and now foreign role in the overall body of work, allow a new arrangement to organically flow around the shifts it inspires, as a river wends its way around the randomly placed detritus of man.'"

"Good Lord, stop. It's like my kryptonite."

Fiona adjusted her guitar case so as to hit as few passing

students as possible. Northwestern was a long, narrow campus spanning over a mile—liberal arts to the south, tech to the north, and business in between. She had yet to make a full pass from Flem to dorm without whacking someone.

Despite all these bodies, the walk was a fairly quiet one—just passing conversations in pairs and threes, the rustle of leaves in the brisk Chicago wind. Not so on Lucy's side.

"I can hardly hear you," Fiona said, pulling the phone closer to her ear. "Where the heck are you?"

"In a café. There are about seven within ten minutes of me. I'm trying them all."

Fiona felt a sudden pang for her coffee shop and best friend. "How's that one rank?"

"Quite low—too hipster. Good one yesterday, though. Had all this cool old movie paraphernalia."

"I didn't know you cared about old movies."

"I didn't either." She paused. "It could have something to do with all the girls there."

Fiona laughed. "So you're not the only one in New York?"

"It appears I am not, thank God." Fiona heard rustling on Lucy's end as her best friend said, "'Kay, I gotta go to class. But, hey, be respectful to the hair band. Despite the bluster, it's a fragile creature."

She and Lucy spoke or texted every day—pretty much the same as with David. Fiona had a standing Sunday night call with her parents, but they emailed and texted about little things during the week. Ryan, however, was another animal altogether.

Either he was lying, or he truly had no free time. The few times he picked up his phone, he was out of breath, running from one place to another. He had mandatory athletic study halls in the library every night, so he couldn't video chat. She got occasional quick texts—*bbq here sucks* or *what's iambic pentameter*—but nothing more.

Now back in her room, she sat cross-legged on her bed and left yet another voice mail demanding he call back, though she didn't think he would.

Ever since the surgery, things felt different with him.

Fine—he had to get to Clemson early, and okay—she spent the first few weeks after her surgery as a useless lump. But what if Ryan was beginning a new life, too? What if he was leaving her behind?

She grabbed her guitar and played around with Flem's assignment awhile. The arrangement was predictable, with lots of opportunities for "reinterpretations." She might make fun of it, but this type of work was perfect for her. After the open mic night disaster, she'd spent a year becoming Queen of the Cover Song. By now, she was a genius with nearly any cover she touched—Beck to the Beatles.

Exposing a stranger's pain to other strangers was much, *much* easier than exposing her own.

In fifteen minutes, she finished Flem's assignment. She'd

ace this class. But that anxiety about Ryan still needled, so she moved on to the meatier part of her therapy. Going between Moleskine and guitar, she picked out notes and fiddled with words—her *own* words and notes—until it felt like a real beginning of something.

My pieces got melted / The edges are jagged

I wonder if they see / Only half the pieces cover me

As always, she got lost in it. She glanced at the clock, and two hours had passed. It was probably time to put this one away, anyway. She'd figured out over the years that it worked best that way. Start it, write it down, then leave it alone awhile.

Plus, she was starving.

She walked out of her room and nearly face-planted, her foot colliding with a body sitting just outside her door.

"Ow! What the—"

A boy popped up, catching her by the elbows. "Sorry. I, uh, heard you playing. Singing." Once sure she was steady, he let her go, ruffling a hand through dark, wavy hair and looking sheepish. "I normally don't sit outside of strange girls' doors."

Fiona kept a wary eye on this eavesdropper. "Wouldn't *you* be the strange one here?"

"I know. It's bad, right?" He cleared his throat. "It's just . . . you sound like Lorde. But like, with maple syrup."

Well, she'd never been compared to syrup before.

He gestured down the hall. "You going somewhere?"

The Eavesdropper was about as tall as Ryan, maybe a little broader. His charmingly imperfect smile played against a background of perfect olive skin.

This boy was *cute*. "Downstairs," she said. "I was getting something to eat."

"You're from the South."

Fiona rolled her eyes. "Memphis."

Her accent was a constant source of amusement up here. Her Yankee friends randomly commanded her to say *pie* or *my*, while giggling at her dropped *g*'s.

The boy gawked at her. "No way. Where'd you live?"

"Uh, Midtown."

"High Point." He rocked back on his heels, giving her an openmouthed, crooked smile and holding out a hand. "I'm Jackson King."

Fiona took his hand. When his skin met hers, an almost-violent case of flutters coursed through her, stomach to throat. "Fiona. Doyle."

"Nice to meet you, Miss Fiona." Affecting a thick southern accent, he folded his hand around hers. "Well, fellow Memphian, would you believe that I was headed to get something to eat, too? Before you distracted me?" He held up his hands, as if proving he wasn't armed. "I'm not a stalker, I swear."

She hesitated—well, pretended to hesitate. Anyway, she had to say *yes*, right?

As they sat across a table from each other, Fiona tried to act like a normal person. It was hard, what with those green eyes. "You *do* look familiar," she said, although she couldn't imagine from where. He certainly didn't go to her high school—he was too cute to forget. Trent-McKinnon-who? cute. "You're not in my lit class, are you?"

He shook his head. "Chemical engineering major."

"I wonder why I didn't see you at orientation. People kept asking if I knew Elvis. Or they called me *y'all*—in the singular. I mean, it's got *all* in it." She took a sip of coffee, shaking her head. "It would have been nice to have some backup."

He laughed, nodding his head. "I got here late—a few days after classes started. I meant to defer but decided last minute to come." He waved his hand, dismissing the question she hadn't asked. "Family stuff."

"I guess I've just seen you around the dorm."

He nodded and wavy hair dipped over green eyes. Looking guilty, he bit one side of his lip, making his smile all the more lopsided. "So, I have a confession."

Oh no. "What's that?"

"I wasn't going for coffee. I was heading to class." He looked at his watch. "Which starts in four minutes."

She laughed, feeling so, so fluttery. "You *were* being a stalker."

The boy hung his head dramatically. "I know. Five minutes in and I've already broken my first promise. It's a bad start."

"A bad start for what?"

He stood and began walking backward as Fiona stayed at the table. He backed nearly all the way to the automatic doors. They slid open, but he paused, those pretty green eyes still on Fiona. With a sly, uneven smile, he answered, "Not sure yet."

FI

Sitting cross-legged on her bed, Fi nestled Panda in her lap and absently picked at her comforter. "Where are you?" she asked, holding the phone away from her ear.

"The common room on my hall." Trent spoke loudly, and still all the background noise threatened to drown him out completely. "There's a party later. People are hanging out."

Fi's dramatic plans for the evening included hiding from her parents' "good intentions" and going to bed by nine, just as she'd done every night since May.

"Sounds fun," she lied.

"And you'd be the expert," he mumbled under his breath.

"What's that supposed to mean?" she snapped.

Critiquing her mourning rituals was Ryan's job. All summer, he and Gwen had tried to coax her out of the house. By August, he was spouting platitudes, like *He's better off now the suffering's over* and *There are other fish in the sea!* All the while, with his arm comfortably around Gwen's shoulder.

"Nothing. Sorry," Trent said. "Hang on, I can't hear anything." Muffled sounds came over—and then the background noise suddenly disappeared. "Okay, I'm back in the room."

"You don't have to leave your party."

"It's not a party yet." She heard the groan of springs followed by a soft grunt. "I want to crash a minute anyway, I'm exhausted. The coach is sadistic. We practiced all day, and it's like a hundred and five outside."

Fi sympathized. Doing anything outdoors in a Deep South summer—which could last till October sometimes—*sucked.* She had swimmer friends who claimed to sweat underwater. "Maybe it's payback," she said. "Remember those awful workouts when you made yourself my personal trainer? *You* never showed any mercy."

"You were in a climate-controlled gym, you wimp." The mattress groaned again, and Fi pictured Trent's feet dangling off the end of the twin-sized dorm bed. He hardly fit in his queen bed at home, always complaining he had to sleep diagonally. "You have no idea—all the pads! Seriously, I could drop dead out there."

Closing her eyes, Fi rubbed her fingers hard across her eyebrows, like she could massage out the dull throb she'd had since Marcus died.

"Man, Fi. I'm sorry. I didn't mean—"

"It's fine. Don't worry about it."

Actually, it wasn't fine. *She* wasn't fine. She was way on the other side of fine—upside down even. But dragging Trent down with her wouldn't get her right side up.

She'd gotten used to the awkward pause that always followed these situations. The thoughtless gaffe—usually something harmless, like *I'd rather die than see that movie* or *A little broccoli won't kill you*—followed by the stammering apology. Then overcompensating conversation immediately after, usually about something trite like the weather or tomorrow night's dinner.

"Tell me about the drills," she said. Her finger looped around a loose thread in the bedspread, and she snapped it free.

"I got the playbook today. Hang on." She heard another grunt followed by shuffling and another groan of springs. "Well, there's the Flip."

For the next twenty minutes, Trent talked her through the Ole Miss lacrosse playbook. Some were pretty clever; a few could even be adapted for a girls' team. She could picture one in particular, a low double cut while the center—Fi—plowed to goal.

Only, when she tried to visualize this happening with her Milton teammates, Fi groaned.

"What's wrong?" Trent asked.

"Nothing." She'd been snapping threads this whole time. Now, there was a knuckle-sized hole in her bedspread. "Just trying to picture the Milton girls trying to pull off the Flip."

"They're really that bad?"

"Some are still trying to keep the ball in their sticks. Which come from Walmart."

"You're kidding."

"Nope. Today, the goalie missed two easy blocks *because she was texting.* After practice, they rolled out a keg."

"I told—"

"Don't. Please."

Milton had always been a hard choice, but it was worth it. Because Marcus was worth it. But then he died, and everything unraveled. It sounded melodramatic but it was true—she'd lost everything.

"So . . . how are classes?" Trent asked. He used the voice he saved for adults—politely non-sarcastic.

This conversation wasn't going to be any better than one about dead boyfriends. "Okay, I guess."

"How's calc?"

"It continues to be the bane of my existence."

During registration, she hadn't paid much attention to her advisor's suggestions, just said "Sounds good" to each one. Spanish and sociology were fine, and creative writing had been a pleasant surprise. But calculus was god-awful.

"I'm sure Ryan could help out," Trent said. "He's how you passed precalc anyway."

"I don't need Ryan," she snapped. "I'll be fine."

She heard Trent snort. "Wouldn't want anyone to know you're not perfect."

"Who said I thought I was perfect?" What a terribly misinformed conclusion.

"Never mind."

With that polite, placating voice, he talked about his classes—Spanish, a geology class he called "Rocks for Jocks," a business class. Some shouts interrupted him, and after a muffled conversation—it sounded like his hand was over the phone—he said, "I gotta go soon."

"Okay."

"Weekends down here are awesome," he said. "You should come sometime."

Fi had no interest in hanging out with a group of people she didn't know. Anyway, Trent would probably abandon her ten minutes into a party, what with all the inevitable swooning girls following him around. "I don't know any girls down there. Where would I sleep?"

"It's not church camp, you dork. You could sleep with me."

For the first time during the conversation, Fi's hands stilled. A thread wrapped around three fingers at once, turning the tips purple. "Uh—"

Trent sighed. "Do you think I'm a total asshole? Your boyfriend just *died*."

It was the first time he'd stated the obvious out loud. It was refreshing.

"I can kick my roommate out," he continued. "He's got a girlfriend. You can sleep on his bed. Anyway, it's only an hour from home. You wouldn't even need to spend the night if your hermit self went into freak-out mode."

She tried to picture sleeping over at Trent's—him sprawled across a too-little bed, snores bouncing against concrete walls. She imagined their comingled body heat in a small, stuffy room; how they'd groggily maneuver around each other the next morning.

"I'm not a hermit," she said.

She heard more muffled in-and-out sounds, like he was pulling on a shirt. "When's the last time you left the house?"

"I leave the house all the time. I've got class."

"To do something social?"

Fi didn't answer. Did the funeral count as a social event?

After another round of bangs and shouts, he said, "Right. Really gotta go now."

"Have fun."

"Seriously, think about it." And then he hung up.

Fi tossed her phone on the bedside table. She slouched down, bringing Panda with her, and swallowed back the need to cry.

Before he left for school, Trent felt almost like a *place* to her—the only place she could just *be*. They watched TV or played Wii or sat around eating popcorn. If she happened to crack a joke or act like an otherwise-normal person, he didn't fake-smile at her and say, "See, it's all going to be okay."

He just let the moment be the moment. Then, when she remembered that everything was terrible and her heart was broken and her life wasn't anywhere near where it was *supposed* to be, he went along with that, too.

Now, he had a new life—without her. And she had what? A school she didn't really want? Helicopter parents? Wallowing?

What the hell was she *doing*?

Fi was an Otherlands regular now. She'd spend her free afternoons there, drinking black coffee—and hiding from her parents—while apathetically studying. Today wasn't so bad, though. Another creative writing assignment.

At first, the assignments seemed bizarre: *Write five hundred words from the perspective of an old lady who's lost her cat, but don't mention the cat. Describe the color blue. Write a conversation where one person talks, and the other only thinks.* But they were fun—and she was sort of good at it.

She pulled the latest topic from her bag. *Write five hundred words around the following statement: I should have known better than to let you go alone. Use the second person and present tense.*

Well, *this* one might be depressing.

"Hey."

She looked up. Jackson stood awkwardly on the other side of her table. He pointed to the chair in front of him. "Can I sit?"

Fi hesitated a moment. Looking up at him, she saw just the littlest bit of Marcus floating around in that doubtful expression and hunch of broad shoulders.

She nodded, and Jackson screeched the chair backward and

sat, putting his mug and a bowl of fruit in front of him. He pointed to the papers in front of Fi, one eyebrow up.

She answered the question he didn't ask. "Creative writing assignment."

He nodded. "How's school?"

"All right, I guess." She shrugged. "I've never been much of a school person, really."

"I like it," Jackson said between bites. "Liked it. Well, the math and science parts. Probably wouldn't have been great with creative writing."

What was happening here? Were she and Jackson *small-talking?*

Fi was even on the verge of confessing her failure with calculus before she stopped herself. She didn't want him to think she wanted tutoring or anything. As much as she hated getting help from Ryan, getting it from Jackson would be twenty times worse.

"Liked it?" she asked instead.

He shrugged. "Homeschool didn't really cut it—kind of a waste. I mean, Ellen King as high school teacher? I don't know which is her bigger weakness—teaching or cooking."

Despite herself Fi smiled, picturing Mrs. King elbow-deep in that battered enamel pot, boiling up some monstrous concoction. Marcus called it the Voodoo Pot. "But you got into Northwestern."

"Good SATs," he said. "The my-brother-is-dying essay probably didn't hurt either."

They looked each other in the eyes then—a steady gaze, with none of the awkward spaces that came when people didn't understand.

"Why aren't you there now?" she asked.

"I deferred."

"Right, but . . . well, there's no reason to anymore."

"I don't know," he said with a frown. "You tell me. You're here, too."

Fi's eyes narrowed. "I go to *school* here, Jackson. I never applied to Northwestern."

Jackson—surprisingly—didn't seem inclined to argue. "I figured I wouldn't be good for much. Maybe next year."

"You think it'll feel better by then?"

"I hope so." She could tell by the way his lower lip dipped in that he was chewing the inside of his cheek. Marcus did that, too. "I don't think I'll have much choice, though. Mom already threatened to rent out my room if I don't go."

"She *wants* you to leave?"

"Yes and no. She and Dad, they're both a mess. When I leave—Jesus, I can't imagine, how *quiet* everything will be. The two of them alone in that big house? But they say I need to get on with it."

"With what?"

"Life."

"Sounds familiar," she said, feeling the scratch in the back of her throat, the sting in her eyes. She supposed this was an improvement, since a month ago, she'd have burst into tears the second Jackson walked up to her table.

He spun his mug where it rested, absently staring into it. "It's surreal to think about. Like I might wake up one day and not think about him till lunch or something. Because right now, he's everywhere." He looked up, gesturing vaguely to the tables behind Fi. "I can't even look at people without making some kind of Marcus observation. That guy's about as fair as he was. The girl's reading a book I checked out of the library for him last year. That fat guy with the cane, would Marcus have been able to beat him up the stairs?"

Fi wiped a tear from her cheek, looked over her shoulder, and studied the people Jackson listed.

"And it gets grimmer," he went on. "Like, who got his organs—or the ones that worked, at least? Who's wearing his clothes that Mom donated to Goodwill?"

Envisioning all these people carrying around bits and pieces of Marcus, Fi lost it.

Jackson's mouth had been open, like he was preparing to say something else. He closed it slowly. "Sorry."

She shook her head, wiping away the tears. She had become nothing but a pathetic lump of wallowing sorrow. "Is this ever going to end?"

She wasn't expecting a response. And Jackson didn't give one.

NOVEMBER

FIONA

"I heard it snowed in May last year," Jackson said. He leaned across the cafeteria table and stabbed her fruit onto his fork.

"Mom has a friend who used to live up here," Fiona said. "She told me a Memphis winter might be gray, but at least it wouldn't kill you. I thought she was joking."

They'd been here nearly an hour, prolonging breakfast and hiding from the weather. Ever since *the eavesdropping*, they'd done this a few times a week. Because of different class schedules, their paths didn't cross often—but when they did run into each other, they'd wind up grabbing lunch or some coffee. She'd started scanning the first floor common room, hoping to run into him accidentally-on-purpose.

They could talk for hours, about everything. Yet somehow, they'd avoided crossing that invisible border into the land of personal information. Just how she liked it.

"Man, I miss greasy southern food," Jackson said, going

for her banana muffin. "When I get back for Christmas, I'm eating my weight in Gus's Fried Chicken."

Dark, wavy hair dipped over one eye. Fiona wanted so, so badly to reach out and touch it.

"I know," she said. "I'm in barbecue withdrawal. Dad's taking me to Corky's on the way from the airport."

"Central's better."

Then followed the "best barbecue" argument, which happened all the time in Memphis—and *never* ended in agreement. "Okay, best record store then," Fiona said.

"That vinyl place on Madison. Shangri-La."

Her heart might melt. She *loved* that place. "Best tourist spot," she said.

"Best? Like as a joke?"

"No. Really the best."

"I've got no idea. I've only been to Graceland ironically." He frowned at his empty fork before pointing it at her. "My brother got me this horrible sequined cape there—a replica of the Vegas concert one. I think it's still in my room somewhere."

"How do you *not* know if there's a sequined—wait, I didn't know you have a brother."

"Had," he said. "He died this past summer."

And just like that, they crossed into the land of personal information. "Oh. I'm so sorry."

"He'd been sick a long time."

She nodded like she understood, which she didn't. The

conversation lagged, their first awkward silence.

"What about you?" Jackson leaned forward, and she let him pick through what remained of her breakfast. "Any brothers or sisters?"

"A brother. He's a freshman, too—at Clemson." She felt guilty suddenly, like having a living brother was showing off.

"You're twins?"

She shook her head. "He's ten months older. It just worked out, how our birthdays fell. He was one of the oldest in our class. I was one of the youngest." She pulled out her phone and held it out to him. "That's him. Ryan."

Jackson took it, eyes squinted. "That girl he's with—she looks familiar."

"Gwen. His girlfriend."

His eyes widened as he studied the phone's small screen. "Otherlands, right? She works there?"

"You go there?"

He wiggled his hand back and forth. So-so. "You?"

"All the time."

"Liar. I never saw you there." He speared a chunk of cantaloupe, pointed it at her, and winked. "I'd have remembered."

Oh, what her body did when Jackson flirted.

With Trent McKinnon, Fiona's fantasies were gauzy and girlish, all smiles and chaste kisses and happily ever after. Not so with Jackson. The specificity of her imagination regarding this green-eyed boy was alarming.

Which then led to guilt. Because, uh, *what about David?*

Since she couldn't handle flirting, she avoided it. Like right now, by getting them back on track with the original conversation. "They've been dating since eleventh grade."

"She goes to Clemson?"

"No, Furman. Nearby, but I'm not sure they see each other much. He's on the soccer team and never has a free second, apparently."

Jackson laughed. "Not that it bothers you."

"It's that obvious?"

"You look like a tractor ran over your toe."

"We were just—are just—really close. But I never talk to him anymore." She looked at Jackson's drawn face and was horrified. "Oh, Jackson. I'm sorry. I shouldn't—"

He held up a hand to stop her. "You're allowed to miss your brother."

"You miss yours."

"He's why I deferred, at first," he said, while idly picking through her fruit. "I didn't want to leave, you know, with him still around. Even after he died I waffled about it, but Mom got sick of me moping. She said stalling didn't change anything. He died and *not moving* wouldn't keep it from being true."

"How did he die?" she asked quietly.

"Heart failure."

"Oh my God. That's terrible."

He nodded. "Four years ago, he got food poisoning, which gave him this fluke infection. Everything just went perfectly wrong after that. By the time the doctors figured it out, his heart was shot."

"It sounds awful."

"Since his immune system was messed up, my parents pulled him out of regular school, to teach him at home. He was so pissed. He wanted a normal life." He gave a short, bitter laugh. "Selfish bastard that I am, I pushed him to stay home, too. I did it with him."

"You were homeschooled?" Fiona imagined sitting with Ryan in those little kindergarten desks that used to be in their playroom, while her mom wrote lessons on an old-fashioned chalkboard. The brief daydream was very unappealing.

"In theory," Jackson said, with a little laugh. "Teaching is not my mother's calling. We pretty much just followed the city school curriculum. I took some classes at U of M," he said. "Marcus kept telling me to go back to school. He said I was missing everything."

"Like what?"

"Football games, clubs, prom. Stuff I didn't care about—but he did," he said. "He always said that even if his life was screwed up, mine didn't have to be. Which is ridiculous. I mean, just because it's not *happening* to me doesn't mean it's not happening to me."

"And you aren't sad?" she asked. "That you missed high school?"

He shook his head. "I got my brother. I was kind of a

jealous girlfriend about it, too. Trying to get all the time with him I could."

Fiona felt that way about Ryan—though she wasn't a jealous girlfriend so much as *jealous of his girlfriend*. "Sounds nice. I mean, not *nice*. But—"

"Don't worry," he said with a cute smile. "I know what you mean. And yeah, it was great actually, having him to myself like that. Although it's come around to bite me, since I really know what I'm missing."

Fiona wanted to know more but felt like she'd been nosy enough already. However, after a few sips of coffee, Jackson offered more up on his own. "This past year, he couldn't even walk up the stairs without getting out of breath. Still, every day he wanted something new."

"Like what?"

"Like, well, like food. But he couldn't stomach much, so *I* had to eat everything and then describe it. And books. He sent me to the library so often, the librarian, Linda, and I were on a first name basis." He shook his head. "We didn't let him out much, but whenever his blood work came back strong—or if he'd had some good days—he'd get a reprieve. And man, he grabbed it."

"What would he do?"

"Anything, really. Sometimes just regular stuff, like bowling. Fishing. Sometimes he got a little goofy. Like—have you ever been to that open mic night at Otherlands?"

Fiona's heart practically stopped beating. She nodded.

Jackson wagged his eyebrows. "All the ways our paths have crossed." For a moment, he just looked at her, all smirky and adorable, before continuing. "He even did that once. Read *Sartre,* of all things. He got booed off the stage, which was probably a first for that place. Still, he was so pumped. Alive." He stared at the table. Suddenly, it looked like all happiness and sarcasm left him. "God, it sucks."

The lump in her throat made her forget her stalled heart. "How did he handle it? Knowing he was dying?"

"He never admitted he was dying." He shook his head, like this still baffled him. "He was the world's biggest optimist. The doctors told him a new heart was a long shot. Like, *long.* Still he thought he'd pull through it."

"You didn't?"

He shook his head. "No. Which felt like crap."

Fiona watched him, this lovely, heartbroken boy. The wavy hair and olive skin and lopsided smile and broad shoulders just the package for all the invisible, real stuff hidden inside.

Gradually, a crooked smile appeared on Jackson's face. "Your turn."

"My turn to what?"

"Share."

Fiona narrowed her eyes at this suspicious question. Just because they were in Jackson's land of personal information didn't mean they had to cross into hers. "I've got nothing."

He pointed to her cheek. "What's the story with that scar?"

Automatically, Fiona dragged her bangs forward. "Nothing."

She hadn't told anyone here about Old Fiona and her life-changing surgery. She hadn't planned it that way, but whenever anyone asked, she remembered her mother's comment in the hotel elevator. *No one would ever know.* And she just kept vaguely deflecting the questions.

"You don't have to do that." Jackson leaned across the table and tucked her bangs behind her ear. His fingertips glanced the skin on her neck, and all the original bits of her erupted in goose bumps. "It's not bad—cool, really. Like there's a little badass lurking under all that cute."

Oh my. "Next question."

Jackson smirked. "You realize I just want to know more now."

Jackson had told her about his dead brother, who'd gotten *booed off a stage.* Who'd fit all the living he could into the life he got handed.

Jackson had told her something true.

"I had some scars growing up," she said. "But surgery this summer fixed them."

"Fixed them?" he asked, eyes widening.

She shrugged. "It's not a big deal."

"What happened?"

She wanted a sip of coffee, but her hands shook in her lap. Acting as relaxed as she could, Fiona gave a two-minute recap of the day when she was five that, theoretically, no longer mattered.

"How big were they?"

She gestured vaguely to the right side of her face.

Jackson whistled. "So you had the scars from five until—"

"Eighteen."

"Wow," he said. "That sounds pretty bad."

Not knowing what to say, Fiona did what she did best— just like with covering other people's songs, she substituted someone else's idea for her own. "What doesn't kill us makes us stronger. Or so they say."

"Spare me the throw pillow mentality," he said, suddenly annoyed. "You're just as likely to end up dead."

Horrified at her gaffe, Fiona said, "Jackson—"

Jackson held up his hand, cutting her off. "All that bumper sticker philosophy. You can't imagine how many old ladies have told me, 'God doesn't give you what you can't handle.'"

"I didn't mean—"

"Sometimes life just sucks," he said, riled up now. "And maybe I *want* to wallow! Maybe I don't want to look for the silver lining!"

She knew it was dumb to argue with him, but he was just so wrong. "Nothing's worse than feeling sorry for yourself. Trust me."

Jackson looked at her a long moment, straight in the eyes. Then his eyes tracked the path of her new scar, from the inside edge of her right eyebrow straight up to where it tucked into her hairline. Like he'd lost the track and couldn't find his way back, his eyes trailed vaguely around her forehead before finding the last leg of the scar's route, below the ear right up to the outside corner of her right eye. Fiona's heart pounded during the slow inspection.

Eventually he winked. "You should tell everybody you used to be a pirate."

Oh, this boy and his weird coincidences. "That's what my best friend told me to say, if anyone asked about the scar. I even did it once—during orientation."

Jackson laughed. "What happened?"

A drunk guy had barely managed to slur, "How'd you get that scar?" When she'd answered, "I'm really a pirate," he'd wobbled forward, said *Aargh,* and planted a sloppy kiss right on her mouth. Before she could get over the shock, he'd hobbled away like he had a peg leg.

Rather than tell Jackson this bizarre story, she dug out a Moleskine. She figured by now, the word had earned space there—plus, she needed something to do with her hands. She wrote *piracy* in a free place.

Jackson nodded his head toward the book. "What's the story with those? You've always got one."

"Just a mess of stuff, really. Song ideas. Notes that wouldn't make sense to anyone but me."

"When do I get to hear one of these songs?"

"I can play you Flem's latest project—'Pour Some Sugar on Me' by Def Leppard. It's horrendous—and a little bit genius, if I do say so myself."

"Sounds like an intriguing combination," he said. "But I'd rather have an original."

"Oh. Um, I've never really played my stuff for anyone."

"Isn't that kind of required? If you're a songwriter?"

"I'm still looking for the loophole."

Jackson tipped his chair backward. "You are an enigma, Miss Fiona."

Fiona gestured to herself as if she were a prize on a game show. "What you see is what you get."

"Interesting choice of words," he said, raising an eyebrow.

She rolled her eyes. "I had scars. I had surgery. Now no scars. End of story."

"You got a do-over," he said, shrugging. "New face, new town. You get to be someone totally different."

"You'll have to take my word that I'm not."

Fiona didn't consider herself scrupulously honest. She didn't sing her own songs. She never told Trent McKinnon how she felt. She never confronted her mother about the long list of grievances. She ran away from uncomfortable conversations with David. Before five minutes ago, she hadn't told a soul at Northwestern about her scars.

Even so, claiming that losing the scars didn't dramatically change her life was the least true thing she could ever say.

"You're a better person than me," he said, with a little

salute. "Life-changing event and staying the same you. Pretty solid stuff."

"The same happened to you."

He held her in a steady gaze, his tone much quieter than before. "I've got the same life, it's just missing a chunk."

Her heart froze in her chest, the rest of her just as paralyzed. She couldn't even open her mouth and pretend to know what to say.

Then her phone rang.

"I can't believe it. It's Ryan," she said, staring blankly at the caller ID.

She looked at Jackson, apologetically asking for permission to abandon this awkward conversation and begin the one she'd been trying to have for weeks. He gestured to the phone—*go ahead*.

Fiona put the phone to her ear. "Hey."

"Hey, do you remember the Faulkner we read, in junior year? What's the thematic premise of 'Barn Burning'?"

Fiona repeated the question back to herself, like it would make more sense that way. "Um, morality I think? No wait—free will?"

"Pick one. I've got to bang this out. It's due in half an hour."

She exhaled all the stale air trapped in her body. "*This* is why you're finally calling?"

"Sorry. I know, I'm horrible." There was a static-y sound on his end, some muffled conversation. "And we need an analysis of the themes in 'A Rose for Emily,' too."

"Who's we?"

"Tony Miller. The sweeper."

"Sweeper of what?"

A pause. "The soccer team, Fiona. You know, that little thing I'm doing down here."

Fiona rolled her eyes, which caused Jackson to narrow his. "Excuse me for not *instantly understanding* your needs, Ryan. As I don't have mental telepathy, sometimes I need things explained. There's an easy fix for that—it's called the damn phone."

"Lord, you, Mom, and Gwen need to form a club or something." There was another static-y interruption. "No, you can't talk to her," Ryan snapped.

"I can't talk to who?"

"Not you, Tony. So the thematic premise?"

Fiona began pulling the phone away as Ryan got louder and louder. "Where are you? The thematic premise to which?"

"The dorm. 'Barn Burning.' Seriously, Fiona, I don't have a lot of time here."

She was about to yell, or hang up, or cause some kind of scene, but with Jackson right there, it didn't seem fair complaining about her breathing brother. "I don't know. Go with the struggle between morality and loyalty." She shook her head, grimacing. "It's been awhile. It's my best guess."

"No, that's great," Ryan said. "'A Rose for Emily.'"

Fiona bluffed something about the mind being both

trapped and free. He repeated it to Tony Miller the Sweeper. After a brief scuffle, a strange voice came on the other end. "Hey, thanks."

Fiona raised her eyebrows. Tony Miller the Sweeper's voice came through the phone so loudly, the girl one table over gave a dirty look. "Uh, you're welcome."

"I'm Tony."

"I figured." This insanely long breakfast was exhausting. She wanted a remedy for the awkward. She wanted her brother back on the phone and possibly a nap—not this Tony person.

"I play soccer with your brother," he said.

"Yes, I got that."

"Your picture popped up on Ryan's phone. You should come visit. Cheer us on."

Fiona narrowed her eyes at Jackson, as if to ask *What the heck?* Jackson just smirked and shook his head.

Another scuffle, punctuated by "Dude, that's my sister!" and Ryan returned. "Don't come visit. They're all pigs." More shuffling. "Hey, I gotta go. Sorry I can't talk longer. I'll call later, I swear."

Fiona gave a skeptical "Okay," but he'd already hung up. "So that was my brother."

"He sounds busy."

She wanted to cry. Flirting with this boy. Learning about his amazing brother. Dealing with her inconsiderate one.

"You're upset," Jackson said.

She put the phone away and looked anywhere but at him. "It's fine. I'm fine."

Third awkward silence.

"I still say you're an enigma." With just the smallest smirk, he leaned forward, resting his elbows on the table. "But I like a challenge."

FI

The coffee shop was packed full. Everyone who was home from college for Thanksgiving break was laughing and hugging and catching up—while Fi sat at a corner table, trying to milk as many extra credit points as she could.

Jackson sat across from her. He'd lost weight over the summer, but his face was looking fuller again. He looked healthier. The girls at the table behind them were blatantly checking him out, but he didn't notice. Either that, or he didn't care.

She was getting used to it. To him. They'd been meeting at Otherlands a few times a week now, ever since that first run-in in September. The company was nice—but they still treaded carefully with each other.

"I can't believe I still have work," she said, sinking in her chair. "Everyone else here gets to relax."

"No rest for the wicked." He looked from his book long enough to nod at the blank paper in front of her. "Anyway, it doesn't look like you're doing much work."

She flicked the edge of the paper. "I'm stuck."

"What's the assignment?"

"Creative writing," she said. "Describe something ugly and find beauty in it."

He frowned a little, kind of sideways. "Like Marcus's urn."

The memory came suddenly—the ornate silver urn centered on the gleaming dark wood altar. "Ugh, that's the opposite. A beautiful thing that's nothing but ugly."

Jackson shrugged and looked back to his book, leaving her to stew in another memory of Marcus. These moments were sneaky little things. They could switch her on and off without warning.

She grabbed her mug and headed up front for a refill, melding into the loose line behind the register. That's when she made eye contact with the last person on earth she wanted to see.

"Hey, Fi." Lucy Daines looked exactly the same. Tall and skinny, even taller with that out-of-control hair and those thick-soled, vintage boots. She acted the same, too, acknowledging Fi only *after* getting ahead of her in line.

Fi took the place behind her. "Lucy."

Lucy ordered three coffees and stepped aside to wait. Fi handed her mug forward and asked for a refill.

"I heard about your boyfriend," Lucy said. "That sucks."

Fi nodded, watching the tattooed barista take his own sweet time with her refill.

"So you're at Milton?" Lucy's voice went higher than normal, and she tilted her head sympathetically.

Fi hated when people did the fake-concern thing. It was even worse coming from Lucy Daines. "Yeah."

"Do you like it?" Lucy asked. She looked uncomfortable, like the small talk was creating some physical constriction.

"It's okay."

"I'm at NYU."

"Cool," Fi said, hoping her jealousy didn't show.

"Yeah, it really is." Lucy got her drinks and used her head to gesture to the back of the room. "Well, I should bring these over."

Fi followed the nod's direction and squinted. "Didn't that guy go to school with us?"

"David Wright. Yeah, we were on the paper. And that's his girlfriend, from UT. She came home with him for the holidays."

After another awkward moment—like neither knew how to relate now that civility had been established—Lucy eventually said, "See you later," and walked away.

Fi returned to her table and nursed the coffee for a few minutes. Then she got her stuff.

"You're done?" Jackson asked.

"Yeah," she said, not sure how to explain her mood change. Not sure she wanted to. "I need to get home."

"Well, have a good Thanksgiving."

"You too," she said, but by his look, she knew that

Thanksgiving at the Kings would be pretty bleak. Jackson had had a tough time with *Halloween*. He'd told her how he and Marcus used to match their costumes.

On the drive home, she kept replaying that conversation about the urn—and then the one with Lucy Daines—wishing she could pinpoint why they bothered her so much.

Seconds after her car keys hit the front hall table, Fi's mother called, "Fiona, come in here, please."

Fi tensed. No good conversations ever started with her proper name.

Lowering her bag to the floor, Fi took cautious steps back to the kitchen. Her mother stood at the kitchen counter, flicking through mail. She held up a single white piece of paper. "This came from school."

Fi took the piece of paper, which read *Student Evaluation: Pre-Probationary*. It looked like a report card of sorts, but finals were three weeks away.

All of her courses were listed, but the writing class was the only one without a note. It was also the only A. Sociology and Spanish were low Cs. Calculus was a D.

From the sociology professor: *From the single time I've seen her during office hours, I could see that Ms. Doyle had the potential to master this material. As we approach finals, I hope she'll show more dedication to the subject and improved timeliness and thoroughness in completing work assigned.*

From Spanish: *Fi began the class with an appropriate grasp of the language for the course level. However, as the term has progressed she appeared to lose ground. I encourage her to make better use of the lab facilities, as well as the optional study sessions offered.*

From calculus: *There have been several optional tutoring sessions available to Ms. Doyle during the semester. I believe her grade would improve should she attend these in the future.*

Fi kept staring at the paper, even though she was done reading. The stalling didn't work. "Do you have an explanation?" her mother asked.

Fi handed the paper back. Her mom took it like it might spread infection. "Um, it's been—you know, ever since Marcus—"

She held up a hand. "Don't blame this on heartbreak."

"It's been a hard semester. What do you want me to say?"

"I want you to do better."

"I've been trying."

Her mother arched her perfect brows. "Not enough, apparently."

"I have an A in the writing class."

"And a D in calculus."

"You know I can't do math."

"All the more reason to use the tutoring."

Fi wanted out of this conversation. The never-ending criticism was exhausting. "My boyfriend is dead!" she yelled, startling herself as much as her mother. "I live with my parents, play for a terrible lacrosse team, take classes I don't care about. I'm just barely treading water here!"

"So grab a vest, Fi," her mother said levelly.

Fi threw her hands up. "A vest. Perfect. That's helpful."

"It's a metaphor."

"I *know* it's a metaphor. I'm not stupid."

Her mother pointed at the grades. "Prove it."

Every part of her body clenched. No matter how hard she worked, she would never, *ever* be enough for this woman. "What do you want from me?"

"I want you to live up to your potential."

"I *had* potential. I was the best lacrosse player in this state in high school. You didn't care about *that.*"

"That has nothing to do with these grades."

"No, but it was *something.*"

"Not enough of a something. You can't make a career out it."

"You sound like Dad."

"That's because I agree with him," she said. "This is your main chance to decide what you want, Fi. After college, things just happen, you can lose track. Before you know it, you're forty and—"

"You're leaping from college to *forty?*"

"It's not that big of a leap, trust me. If you don't plan *now,* you might not get another chance."

"Are we talking about me or you now?"

"Watch the tone," her mom said, pointing to the grades. "We both know you are smarter than Cs and Ds."

"I have an A!"

"One A, Fi. Just one."

Fi sank onto a counter stool, head in hands. "I'll never measure up. You want too much."

"All I want is for you to have the best life you can."

"Well, that life died."

"Then get another one," her mother said—and then she walked away.

DECEMBER

FIONA

"You only just got home," her mother said, standing at the kitchen counter, wrapping her annual Christmas banana breads into pretty cellophane packages. An artful snack plate sat on the kitchen table, with decorative rings of sliced apples, cheese, olives, and crackers.

Just to annoy her, Fiona took an apple slice right from the middle.

The doorbell rang. From the front of the house, her dad yelled, "It's David."

"We won't be late," Fiona said, popping an olive.

"You aren't going out in that?"

"What's wrong with this?" she said, looking down at her long-sleeved tee and favorite black jeans. "I'm just going to the coffee shop."

"It's freezing out, Fiona."

"It's, like, fifty degrees."

"I hope you don't wander around school like this, hardly dressed."

"At school, it's actually *cold*." When she got in from the airport, Fiona's bed was layered in enough thermal gear to overheat a Sherpa. Fleece was the new frill.

Her mom grabbed Fiona's denim jacket from the back of the chair and shoved it at her. "At least wear this."

David walked in the kitchen before Fiona could shove it right back. He kissed her long on the lips—her mother was standing *right there*!—before wrapping her in a hug. "Hey, you."

Her mother's heels clicked away down the hall, thank God. "Hey," Fiona said, hugging him back. It felt good pressing against this familiar chest, feeling those arms around her back, breathing in his fabric softener smell. There was relief, too, that it still felt good.

Leaning away slightly, she asked, "Did you get taller?"

"A little, I think." He smiled. His hair was longer, falling over his eyes. "You look great." He rubbed the back of his fingers along her new cheek. She felt only the pressure, not the touch. "The scar's so faint now."

She drew his hand down from her face. "We should go."

David looked at their hands knotted together. "You sure you want to go to the coffee shop?"

"I already promised Luce. And Ryan will be there. He wasn't here when I got in."

"Didn't he get back yesterday?"

Why, yes he did. "You'd think he could have at least been here to say hello," she said. "I haven't seen him in months."

"*I* haven't seen *you* in months," he said with a little smile. "What about some time alone?"

She pecked his cheek. "Later. I promise."

When they got to the coffee shop, they had to park down the street, there were so many cars already there. "Who the heck's playing?" she asked.

"Just open mic night, as far as I know." He smirked, nudging her shoulder. "Maybe they're anticipating you finally getting up there."

Fiona gestured to the empty place against her back, where her guitar wasn't. "Then they know something I don't."

She'd gotten through the whole semester without having to play for anybody. Luckily, Flem wanted to hear himself more than his students. But from the description of next semester's music class, she doubted she'd get so lucky again.

David shrugged. "It's probably just people home from school."

They found Lucy in the nook, sprawled across the futon, her battered boots clamped on the chair across from it. "Nice of you to finally get here," she said, sitting up. "I'm like the cranky old lady saving seats on Christmas Eve."

"A cranky old lady," Fiona said, hugging her much-missed best friend. "Such a stretch."

Lucy and David did a sideways, back-pat kind of hug before settling in. Because of the crowd, Fiona had to raise her voice. "Where's Ryan?"

Lucy pointed to a crowd at the bar. A few people separated him from Gwen, who now stood on the customer side of the counter. Her back to Ryan, she appeared to be in an animated conversation with people Fiona didn't know. Ryan was talking with a neighboring clump of strangers.

She couldn't believe he hadn't waited at home for her. She thought of their dad and uncle, who spoke only three times a year; they exchanged birthday and Christmas cards. It hurt her heart that she and Ryan might end up like that.

"Who wants what?" she asked, leaving David and Lucy so she could go claim her brother.

She said hello to Gwen and her friends. Then she hugged Ryan and asked if he'd grown, it'd been so long since she'd seen him. He rolled his eyes and poked the guy next to him, whose back was to them both. "Hey, this guy goes to NU. He said he knows you."

Oh crap, she *knew* that wrinkled button-down, those jeans, which looked so comfortable she'd considered stealing them on more than one occasion. Fiona's heart began to pound and would not listen to her commands to calm down.

The dark, wavy hair slowly turned. Jackson faced her, smiling lopsided. He pointed a thumb at Ryan. "I met the brother."

"So I see," she said.

"Did you really cry in the cafeteria last week?" Ryan asked, laughing. "When it snowed?"

"I did not *cry*."

"Please," Jackson said. "You were totally watery."

"Watery is not crying." The coffee shop guy handed her three mugs from his side of the counter. She picked up two, frowning at the third. "Ryan, help me with Lucy's."

"A very fine hair to split." Jackson stepped forward, picking up the third mug. "Point me toward this Lucy person."

Ryan nearly spit out his coffee. "Dude, you don't know what you're getting into."

"Now I'm really curious." He leaned close, whispering conspiratorially. "It might be a clue to the enigma of Fiona Doyle."

It was ridiculous how quickly her traitorous body reacted.

Jackson motioned her forward with his head. "After you."

Fiona widened her eyes at her brother, hoping he would correctly interpret her desperate look, which said: *Grab that cup from him. Jackson belongs to Northwestern Fiona, not Memphis Fiona.*

Unfortunately, he did not correctly interpret. Instead he turned toward Gwen and asked, "Babe, are those two with the dueling harmonicas playing tonight? They're hilarious."

Taking a deep breath, Fiona headed to the nook and tried to convince herself she was overreacting. When she handed David his mug, he looked to the stranger at her side—and back to her. She couldn't make eye contact with him. Instead, Fiona focused on her best friend. Lucy, too, was glancing between her and Jackson.

"So this is Lucy," Fiona said. "And David. Y'all, this is Jackson King. He goes to Northwestern, too."

Fiona cringed at the slow, totally inappropriate smile spreading across Lucy's face. "Well, Jackson King, it's nice to meet you. I've heard—"

Fiona coughed. Lucy caught her eye and let the rest of her statement fade away.

Jackson handed Lucy her mug and plopped down beside her. "Now, *you* look familiar." He looked up at Fiona, who stood helplessly at the end of the futon. "How could I possibly recognize your friend and not you? It's so wrong, the world's off balance—like a cat with a bandanna around its middle."

This was not happening. "It's the hair," Fiona said.

Jackson got another look at Lucy's wild, tall hair. Hair that "possessed its own soul," Lucy liked to say.

"It is pretty memorable," Jackson said, his eyes a little wider.

Fiona closed her eyes, took a breath, then opened them in David's direction. "He's sort of replacement Lucy. At school, I mean. It seems I'm a glutton for abuse . . . and strange metaphors."

"Another clue!" Jackson said. Then his eyes moved between her, perched on David's armchair, and David.

Fiona gestured to her unhelpfully silent best friend. "Feel free to take over any time."

"I don't have the heart, my friend," Lucy said, staring past Fiona's right shoulder.

Fiona followed Lucy's gaze. If she weren't hovering near a meltdown, she might have laughed. Because *of course* this was the perfect moment for Trent McKinnon to walk over and say hello.

Oh, but college had treated him well. Trent filled out his shirt like the fine male specimen he was. Given the bronze color of his face, she figured he must train outside most of the time. Wide, natural swipes of light blond highlighted his hair. The boy was, indisputably, part god.

But he wasn't Jackson King, was he?

"Hey, partner," he said, smacking Fiona on the shoulder. "Long time no see." Trent nodded to the others before turning back to Fiona. "Man, you look *awesome*."

"Oh. Thanks."

Trent bent his knees and brought his face inches from hers. Their eyes lined up—and then he *looked* at her like she'd never been looked at before. Her attraction to Jackson notwithstanding, she wasn't made of stone. Trent McKinnon was her first love, and they were close enough to kiss.

She was The. Worst. Girlfriend. Ever.

However, as his eyes continued to rake from left to right, she stopped swooning—and started feeling like a science exhibit.

"Seriously. I mean, it's incredible," he was saying.

David's hand tightened around her waist. Jackson leaned forward, his eyes darting between Trent and Fiona—not that they had far to travel. No one said anything for several long seconds as Trent continued scrutinizing her face.

The other three interrupted him at once.

"Dude, how about you give her some air?" said Jackson. "All right, show's over," Lucy said. And David: "Trent."

Trent straightened, rubbing his hand along the back of his neck. "Sorry. It's just . . ."

"Incredible. Yes, we know," Lucy said. "Hey, could you send Ryan Doyle over here?"

"Oh. Yeah," Trent said. After an awkward second, he pivoted toward the bar. "See you later, partner."

"Trent," Fiona called, because despite the inspection, she'd always have a soft spot for him. "Don't lose touch with the soil."

He smiled, fired a finger-gun at her, and disappeared into the crowd.

David's hand was still clenched around her waist. "I know you're friends with him, but Jesus, Fiona. That was ridiculous."

"He was being nice," she muttered.

"It was like you were a freaking science fair project." His voice came out louder than normal. It made Fiona look at him twice.

Ryan walked up. "What's going on? Trent McKinnon said I had to come over."

"I needed to give him an activity," Lucy said.

Jackson's eyes hadn't moved from Trent. "That dude's an asshole, right?" he asked no one in particular.

Ryan and David said *yes*, Fiona *no*, and Lucy *meh*.

"Okay, it's girl time," Lucy said, standing and pulling Fiona up with her. "See you boys later."

She dragged Fiona outside of the coffee shop, to the battered back porch by the parking lot. The night felt colder than when she'd left the house—and she'd left her jacket in the car, out of spite.

"He doesn't know, does he?" Lucy asked.

Sinking down onto the stairs leading to the parking lot, Fiona dropped her head in her hands. "The most awful thing is, I don't know which *he* you mean."

"It'll be fine. Just tell him."

"Tell *who what*?"

"Well, I imagine you'll have to tell both *whos*." There was a pause. "Just to clarify, we're talking about David and Jackson, right?"

Fiona nodded into her hands.

"Do you like him? Jackson?"

"I don't know. Maybe?" But the answer was noncommittal. She buried her face deeper into her hands. "I'm such a bitch."

"Why are you a bitch?"

"I don't want to be that girl. The *something better comes along girl*."

Lucy snorted. "That's life, Fiona—just a strung-together series of abandoning one thing for another."

"That's terrible! You'd just ditch me if someone better came along?"

"Best friends don't count," Lucy said, nudging her shoulder.

Fiona shook her head. "Everyone counts—well, everyone important. Loyalty matters."

"Does their loyalty matter more than *you*? Does what David wants—what he *deserves* or whatever—count more than what you want?"

Fiona looked away. The car directly across the parking lot had those silly stick-figure bumper stickers, one per family member—a mom, dad, girl, two boys, three dogs, and a cat. By stickers alone, Fiona knew the family's school, soccer and cheer teams, and that they didn't like the previous president. One sticker said *Mean People Suck.*

Fiona wondered why people felt the need to advertise their lives, their politics, and causes. It was like what Jackson said that morning in the cafeteria back in November—you shouldn't fall back on catchphrases. You should speak your own philosophy.

Still, she couldn't look away from *Mean People Suck.* "David liked me when I was a mess, Luce. Breaking up with him after, once I've been fixed—how's it different from someone divorcing his wife when he gets rich? Or famous or whatever?"

"First off, you're eighteen, so the marriage comparison is a stretch. Second, what? You've got to stay with David the rest of your life because he *noticed* you first? Don't get me wrong—good for David—but seriously, Fiona. It doesn't give him lifetime possession rights."

"It sucks, feeling like this."

"Yeah, I know."

"You do?"

Lucy gazed across the parking lot, too. "On the flip side. A girl I like at school likes somebody else more than me."

"Why didn't you tell me?"

"It's weird talking about it." Lucy shrugged. "It's just not me, the brokenhearted thing. Honestly, the whole fluttery-crush action isn't much better. All that up and down—it's too much emotional turmoil. I prefer to remain uniformly crotchety."

"Oh, Luce. I'm sorry."

"It was fair, though, her choice. Doesn't make her—or me—*less*. Decent people break up with other decent people all the time."

"You're a better woman than me."

"Agreed." Lucy shifted back, resting her hands behind her and leaning into them. "So let me ask you this—what if David broke up with *you*? How would you feel about it?"

Fiona frowned. "Annoyed—like, about why. Worried we couldn't be friends anymore."

"And Jackson? If nothing happened there?"

"Oh." The idea was worse than that rusty-nail feeling she got when Trent McKinnon broke her heart. *This* felt like a chunk of her getting sawed off by an old, dull knife.

She looked at her friend and whispered, "He smells like cantaloupe."

JANUARY

FI

Fi slogged to the sidelines, cold, wet, and irritated. For the past three hours, the Milton women's club lacrosse team—go Badgers!—had put forth the saddest display of skills and teamwork Fi had ever seen.

"Fi, got a sec?"

Fi looked up from her bag. Mandy Pittman, the coach who wouldn't let the team call her "Coach" since she was, in fact, only two years older than the seniors, stood a few feet in front of her. "Sure," Fi said.

Mandy sat beside her. "You doing okay?"

"I'm fine. Why?"

"The growling made me suspicious."

"I wasn't *growling*," Fi muttered.

"I'll be sure to clarify that with Kristin. She's worried you're going to come after her in her sleep."

Fi scowled, thinking about Kristin, the sophomore attack

who couldn't catch a ball if someone *handed* it to her. By some miracle, the girl had found herself in the perfect position for an assist from Fi—smack in front of the goal with no defenders near her. Fi even tossed her the ball at about a quarter strength, and Kristin missed it. How she managed to bounce the ball off her toe, Fi couldn't guess.

Still, she didn't want anyone to be scared of her. "She's upset?"

Mandy waved her off. "She has a brother here, two years ahead. They have disturbing wedgie battles in the cafeteria. I think she can handle a little growling from a freshman."

Wow. Ryan might be annoying, but at least he'd never tried to wedgie her—privately *or* publicly. A few years ago, she might have taken him, but he was about six foot two now.

Mandy pointed across the field, where the rest of the team was heading to the locker room. "They're doing their best, you know. Most of us are just here for the fun of it."

Fi zipped her bag and sat up, looking past the gray, soggy field to the campus beyond it. The buildings were pretty—stone, ivy-covered—and flanked by cobblestoned paths and sweeping bright-green lawns. "Yeah. I know."

Mandy turned to look at Fi. "Not to be nosy, but—why are *you* here?"

Fi's heart broke a little at the question. Did the "fun of it" part not apply to her? "Because I love it."

Mandy shook her head. "No, I mean why are you on *our* team? Why are you playing for Milton?"

"It's a good school," she said. "I wanted to be close to home."

"You didn't want to play, like, for a *good* team?"

"No, I did," she said, fiddling absently with the zipper on her bag. "I was talking to Northwestern, actually."

Mandy whistled. "Great school."

"But far."

"And that was bad because . . . ?"

Fi took a deep breath. She was partially tempted to reveal the whole story—the dead boyfriend, the blown chance at Northwestern, her multiple-personality emails to Candace Starnes, the head coach. "Personal reasons," she said instead.

"Look, Fi. I'm sure everyone on the team would love to learn some tips from you—but we are what we are. We're not trying to win the league. We're playing some lacrosse and having a beer after, okay?"

Fi nodded.

"If you want to talk to other teams, I'll help however I can."

Nice. I'm getting pushed off a bottom tier club team. She stood up, flinging her bags over her shoulder. "Are we done?"

"Yes, we're done."

Without another look at Mandy, Fi walked across the muddy field, flung her stuff—and then herself—into her car, and clenched the steering wheel.

Her. Life. Sucked. Lacrosse at Milton. Pathetic grades. Her best friend was currently a stuffed bear.

She wanted to see Trent.

It was such an urgent, unexpected thought. But what was she going to do? Just pop in? Vent? Cry on his shoulder? It wasn't like he would comfort her, tell her everything would be all right. Trent might offer his shoulder, but he couldn't stomach wallowing.

A muddy, sweaty mess, Fi cranked the engine and headed south anyway. A little over an hour later, she was following Highway 6 into Oxford. She took a right when the green University of Mississippi sign told her to. At first, the road was all sprawl and chain stores, but eventually, Fi was driving past big old trees and pretty buildings.

She'd been down here a few times before—some football games with Ryan and her dad—but she didn't know the campus well. She rolled down a window and yelled to a runner on the sidewalk. "Hey, is there a dorm around here called Stockman? Strockman? Something like that?"

The guy pointed to two tall buildings peeking over the trees. "Stockard. Take a right on Rebel Drive. You'll be right there."

She pulled into the lot, but couldn't get into the dorm without a card, and the desk appeared to be empty. Trent wasn't answering his phone, so she did the only thing she could think of—buy some bad coffee at the little mart across the street and wait on her hood until he came back. There better not be a back entrance he could slip into without her catching him.

Thirty minutes later, Fi was still on the hood, curling in on herself against the cold and wishing she'd brought a coat, or at least dry clothes. At four thirty, the sun was setting. Winter sucked.

She'd about given up and was digging through her bag for her keys when from behind her a voice said, "Fi?"

Trent stood at the side of her car, a few guys behind him, a girl right by his side. He looked older—collegiate—even though he wore only jeans and an Ole Miss sweatshirt that looked comfy enough to steal. He had the same backpack from high school.

"Hey," she said.

"Uh, *hey,*" he drawled, looking at her like she was unstable. "What the heck are you doing here?"

Fi looked past him to the people she didn't know. "Um—"

Trent followed her gaze. Quickly he gestured to the guys. "This is Zach, Brian, and Chris. Lacrosse." Then to the girl. "And Lindsey."

Fi held up a hand. "Hi."

Trent waved his friends on, saying he'd catch up with them later. Lindsey looked over her shoulder at Fi as she went to the dorm.

Hopping onto the hood, Trent slid beside her. "So, Crazy, why are you here?"

Fi sighed and slumped against the windshield. Trent followed suit. Her shoulder rested against his upper arm; her head lolled onto it as well. "I don't know. Bad day, I guess."

"How bad are we talking?"

Fi sighed. "My grades suck. Mom and Dad harass me daily. The lacrosse team hates me."

"Why do they hate you?" he asked.

She groaned, looking up at the sky. "They are *terrible*."

Trent was silent a moment. "And my role here is?" he eventually said.

"I don't know. I just drove down. I needed to . . . get some fresh air or something."

"The hermit has left its—what do hermits live in anyway? Tree trunks? Shells?"

"That's a crab. And I'm not a hermit."

He looked sideways at her, smirked, and then slid off the car. "Time to find out," he said, holding out a hand.

She studied his hand a minute before taking it. He gave a quick tug, pulling her across the hood to land just in front of him. "There's an ice cream social in the dorm lobby."

"An *ice cream social*? Have we time-warped back to 1923?"

"Every second Thursday. It's some crazy old tradition—maybe since 1923, I don't know. Anyway, they don't skimp on the sprinkles, so what do I care?"

Fi walked beside Trent, her hand still in his. She felt like a fourth grader, holding hands while crossing the street—on the way to an ice cream social, no less.

Trent scanned his card, and they left the cold of the parking lot for the overheated warmth of the dorm. They turned the corner and walked into a *packed* lobby—there had to be at least a hundred people.

She'd forgotten what her mom had told her about Ole Miss, how the girls went to football games in dresses and heels, the boys in coats and ties. People *dressed* here, and everything— even an ice cream social, apparently—was an event. There were maybe forty girls, all with updos and makeup and designer tops over skinny jeans. The place looked more like a club in Manhattan than a dorm lobby in Oxford, Mississippi.

Fi still had on her sweats.

Glaring at Trent, she snapped her hand out of his. "I can't go in there."

He grimaced, looking down at her and back to the room. The girl he'd been walking with, Lindsey, looked back at them. She'd shucked her coat to reveal a cute, off-the-shoulder tunic over leggings. She flashed Fi an unfriendly look.

Trent frowned. "You can't be mad at me! I would have told you to shower at least."

"Never mind." Fi turned back to the door. "I'll call you later."

He stepped in front of her. "Stop being melodramatic. We'll go to my room."

"What about the sprinkles?"

"Hey, Lindsey," he called. "Bring me some later, okay?"

Lindsey gave a fake smile and a quick nod. As they climbed the stairs, Fi asked, "What's up with the girl?"

"Nothing. We're just hanging out," he said, unlocking the door.

Trent's dorm room smelled like a larger, less-ventilated

version of his car—old food, dried sweat, and boy. Dirty clothes sat in messy clumps on the floor, and take-out containers overflowed from the trash can. Fi picked her way through the mess, looking for a semi-sanitary place to sit. "You are a pig."

"It's my roommate." Trent kicked a few clothes piles toward one wall, making a path, and pointed between the two desks, one fairly organized and the other lost in the mess of papers, convenience store cups, books, and Fi couldn't even tell what else. "He's disgusting. And hardly ever here, only long enough to deposit more crap."

"Open a window at least."

Trent cracked a window. Cold air blew in, but at least it took the smell back out with it. He pointed to the neater of the two beds, and Fi sat, scooting across to rest her back against the wall. Trent joined her, the two of them side by side against cold, painted, concrete blocks. "It's a Doyle kind of day," he said. "Ryan called this morning."

"Yeah? What'd he have to say?"

"He quit the lacrosse team," Trent said.

She jerked straight up. "What?"

"Can't say I'm shocked. All Christmas break, he wouldn't shut up about that intramural soccer team over fall semester. He'd never talked about lacrosse like that."

"When did he talk about soccer?"

"Uh, the *entire* break."

"Not with me. I only got the here's-all-the-ways-you're-screwing-up-your-life lecture."

"He's just worried about you"—Trent nudged her shoulder—*"because you crazy."*

"I'm not crazy," she mumbled. *Just pitiful.*

"Anyway, he said lacrosse was a ton of work and a pain with his schedule, and since he wasn't getting a ride either way, he'd rather play soccer."

"How could he just give it up like that?" she asked.

Trent looked at her with a single raised eyebrow.

"Shut up," she said.

Someone knocked on the door. "Trent? Are you in there?" a girl's voice called from the other side.

Trent slid off the bed and opened the door to Lindsey. She held a cup of ice cream out to him with a perfectly manicured hand.

"Thanks, Lindsey," he said, taking it. "Hey, we're still, uh, talking and stuff. Catch you later?"

Lindsey forced a smile across her face. "Sure. I was on my way to Chris's anyway." She waved bright-pink fingers toward Fi and drawled, "It was nice to meet you."

The Chris comment—a pretty blatant attempt to get him jealous, Fi thought—didn't hit its mark. "Great. Thanks again for this," he said, over the spoonful of ice cream in his mouth. He closed the door on Lindsey's pageant queen smile.

"She's so going to dump you."

He offered her the spoon. "She can't dump me if we never dated."

"Well, she wanted to."

Trent shook his head, looking dramatically forlorn. "Wanting does not a relationship make."

"So profound." She took the spoon from him, scraping another bite. "You weren't lying about the sprinkles."

"I know, right?"

"She's cute, though. Why aren't you interested?"

He spooned the last bit directly into Fi's mouth. "Not my type."

Fi took the cup from him, running her finger along the inside rim and sucking off the captured sprinkles. "Have you figured it out yet?"

"Getting there." He stretched out, so that Fi nestled between the wall and the nook created by his hips. She draped her legs over his—which hung over the edge, just like she'd imagined. "A girl who's naturally pretty, without tons of makeup and hair spray but not all hippie either. Funny. Sophisticated but not stuck-up. She has to be an impossible mixture of high and low maintenance—easy but not too easy, so as to keep me on my toes."

"Sounds complicated." She tossed the empty cup toward the trash can. It clattered to the ground, since there was no room.

"I'm a complicated man, Fiona Grace Doyle."

"You didn't used to be, Trenton Alexander McKinnon the

Third. There was a time when you thought fart jokes were the height of comedy."

He wagged a finger at her. "Never underestimate the time-lessness of the fart joke."

"Remember when we played in the backyard, and Ryan and I would trash-talk each other, and you'd try to keep up with those sad yo' mamas?"

Trent smiled with that single raised eyebrow. "What do you mean, *you and Ryan* trash-talked each other? The only one I remember doing the trash-talking was you."

Fi shoved him with her foot. "Figured you'd take his side."

He rolled his eyes before looking at his watch and holding it out to Fi. "Not that this impromptu playdate isn't the high-light of my day, but shouldn't you be getting back home? It's at least an hour drive."

Fi frowned at the pitch-black winter sky. "Ugh. That's going to suck."

"You could sleep here." He frowned at his roommate's bed. "Though I couldn't swear how clean those sheets are."

"That's nasty." Fi pushed herself up, stumbling over Trent's legs as she got off the bed. "I have an early class tomorrow anyway."

Trent stood and opened the door. "I'll walk you out."

"Maybe I should ruffle up your hair. In case Lindsey's lurking."

Trent paused to look at her. "You're awfully concerned about Lindsey."

"I'm not concerned," she mumbled.

He studied her another moment or so before taking her hand and dragging her down the stairs behind him. Once outside, both hunched over, drawing their thin sweatshirts further up their necks. Trent pulled her a little closer, wrapping an arm around her as people do when they're cold. At the car, Fi fumbled with her keys, her fingers stiff and shaky. She popped the door and slid in, cranking the heat. Trent squatted just in front of the open door, his face nearly the same level as hers. "If I make the slob wash his sheets and throw his crap away, will you visit one weekend? I could show you around."

"Um, maybe." Fi looked away from Trent to the steering wheel, her hands sliding up, down, and around it. It surprised her that the idea sounded good, suddenly. "Yeah. Okay."

"You'd have to shower. It's not required—I know you have an aversion—but I recommend it."

She smiled at her hands. "I think I can handle a shower."

Trent put his fingers under her chin, gently turning her face to him. "I'm glad you came down."

"Me too."

"It's going to be okay," he said, still crouched in front of her. Still holding her face so she couldn't look away from this heartfelt Trent McKinnon who made her uncomfortable and awkward and not sure what do with her hands. "You'll be okay."

Fi swallowed a sudden lump in her throat and nodded.

He dropped his hand and smiled just barely. "It's because of you, you know."

"What's because of me?"

"My evolution past the fart joke. And if you can wield that sort of magic on a dumbass such as myself, then it's only a matter of time before you pull yourself out of this funk."

They stared at each other a long moment. Trent slowly leaned forward—probably to hug her, she was sure it was just to hug her—but Fi immediately tensed, gripping the wheel. Trent paused, his eyes leaving her face to take in her rigid posture. He took a slow breath, shook his head, and slowly placed his lips on her forehead.

FIONA

Fiona hadn't taken a word of Lucy's advice. All break, she had avoided Jackson—and real conversations with David. Now back at school, she had a new semester with new classes—and the same old problems.

For example, she *should* be thrilled about her music class. Professor Weitz was a published jazz composer, played guitar beautifully and—unlike Flem—she'd yet to bow to anyone's clarinet. However, the class had One Major Flaw—or *opportunity*, as Weitz called it.

"Each of you will perform an original composition," she had said in the first class. "And benefit from the feedback of your peers."

"So," Weitz was now saying. "Who's up?"

A tall, pretty blond girl—Fiona recognized her from the dorm—walked to the front, oboe in hand. She sat on what Weitz called the *individual critique stool*. "I call this Interlude in

D," Oboe Girl said.

She played about five minutes. The piece was a little old-fashioned, but man, the girl's fingering was crazy good.

"Comments?" Weitz asked, when the girl finished and rested her oboe on her lap.

Fiona braced herself. The redhead held up her hand to go first—of course.

"Isn't the point to bring classical elements to modern compositions," she said. "Not the other way around?"

Redhead always went first. She had been the first to play for the class—cello—and had therefore escaped the bloodbath that these critiques had slowly descended into.

"It didn't sound very original to me," Flute Guy was saying, nodding toward Redhead. "It was just Brahms and Mozart squished together."

"Three hundred years later," Yankees Hat added.

And the ball was rolling. Oboe Girl sat up there, enduring the "helpful feedback" free-for-all, while Fiona broke into a sweat.

If she couldn't handle someone else being criticized, what was she going to do when it was her turn? Where was Flem and his eighties covers when she needed them?

After class, Fiona merged onto the path back to the dorm, biting her nails and wondering how to *"divide one of her existing melodies into phrases, making sure the cadence in the second phrase completes the incomplete cadence in the first."*

She called Lucy to whine. "It's negative ten outside. My

coat is freaking enormous."

"And I was just wondering about the weather in Chicago. And your coat."

"Sorry. Bad class."

"Let me guess," Lucy said with a sigh.

Okay, Fiona might have complained about this class a few times already. "Those people are *insane*. They'll eat me alive."

"It's only opinion. You don't have to listen to them."

"I just can't do it."

"Fiona Doyle," Lucy said. "You are the most ridiculous person I've ever met. *What kind of singer doesn't want to sing?*"

Fiona wished she knew. In theory, her fear should have been cut out of her, left on the operating room floor with the scars. She was fixed now. She should be able to do this.

"I know. I know, it's crazy," Fiona admitted. "I just don't know how to, you know, fix it."

"Well, you could always just *sing*."

"They'll all be looking at me."

"And lucky they will be, my non-scarred friend."

"I'm not *un*scarred."

"Oh. My. God. Get over yourself and sing a damn song."

"I can't."

"Why not?"

"None of them are ready."

Fiona had to pull the phone away from her ear, Lucy's exhale was so loud. "Right. New rule à la Tough Love. You can't call me again until you've sat someone down across from you, looked them in the eye, played your guitar, and sung one of *your* songs."

"What? That's not fair."

"Oh, it's totally fair—and a requirement for my sanity."

"But, I *have* played for people. I've sung for you."

"Amy LaVere covers don't count."

Curse Lucy and her Tough Love. "Okay. I'll sing one of mine for you. Tonight."

"What, over the phone?"

"Yeah. It'd be better anyway. Baby steps."

There was a painful pause. "Nope," Lucy finally said. "I've waited six years to hear an original Fiona Doyle. I want it in person." Fiona heard another deep breath. "So this is where I tell you good-bye and say I truly hope to hear from you soon."

"Lucy—"

"Hanging up now." And then she did.

Fiona stared at her disconnected phone—then trudged back to the dorm, numb. She didn't notice the biting cold or the slippery path or the ugly gray-white snow.

She was Lucyless. She felt like a cat with a bandanna around its middle.

She was almost to the top of the dorm steps when she looked up. The person she wanted to see most—and least—stood on the landing, looking down at her.

This was the first she'd seen Jackson since the disaster that was Otherlands. He'd texted a few times over break—asking her to meet him at the coffee shop, to help him spend his Christmas money at Shangri-La, to come with him to the Harry Potter marathon at the bargain theater. She gave lame excuses each time—rather than saying, *I have a boyfriend but I like you more, which makes me feel like the most horrible person ever.*

"You look like you lost your best friend," he said.

"What a perfect summary."

"What happened?"

"Something with Lucy. Music assignment thing." She shook her head. "Nothing."

Jackson opened the door and followed Fiona up the interior stairs.

"So," he asked. "How was the rest of your break?"

"Good." This was such a lie. "You?"

"Kind of sucky, really. First Christmas without Marcus."

Fiona drew in a long breath, looking at Jackson. "Oh, I'm so sorry. And all those texts—you needed a distraction."

"Looked like you had all the distraction you could handle."

So much for hoping the Coffee Shop Awkward hadn't been obvious. "Your schedule's good?"

He stopped and looked at her with that Jackson-y smirk. "What a lame subject change—you're as transparent as a well-dressed preacher."

"I have no idea what that means."

He laughed. "Yeah, classes are fine."

A few dark curls escaped his hat. She wanted to tuck them back in—or tug off the cap and wrap her hands in his hair.

She got them walking again, instead.

"What else are you taking?" he asked.

"Statistics, which is *ridiculous*."

"Why?" he asked, looking adorably baffled. "It's just common sense."

"Uh, no. I'm very sensible—and I still get the alternative and null hypotheses mixed up."

"Null assumes that the event you're hypothesizing has no effect. Alternative assumes the event created some change." He rattled this off like *everyone* had this information memorized. "Just remember null means no."

"Okay, math genius. Explain Bayes' Rule, then."

"The conditional probability of event A given event B—and then the other way around. It links the degree of belief in a proposition before and after accounting for evidence."

"Can you pretend you're me and take the tests?"

"Miss Fiona, really!" He laughed. "I can help you study, though."

Fiona reached her floor but stopped just outside the door. She adjusted the strap on her guitar case and took a deep breath. "Can I ask you a favor?" she said.

"Sure."

Fiona pointed toward her room. "I need an audience. For practice."

"An audience?"

"It's a requirement for one of my classes—to perform one of my own songs. I'm kind of freaking out."

"You weren't kidding, about not singing your own stuff?"

"Nope. I have a serious hang-up about it in public."

"Because?"

"I don't know, just because. But my grade—and scholarship— depend on it, not to mention Lucy won't talk to me until I do it."

Jackson wagged his eyebrows. "So I'd be your first?"

Oh my. "Forget it."

"No. No. I want to. Please. Please let me be your first." He knelt right in front of her, clutching his hands together in front of his heart.

"Let's get this over with," she mumbled and led him into her room.

Pointing to the chair by her desk, Fiona assumed her usual guitar-playing position—cross-legged on the bed. She took a few moments—longer than she needed, really—to tune, humming herself into pitch. She took a deep breath, hit the first chord, and sang.

> *If I'm inside out / And upside down*
> *When I'm piece by piece / And pound by pound*
> *How do I measure the melted?*
> *How do I know what's left is enough for you?*

Now came the instrumental part. As her fingers picked out the melody, she glanced up. Jackson was watching her with an intensity that made blood thrum in her ears. She looked back to her fingers and promised herself she wouldn't look back up again. She even closed her eyes, for extra security.

When I'm inside out / And upside down
When I'm piece by piece / And pound by pound
After the stitches have faded.
How will I know what's left is enough for you?

She kept her eyes closed nearly a full thirty seconds after she finished. Slowly, she opened one eye then the other, too stressed out to glory in the fact that she'd done it. Finally done it.

Jackson leaned forward in his chair, elbows on knees, hands joined in front of him. "You wrote that?" he asked, quietly.

Fiona nodded.

"Is it about that guy in the coffee shop?"

Ugh, *this* was why she didn't sing. "No, it's not about him." *It was about her, damn it.*

"It was really good," he said.

"You don't have to do that."

"Do what?"

She pulled her hair from its ponytail, dragging it over her face out of habit, and studied the pattern of her bedspread. "Compliment me or whatever."

"I'm not really a false praise kind of guy."

The lump in her throat made it impossible to speak. She

felt like a biology frog, flayed out and pinned down, all her insides open for inspection. She swiped her hands over her eyes, hoping he hadn't noticed the tears welling up.

He sat beside her. "I get the feeling I'm handling this wrong."

"It's not you," she said, shaking her head. "I don't think I was ready."

"You did just launch into it. No foreplay at all."

She looked sideways at him. "Why does it always feel like a double entendre with you?"

"Well, I'm not that subtle." He sat up and tucked her curtain of hair behind her ears, left side, then right. His fingers lingered on the skin of her neck while his eyes lingered on the scar.

"Seriously, let me make it up to you," he said. "Play something else. I'll be better this time." He leaned in and whispered dramatically, "More attentive to your needs."

Performance jitters flowed away, like someone had opened a tap—but stomach flutters immediately took their place. Her heart pounded like it might break through her ribs.

Surprising herself, she picked up the guitar and smirked right back at him. "They say it's never good the first time, anyway."

FEBRUARY

FI

Fi knocked on her advisor's door. The loose glass pane in the chipped, wooden door rattled. The door swung open, and Fi faced Brenda Lyon, cochair of the English department and Fi's assigned freshman advisor.

"We said four." Professor Lyon glanced at her watch.

"Right. Sorry, lacrosse practice went a little long."

Fi sat down on an unforgiving wood chair on the "guest" side of the desk. Lyon settled into a plush, leather one on hers.

This would be their fourth meeting—one each for first and second semester course selection, one in between to discuss Fi's uninspiring academic performance. Lyon always looked exactly the same—tightly pulled back graying hair, starched blue button-down, black skirt.

For the next three to four minutes, Lyon clicked through her computer. Fi eyed it from the back, as it coughed up her secrets like a traitor.

Finally, Lyon looked away from the screen. "I thought we'd come to an understanding about this semester, Fi."

"I'm sorry?" Fi asked, playing innocent.

"We're almost to midterms, and you're barely keeping your head above 2.0."

"Spanish and sociology should be Bs."

Lyon glanced back to the screen and raised an eyebrow. "How do you figure that math?"

"Well, I mean I'll get there by the end of the semester. Not immediately."

"It'll take an incredible amount of work. Dedicated work." Lyon looked back to the screen, shaking her head. "You'll forgive my skepticism."

"It's been a hard year," Fi muttered.

"Fi, *every* freshman has issues with transition. It's tough to adjust to the independence and responsibility. But you still have to."

"My issues are a little different."

"How so?"

"My boyfriend died nine months ago." She felt a wave of nausea the second the words were out of her mouth. Why did she keep using Marcus as a bargaining chip?

"I'm sorry to hear that," Lyon said, considering her a moment. "Have you thought about taking some time off?"

"Um, no." She only needed a second to mull over the idea. "But I don't want to do that."

"I can't give you another chance, Fi. You have to buckle down here."

She looked Lyon in the eyes. "I can work."

Lyon drummed her fingers against the desk, watching Fi. "Okay. But it's going to be hard." She angled back to the computer, clicking on a few screens. "You're on academic probation."

"Oh. Okay." After a moment, she added, "What's that mean, exactly?"

"You have until the end of this semester to get a minimum of 2.25 in all your courses. If you skip any classes or fail to complete assigned work, your professors will be required to notify me. And you cannot participate in any extracurricular activities until the probation period ends."

Fi nodded as Lyon went through the rules. A little extra work, a tighter rein on her schedule—she could do that. She *would* do that. But at that last bit, Fi held up a hand. "Wait—um, what qualifies as an extracurricular activity?"

"Any school-sanctioned groups that aren't linked to your academics. Student government, academic organizations, service clubs."

"Does that include the lacrosse team?" she asked as calmly as she could manage.

"Yes."

"Can we come up with other terms? So I can stay on the team?"

"There *are* no other terms. Probation is the only option you've got left."

"Right, I just think I can handle the work *and* the team."

"If you're on probation, your coach cannot *allow* you to play. It would violate a handful of school rules—and jeopardize the team's standing within their athletic league."

Fi dug what was left of her fingernails into her palm. She could feel skin peel into them. "And if I fail probation?"

"The fact that you're considering that as an option isn't giving me a lot of confidence, Fi."

"Lacrosse is all I have right now."

"So finish probation and get it back. But if you fail probation," Lyon said, leaning forward, "you won't have Milton either."

Fi closed her Spanish book with a smack. Both her and Jackson's coffee mugs trembled on the table. "I'm done."

"Are you fluent yet?" he asked, frowning at the coffee puddle under his mug.

"Only if you need directions to the library—or to buy cheese." She stretched, speaking through a yawn.

"Is it totally pathetic I want to go to bed"—Jackson yawned back, looking at his watch—"and it's only four?"

She had gone to bed at four for weeks after the funeral. Thankfully, it'd been a while since she'd been that bad off.

She stood, throwing her books into her bag. "I feel like a slug. I need to work out or something."

Even though she was teamless, Fi had started running ladders and throwing against brick walls. All the parts of her that had softened were slowly hardening. It was kind of lonely, though—no other girls, no Ryan, no Trent.

Jackson was still leaning like a lump over his chair. "Want to learn lacrosse?" she asked him.

Jackson raised his eyebrows. "Why not?" he said, and piled his things together.

In the coffee shop parking lot, Fi tossed her bag in the trunk and fished through the pile of lacrosse gear. After grabbing one of her sticks, an old one of Ryan's, and a few balls, Fi and Jackson walked in perfectly parallel paths to the neighborhood park across the street. Good thing it had lights, because it was already getting dark.

"So this is a stick." She handed him Ryan's, pointing to the different parts. "The shaft. The head. The ball goes in the pocket. See how your pocket is bigger than mine?" Jackson's eyes raised, and Fi shook her head. "No jokes I haven't heard. Grow up."

He smirked. "The guys have big balls?"

She groaned. "We use the same ball. But you're allowed to check in the men's game and not in the women's. The deeper pocket helps."

Taking a ball and her stick, she walked a few feet away. "Put your hands here and here. Bend your knees as you catch." She tossed the ball lightly. Jackson caught it. "Now shift your hands to here and here to throw. Like this."

He watched her and did a fairly good imitation. They tossed back and forth a few minutes, and as he looked more comfortable, she showed him how to cradle so he could run without losing the ball, and how to reach out and catch with one hand. They talked rules, teams, leagues, the differences between the men's and women's games.

"You're not bad," she said. "It's awkward at first for a lot of people."

"How was Marcus?"

"I never taught Marcus."

He looked surprised. "He wasn't interested?"

"He never seemed up to it."

Jackson sighed, shaking his head. "He never got to do anything."

"Because of y'all." Fi was only half-surprised when this blatant challenge came out of her mouth.

"We didn't have much choice," Jackson said, narrowing his eyes.

Fi frowned slightly. "I keep waiting for a hateful comment."

"Believe me, I'm biting my tongue."

"Why?"

Jackson studied her for a long moment. Then he took a deep breath and slowly lowered the head of his stick to the ground. The ball rolled out of it, resting at his feet. "The day before he died, he wanted me to read to him. We'd gone through everything in the house, so Mom had to scrounge up some old poetry book for us."

"Okay." She had no idea what this had to do with anything.

"So there was this poem. I can't remember much of it, but I'll remember those last two lines the rest of my life. He made me read them over and over."

"What were they?" she asked, a little terrified of the answer.

"*The winter of love is a cellar of empty bins / In an orchard soft with rot.*"

The *soft with rot* part sounded so familiar, but it took a few moments before she made the connection as to why. "He was mumbling that to me," she said. A clear image of Marcus, gaunt and pale in his dining room deathbed, lit up her brain. She hadn't thought of him like that in so long. "The last time I saw him."

"He said it was you," Jackson said, suddenly looking as somber as she felt. "You were going to be those empty bins, once he died. And it was maybe the saddest thing I had ever heard."

"The poem?"

"No, his voice. How he sounded. Like—like, all the joy he always felt just got sucked out of him all at once. It was tragic." He looked at her now. "It was the same way you looked, at the funeral. You looked just as tragic as he sounded."

She swayed on the spot, either because she might faint—or the earth was actually shifting beneath her.

How could her heart keep *breaking*? It was the most fragile, delicate thing. Why wasn't it more like her broken ankle— stronger when it healed? "I don't need your pity, Jackson."

"It's not pity," he said. "It's guilt."

"Is that supposed to be *better*?"

He shrugged. "It's the best I can do by way of apology."

As backward as their friendship seemed, she thought they'd been drawn together because each *understood* the other. "So being friendly now is just an apology for how mean you were to me before?"

He sighed, spinning his lacrosse stick where it rested on the ground. "You're right, we did keep him on a pretty tight leash. He bitched, complained, tried to find loopholes, but three able-bodied control freaks versus one guy who gets out of breath eating cereal—not a fair fight." He shook his head. "But, no, it's an apology to him—not you."

"Do you even like me?"

"You're fine. I mean, I don't really know you." He held up the stick with a shrug. "Besides your obsession with this weird sport."

Fi looked from her stick to his and back. She remembered sitting in Ryan's room years ago, asking him what she was good at, what defined her. The list was just as pathetic now as it was then. After all this time and all this pain, she added up to nothing more than Marcus and lacrosse. The two things she loved. The two things she'd lost.

For no reason she could explain, she spontaneously let out a cry—a guttural yell—and hurled her stick as far away from her as she could. She even took a few steps for momentum, like she was throwing a javelin.

She sank down to the grass, pulling her knees into her

chest and wrapping her arms around them. She saw Jackson's feet in her peripheral vision—how they turned away from her, hesitated, then turned back and walked over.

He sat down a few feet away, kicked his legs out straight, and leaned backward against his elbows. He didn't speak, so Fi didn't know if this was one of those coffee-shop-comfortable-silences, or if he was waiting for her to say something first.

"If I never met Marcus, I'd be at Northwestern. I'd still have it," she said.

"Have what?"

She pointed in the general area of her thrown stick. "I couldn't love them both at the same time. I had to pick one."

"Looks like you picked wrong."

Fi groaned and buried her head in her knees. "Do you really think so?"

"God, I don't know." He sighed. "He was happy. I was furious. Now you're miserable, and I feel guilty. Flip side—what? Y'all never met? He and me, we'd have been the same we always were. You'd have been the same as you were before you met him. You and I could have avoided this weird . . . friendship or whatever."

"I'd have been the same," Fi repeated. She wished she knew which was better.

Since May, it had felt like horrible, cancerous thoughts had been eating her from the inside out. "A few months ago, you said that everywhere you looked, you saw some connection to him."

"Yeah," he said cautiously. "So?"

"Do you think anyone, you know, got his organs?"

"I know Mom and Dad signed the papers, after. I don't know what actually got donated, though."

"Do you think it would have hurt him?"

Jackson exhaled. "He was dead."

"Do you think he's happier now?"

"I don't know."

She looked at the sky, like she could squint out the view past the clouds. "Do you think he can see us?"

"Jesus, Fi." Jackson flopped backward in the grass with a groan. "What do you want from me here?"

Marcus would have answered. He would have talked for hours about all of this with her, analyzing all the philosophical angles. "I want you to be him."

"Well, he's dead." Jackson stood up from the grass. Bits of it stuck to his holey, worn jeans. "I'm not a substitute."

That's obvious. "What are you then?"

Jackson shook his head and turned. He spoke over his shoulder as he walked away. "Just a bitter, alive guy without his freaking twin."

FIONA

Fiona was looking out the common room window. The sky was a smooth, cloudless blue, and the trees stood perfectly upright. Usually, the wind blew them around so wildly, they might javelin themselves through the window.

"You're not coming home?" her mother was asking, over the phone.

"Everyone else has a different spring break. No one will be in town."

"Your father and I will be here."

As tempting as that *sounds . . .*

A few weeks ago, she'd had the same conversation with David, only he was asking her to visit UT. "I can't afford a ticket," she'd said. If she wasn't going home, her dad sure wasn't going to fly her to Knoxville to see her boyfriend.

"I could come to Chicago," he'd said. "During my break.

We could see a Cubs game. Try that stuffed pizza you talked about over Christmas."

"Yeah, you'd like it."

"Great. So, should I buy the ticket?"

"Sure," she'd said, wishing she felt more enthusiastic about the idea. "That'd be fun."

She hadn't shared David's travel plans with her mother, who was still complaining, long distance. "You're just going to stay up there, alone?"

"Lots of people are staying on campus," Fiona said. Jackson, for example.

"I wanted to take you shopping."

Good Lord, the woman had a one-track mind. "I have plenty of clothes."

"Everything has holes. It looks ratty."

"I'm in *college,* Mom. No one cares how I dress."

"You should care," she said. "You have so much to show off now."

Translation: You really looked like crap before. "Mom, will you just give it a rest?"

"Watch the tone, young lady." After an uneasy pause, her mom added, "I didn't push you before, because you were self-conscious. But now, I don't see why—"

"You didn't push me?" Fiona gave a bitter laugh. "Are you kidding?"

"I'm sorry?"

"You've been trying to improve me since I was *five.*"

"I am your mother," her mother said. "It's my job to make your life better."

"Make *me* better, you mean."

"I didn't say that."

"You didn't need to. You've had thirteen years to make it clear."

"Fiona, what on earth are you talking about?"

As her mom spoke, Jackson walked in. He leaned against the common room wall, watching her. She must have looked as angry as she felt, because after a second he mouthed, *The best friend?*

How many of her dramatic moments was this boy going to witness?

"Forget it. I gotta go," Fiona said—and then she hung up *on her mother.* She stabbed the phone's *off* button and threw it to the couch across the room.

"Are you okay?" he asked.

"My mother. She drives me crazy."

"It's fifty degrees outside." He pointed out the window. "That should cure you of just about any negative emotion."

"It's not even windy," she said, like it was the *weather* curing her—and not Jackson, standing there, looking adorable. He wasn't bundled up, just in a long-sleeved Henley and those jeans she coveted.

"I'm giddier than a twelve-year-old girl at a boy band concert," he said.

"That one actually made sense," she said.

"We should go out before the arctic tundra returns." He held out a hand, hoisting her up.

Mother, shmother. Grabbing a fleece, she followed him down the stairs and into the unseasonably balmy weather.

They walked side by side on the crowded campus path, squeezing close together since lots of other people had the same idea. Jackson suggested they head to the lake.

"What's the update on your music class?" he asked.

"It's my turn on Friday." This was the last thing she wanted to talk about.

"So that's great, right? Finally get to show off your stuff?"

"It's going to be awful." Fiona nearly threw up when Weitz handed out the performance date. February 27.

Jackson nudged her in the side. "Man, you're dramatic about this whole thing. It's just a bunch of other students and a professor. How bad could it be?"

"The class is sadistic—and the professor isn't that much better. Last class two people played. She called the pianist's arrangement 'sophomoric' and told the girl on guitar to keep working and perhaps she'd stumble onto something worthy of revision."

Jackson snorted. "Statistics doesn't look so bad now, huh?" Then he spread his arms toward the beach in front of them. "I gotta say, before I got here I was skeptical about the whole *beach in Chicago* thing. But when it's not subzero outside, it's pretty awesome."

"It's a nice perk." Fiona took in the view—clean beach

with a blue lake so big, it looked like ocean.

He walked onto the sand, stopping a few yards away from the line where wet met dry, and sat down. Looking over his shoulder, he patted the space beside him.

She sat next to him, arms wrapped around knees, but eventually both lay back, heads only inches apart in the sand. He smelled like some combination of wool, coffee, and soap—and just the littlest bit of fruit.

Fiona closed her eyes and willed her fair skin to soak up the vitamin D. She wondered if her new skin would color the same as her old skin. She'd never even thought to ask the doctor.

She turned her head toward Jackson and was surprised to see him lying on his side, elbow propped up in the sand. He was looking at her, his head resting in his hand. For a moment, that's all they did—lay there and stare. A border of deep cobalt blue rimmed his green irises. His jaw and cheekbones looked sculpted, like they belonged on a statue in a museum somewhere, not on a boy who was looking at her *like that.*

God, but he was beautiful.

After a time, Jackson lifted his free hand and slowly ran a finger under the length of her scar—from the space between her right eyebrow and nose, up her forehead, then repeating the path from under her right ear, up to the outside corner of her right eye.

She didn't speak, her breath unsteady from watching him,

from feeling the gentle weight of his finger against her face.

The circuit complete, he gently rested his palm on her cheek and began tracing the scar once more—this time with his thumb on the new skin.

Under the gentle weight of his thumb, her skin felt tingly. Like a foot that had fallen asleep and was 90 percent awake again.

Oh. *Oh.*

She could feel it.

She could *feel* it.

Her whole body tensed at the sensation. His gaze moved from her skin to her eyes. His palm still rested on her cheek, and his thumb rubbed lightly back and forth against the actual scar line. "Go out with me," he said.

"We are out." Her voice came out as husky as his, like they were in a crowded library, not alone on the beach.

"*Out* out. Friday night, after you play." He smiled, leaning in a little closer. "We'll toast the standing ovation."

She frowned at this reminder. "More like drink away my sorrows."

"Or that." He leaned closer and said again, "Go out with me."

Fiona's previously-numb-and-now-tingling skin screamed *yes!* Her heart and spine, her muscles and bones and nerves— all her real, tangible pieces pushed her toward *yes*. But her invisible parts—those bits that felt guilty when she actually enjoyed herself; that chunk of her that knew what Friday held in store—answered first. "I'm not sure—"

Jackson interrupted her, shaking his head but not taking his hand from her face. "Look, I get it. You've got some *complications*. Go out with me anyway."

Fiona swallowed her fears and guilt and nodded. Jackson smiled. She smiled back. And then they were covered in the sudden, cold shadow of an enormous, fluffy cloud.

"They look so harmless up there, don't they?" Jackson said, looking up at the single cloud blocking all the sun.

Fiona wanted to spend hours out here with Jackson, but instead she stood and held out a hand. "We should get back anyway."

It felt fifteen degrees colder on the way back. Both walked hunched over with hands crammed into pockets. The pace was faster than on the way out—their bodies a little closer, too.

Jackson cracked jokes as they went, coming up with stranger and stranger suggestions for their date. Dinner was too predictable, what about visiting the International Museum of Surgical Science? Trying to climb the Bean in Millennium Park? Throwing plates at a restaurant in Greektown?

Fiona laughed at first, going along with it. A little giddy from the idea, but then her reality came knocking. "You know, maybe we should do it another day. Not Friday."

He gave her a careful look. "Why?"

"That day's not a great one for me."

"Right. So we give you something to look forward to—a

light at the other end of the performance tunnel."

She shook her head. "It's not that, really. It's . . . well, this will sound stupid, but the date? February twenty-seventh? It's historically a bad one for me."

"You have an unlucky *date*?"

Fiona nodded, feeling silly.

"That's intriguing," he said. "Is this part of the Fiona Puzzle?"

"Like I said, it's stupid. But maybe another day?"

Jackson stopped, his expression suspicious. "Look, if you don't want to—"

"No, I do," she said quickly. She looked at the sky, now covered in sheets of clouds. "It's just . . . I'm usually—always—cranky that day. Like . . . bitchy. I'm trying to save you. By Saturday I should be fine."

"Tell me why."

She took a breath. They were still stalled there, blocking the path as all the other people who'd had the same great idea fled the weather change, too. "It was the day I had the accident." She gestured toward her face, in case he needed clarification. "I hardly remember it—the accident, I mean. And theoretically this year should be different—you know, since I'm all fixed. But—"

Jackson studied her a minute then gestured to the path, getting them both walking again. "Let's keep it Friday. If the day really is terrible, I'll grant you permission to postpone till Saturday."

"You'll *grant* me?"

"You're welcome."

She laughed. "I really hate it. I wish I'd just get over it already."

He nudged her shoulder, staying closer than ever once the nudge was over. "You got some weird hang-ups, girl. Audiences *and* calendars—oh, the horror!"

"You sound like Lucy. And Ryan."

"What you need is some Good Day Replacement Therapy."

"Which is?"

"Balance it out. If you're destined to have this sucky day, designate a really good one, too. The day you'll always wake up ridiculously happy." He shrugged and looked over at her, smiling lopsided. "So, what's the good day?"

"I don't know. Maybe May eighteenth?"

"What happened then?" he said, frowning.

She gestured to her face again. "The surgery. Seems appropriate, if the goal is balance."

Jackson stopped again, eyeing her differently than before. After a breath, he pulled her off the path with him, getting them out of the way of the others en route to countless places. He narrowed his eyes, asking carefully, "So . . . what *was* the surgery?"

She touched her cheek, feeling it more in her fingertips than on her face. She *had* felt Jackson's touch on the beach, hadn't she? "A deep tissue skin graft."

"Which is?"

"It's pretty technical."

His brow arched upward. "Said the artist to the engineer."

Fiona sighed. "It was a transplant. They took out all my bad skin and replaced it."

His eyes traveled to her face, following the line of scar circling her eye. Slowly he asked, "Replaced it with what?"

"Uh, new skin."

"Which came from?"

"Oh—an organ donor." It was odd, how easily she let this information out. When had she become so blasé about wearing someone else? She hunched further over, feeling the cold more and more. Trying to get them back on the path, she said, "I'm freezing. Let's head back."

Fiona turned back to the path, but Jackson didn't follow. She pointed her head toward their dorm a few times, but Jackson stayed put, his eyes locked on her face. Even so, he had a faraway look.

"What did you say the date was again?" he asked.

"May eighteenth." She stomped her feet. "Seriously, let's go."

He shook his head, still focused on her but not at all. "What time?"

"What?"

"What time was your surgery?" His tone was so weird. Like a strangled yell, as if the words forced their way out on their own.

The clusters of people passing looked over their shoulders at him—and she gawked right along with them. "What the heck is wrong with you?"

"TELL ME THE GODDAMN TIME!"

She recoiled back. "Afternoon. I don't know! I got there at three maybe. Why are you yelling at me?"

"When did you get the call?"

More people were looking now, whispering to each other about this one-sided public argument. Fiona wished they'd clue her in. She had no idea what was going on. "What call?"

"That there was a donor! When did you get the call?!"

Fiona stared at this boy who'd replaced funny, easygoing, sarcastic Jackson. *This* boy looked like he was drowning, right here on the snowy path. Like some great burden was pushing him under a waterline no one else could see. Like some horror, some awful thing, was suffocating him.

And suddenly, she couldn't breathe either.

She began backing away. "We shouldn't talk about this . . . we can't . . ."

In two steps he closed the distance and grabbed her hand, holding her still. Quieter now, like he was forcing himself to stay calm, he said through clenched jaw, "When did you get the call?"

Eyes wide, Fiona shook her head back and forth. She felt the tears—only on the one cheek, though she was certain both were damp. "There are rules," she choked out. "We're not supposed to know."

Jackson let her go. His eyes did not leave the right side of her face as he began walking backward. Fiona stayed in place, watching him retreat farther and farther until he eventually turned and walked away.

FI

Trent jogged into the lobby, rounding the corner less than a minute after Fi gave her name to the check-in counter guy. His wet hair had dripped a dark ring along the collar of his shirt, which clung to him unevenly. Even so, he grabbed Fi up into a damp hug. "I thought you'd bail."

Fi hugged him back. She couldn't remember the last time she'd really *leaned into* someone. This proximity to skin and smell, body and life, was a surprising comfort.

He let go first, and Fi pulled back quickly, embarrassed by her clinginess. She gestured to herself. "I even showered."

He took a step back, getting a bigger view. "Yes, you did." Then Trent grabbed her hand, dragging her behind him as they went upstairs.

In the common room on his floor, mostly guys, a few girls—including Lindsey—sat on battered couches or perched on beat-up coffee tables. Plastic cups and an assortment of glass bottles littered the few open spaces.

As Fi and Trent passed the gathering, maybe half looked up. Pausing in the hallway, Trent gestured to Fi with his free hand. "Y'all, this is Fi, a friend from home."

There were a few "Hey, Fi's," and she waved in response before Trent pulled her onward to his room. She sat on his bed as he rubbed a towel through his hair and frowned at his dampened shirt. "I was still getting dressed when you got here," he said, pulling his shirt over his head and tossing it on the bed before rummaging in his closet for a fresh one.

Fi looked away from Trent's half-nakedness. She'd seen it a million times before—even so, it felt weird all of a sudden.

He'd buttoned up by the time she turned back. The mattress dipped from his weight as he sat beside her to pull on socks and shoes.

"So, what's the plan?" she asked.

Still bent over his feet, Trent gestured back toward the common room with his head. "We can hang in the lounge if you want. You can meet some people. There are a couple of parties later."

"How much later are we talking?"

Trent raised a single eyebrow. "You going to turn into a pumpkin or something?"

"She didn't turn into a pumpkin, her carriage did." Fi looked at her watch. "I just don't know how late I want to drive home. Highway and all that."

Trent looked at her with a long, steady eye before saying,

"Just see how it goes. We can always come back."

"All right." Fi stood and straightened her top—one that Caroline Doyle had picked, no less. When she left the house, her mother actually froze for a second, as if seeing Fi in cute clothes—with makeup! And blow-dried hair!—caused her temporary paralysis.

Trent smiled and stood. Standing just in front of her, he actually leaned in and kissed her head before pulling back with a confused frown. "Did you get taller?"

Fi held up her right foot, showing off her boots. "Two-inch heels."

"The world's gone lopsided," Trent replied with a laugh. "Come on," he said, grabbing her hand again.

As she'd gotten ready that night, Fi had wondered why she was driving over an hour to go to some parties where she wouldn't last twenty minutes. But by the time everyone in Trent's common room started grabbing their sweaters and keys to head out, it was almost ten. She'd spent two hours having fun with strangers.

Chris, one of the lacrosse players Fi had met during her parking lot freak-out, gave her a hand, pulling her up from the couch. "You coming?" he asked with a smile.

"Oh. Um—" She paused, not actually sure *what* she wanted to happen next.

On the one hand, she was having fun. Trent's friends were nice; hanging out with her best friend felt like the perfect kind of therapy.

On the other hand, as nice as this couple of hours had been, she felt . . . out of shape for it. Like the day when she met Marcus, just hobbling up the handicap ramp in a cast and *standing* for ten minutes had worn her out.

"No," she said. "I should probably head out."

Before he could speak, Lindsey passed, and, with a look Fi could only describe as feline, she idly dragged her fingers across Trent's chest and asked, "You're coming though, right, Trent?"

Trent gave Fi what Ryan called "the look." Both had used it over the years, and though it was just a glance, it communicated many things. Not the least of which was You Drive Me Freaking Crazy. "Guess so," he said.

"I'll get my stuff," Fi said.

Trent mumbled for them to go on ahead, he'd catch up. Trying his doorknob with no luck, she waited for him to come up the hall. "It's locked," she said.

Fishing keys from his pocket, he held open the door. "Looks like the roomie didn't need to clean his crap after all."

Fi decided not to point out that the room wasn't really *clean*—just mildly less disgusting. "I never promised I'd stay."

"Whatever."

She put on her jacket. "I was going to end up the third wheel anyway."

"Wonder what that's like." He took a sip from his plastic cup, watching her over the rim. "What are you talking about? Third wheel to who?"

Fi walked up to him, dragging her fingers across Trent's chest just as Lindsey had. Okay, it was snide. And her fingers lingered on the edge of his muscles longer than necessary. She pulled her hand away. "Sprinkle girl."

"I don't care about Lindsey." He watched her for a long, *long* moment. Fi couldn't decipher his expression—even so, her heart beat faster.

"I should probably get going," she said, faking a lame yawn.

"Don't do that," he snapped. "Just go if you want to."

"It's not like I didn't have fun," she said, sounding whinier than she meant to. While having the same best friend for nine years definitely had perks, the "seeing right through you" part could be annoying. "It's just, you know, I have to work up to it."

Suddenly, Trent's whole body tensed. He yelled—growled, something—and threw his cup against the wall. Frothy liquid splashed upward, splattering against the painted concrete blocks, before the cup fell to the floor with a little *tink.* "That would have been more impressive with a glass," he said, frowning.

Fi stared from Trent to the cup. "And just as crazy."

"Since when are you Queen of Sanity?"

"Yes, that's helpful," she snapped. "Tell me I'm crazy. Call me a hermit. Smugly look down your nose at me. While. I. Grieve."

"Are you kidding me? I have listened to you whine for almost a year! Months longer than anyone else has been able to. Your own *mother* is sick of it!"

"Oh no, Caroline Doyle is disappointed in me! What shall I do?"

"Right, because no one else's feelings matter anyway, do they?"

"No one else has a dead boyfriend in a jar!"

"I am *sick* of your dead boyfriend." Trent's nose flared at the corners as he yelled. "And your crappy lacrosse team! And your stupid issues with your brother!"

"Just say you're sick of *me,* Trent. It's all the same thing."

"Yeah, okay, sometimes I am sick of you. You're a hell of a lot of work, Fi."

"And you're a horrible best friend!"

"I never wanted to *be* your best friend." Scowling, he picked up the cup and chucked it into the trash can. "And if this"—he gestured between the two of them—"is what we are now, I'm not interested anymore."

Fi's head snapped back like he'd hit her. "Are you breaking up with me?"

"I already told you," he answered quietly. "You can't dump someone you never dated."

"We dated," Fi answered weakly, not sure what they were fighting about anymore.

"No we didn't—because *you never let us.* And *you* are always the one who gets to decide." Trent watched her a long time, his chest pulling in big, heavy breaths. "This is the last time though, Fi. Last chance. Tell me what my role is here. Pick one."

"I can't." She wiped away the sudden tears with her fingers. "I can't."

"Pick," he demanded, his teeth biting down on each other.

Fi was full-out crying by this point. Mascara coated her fingers. Grabbing her bag, she wrenched open the door. As it closed behind her, she choked out, "Why bother? I never pick right."

FIONA

Fiona had not seen or heard from Jackson since he left her on the path. She'd stood there, watching him slowly disappear, and hadn't had a call, text, note on the door, or "accidental run-in" since. She'd brooded about going to his room, but couldn't stomach all the potentially awful outcomes. He might refuse to speak to her or slam the door in her face. Or demand back what was his brother's.

Or might be his brother's.

They would never know. The big question—*Did Fiona Doyle wear part of Marcus King?*—would never get answered. Even if she *wanted* to find out, which she very much did not, the hospital wouldn't tell her. As she heard over and over before the surgery, the anonymity of donor and recipient was nonnegotiable.

She'd thought about calling her parents, just to double-check. But then she'd have to deal with her mother, and she had enough major life crises at the moment.

Because today was February 27—the day nothing good ever happened. The day she would perform an original song in public for the first time ever. The day she may or may not be going on a date with a boy who may or may not despise her.

She procrastinated in bed as long as she could—counting the ceiling's acoustic tiles, attempting to find a pattern in the floor's linoleum speckles. Each minute wasted was one less to worry about.

When the phone rang with Ryan's programmed ringtone, Fiona hesitated. Of course he'd pick *today* to finally call. After three rings, she answered. "Hey."

"How you doing?"

Fiona stared at the ceiling.

Ryan tried again. "I got the message about the critique. I was calling to wish you good luck."

"That was days ago."

"Sorry. It's been busy."

She did not say *We're all busy, Ryan* or harass and scold him like their mom—she didn't reply at all.

Ryan sucked in a big gulp of air and exhaled the statement, "I'm dropping off the team."

Fiona shot upright. "What?"

"It's too much—my grades are mediocre, I'm constantly canceling on Gwen, you're always mad at me. I never have time for *anything.*"

"But you love soccer."

"I think I'd love it a lot more if I played club. Had some *fun*, you know? Coach kids or something." He sighed. "Mom and Dad will probably kill me. Walking away from the scholarship."

The scholarship reminder felt like a gut punch. One more reason to stress out about the critique. "They'll understand," she said, hoping it was true. "Mom wasn't big on you playing Division One anyway."

He said "yeah" noncommittally. "Enough about me. How are *you*?"

"I'm playing for a group of music and theater majors— who are quote, *encouraged to comment,* unquote. Which is just code for ripping each other to shreds."

"You'll do fine."

"I really don't think I will."

"Then you'll just *do*. And that's okay, too."

Despite herself, Fiona smiled. Then she looked at her watch. "Crap, I'm late!"

Ryan called "Good luck!" as she hung up. Grabbing her guitar and a stack of Moleskines, she ran through campus. Mounds of dirty snow lined all the paths.

At class with seconds to spare, she leafed through her books, still not certain which song to perform. She'd re-arranged five, not sure about any of them.

Weitz consulted her list. "Are you ready, Jacob?"

Jacob had been in Flem's class, and Fiona knew he was

good. He sat on the stool, looking cooler and more relaxed than Fiona could ever imagine being. He put his violin on his shoulder and said, "This is just something I've been working on."

A few minutes later, he lowered his violin. Fiona couldn't say if he'd played a waltz or a pop song. He could have sprouted horns and danced an Irish jig, for all she knew. But when Weitz said, "Thoughts?" Fiona was all ears.

"I'm not familiar with that technique," said Redhead. She tilted her head, like she found this discussion oh, so interesting. "It seemed almost self-taught. Did you train with any *trained* musicians?"

"Several," Jacob said calmly. "I was first chair in the Boston youth symphony."

Normal people might have been impressed, but not Redhead and her bloodthirsty friends. Flute Guy, Yankees Hat, and a few black-clad drama majors offered the following helpful insights: *Your fingering looked awkward. Was that intentional? Are you certain your violin was properly tuned? I didn't really hear anything original.*

Ten minutes later, when Jacob's work had been picked apart until it was nothing but a senseless pile of quarter notes, Weitz let him go and called Fiona up.

With shaking hands—her cuticles were a mangled mess by now—she pulled her guitar from its case, brought the whole stack of Moleskines up front, and sat on the stool.

"You're a singer *and* musician, yes?" Weitz said, looking at her notes. "Your composition will come with lyrics, I assume."

"I was only going to play," Fiona said. She was near enough meltdown from just that.

Weitz raised an eyebrow—then nodded to Fiona's guitar. "When you're ready, Ms. Doyle."

Fiona clenched her jaw, swallowed, and began to strum.

It didn't start well. She played like someone taking a test. She *sounded* like a paint-by-numbers painting—formulaic, emotionless, and without any nuance at all. As she picked the melody, it only got worse. Each note was a painful *and-now-I'm-going-to-play-the-A* experience.

She sucked.

When she finished, Fiona kept her eyes on the strings, terrified to look up. There was complete silence.

Professor Weitz cleared her throat. "Yes, well. That was . . ." She looked at the class. "Anyone have thoughts to share?"

It was an assault.

There was a glimmer of something intriguing, but it was hard to pinpoint it in the mess. The progressions came off stale. It's a case of proficiency without spirit. I wasn't sure of the point. I found myself craving more emotion. It was trite. It had no soul.

You're really a music major?

It wasn't just Redhead and her ilk, either. Almost everyone— even French Horn Girl, who was normally as quiet as Fiona— had something to say. "I think it needed a little something more."

Fiona sat on the stool, paralyzed and taking it.

"Did you write lyrics to go with this composition?" Professor Weitz eventually asked.

Fiona nodded, forcing herself to say, "Yes."

"Play it again, please. With the lyrics. We might get a better sense of intention."

The students murmured lukewarm agreement to this idea.

Fiona's eyes darted from her persecutors to their leader. "Um, I hadn't really prepared—"

"You've had weeks to prepare." Weitz leaned back in her chair. It creaked in a sharp D. "As this is a significant portion of your grade, I suggest you try once more."

Fiona exhaled, sucked as much air back in as she could, and tried again.

I got ripped down the middle / Accidentally

Her voice creaked as she reached for the A. She hadn't warmed up her vocal cords at all.

I heal little by little / Coincidentally

The chord change worked better here, now that it was paired with words. Still, it highlighted some awkward spots in the phrasing.

It's piracy / It's mutiny / God I hate the scrutiny

What was she thinking, putting this chorus with these lyrics? They didn't make any sense together. She wished she'd worked with the words, when she'd done the rearranging.

Dates create me and narrate me / Fate dictates me and negates me.

And back to the ridiculous refrain about pirates.

As the last note bounced around the room, Fiona forced herself to face her tormentors head-on. She hadn't looked up the first time, so she wasn't sure if these expressions were any better.

"Anyone?" Weitz said, and it began again. *I wasn't sure how the phrasing was meant to underscore the lyrics' intentions. The meter was off, it distracted me. There wasn't any real marriage between the lyrics and the composition; they just felt put together without much thought; it was like three different songs. It didn't make sense.* And then the worst one of all: *The lyrics confused me—was I meant to feel pity?*

"I agree with the class, Ms. Doyle," Weitz said. "I think you have some work ahead of you."

Fiona nodded. Weitz looked at her watch. "Okay, everyone. Next week then."

Fiona kept her head down and gathered her things. She zipped her guitar up as quietly as she could and slid it on her back carefully. She took each step from the music building to her dorm as if the path was covered in ice, walking as if to minimize the impact of her every move.

Her throat burned—not from singing with cold vocal cords but from the lump stuck right in the middle. Her mind may have been numb from the whole thing, but her eyes seemed to work fine. Warm tears spilled freely down her cheeks as she walked home.

She'd go back to her room and stay in bed the rest of the day.

Head down in the dorm lobby, she collided with another body on the way. Books slapped to the floor. She and her victim stooped to pick them up. "Sorry."

And *of course* it was Jackson.

One of her hands clutched the Moleskines as the other went to wipe her cheeks. She wanted to erase the evidence. Why did she always cry in front of this boy?

"It was bad?" he asked.

Fiona didn't respond. Surely the answer was clear enough.

"Sorry," he said.

She shrugged. His eyes went to her face—to the area that always seemed to mean everything. Slowly, he began to back away. When a good ten feet separated them, he said, "I can't make it tonight. Something came up."

She watched him continue his path backward, her hand on her cheek. Then, like he'd done the day they'd discovered their "coincidence," he turned away. Through the glass doors, she watched until he'd disappeared down the path, swallowed by the icy branches on the leafless trees.

She turned toward the stairs. On the way, she passed the row of three trash cans—brown for garbage, green for glass and aluminum, blue for paper. She took only the briefest look at her Moleskines before dumping the lot of them in the blue one.

Maybe one day, they'd be turned into something useful.

FI

Fi was still in her pajamas—well, sweats and a T-shirt—when she opened the door. Jackson stood on the porch, more appropriately dressed in jeans and a button-down. It was three in the afternoon, after all.

"Late night?" he asked with a smirk.

Fi glared back. It was after one in the morning when she got home from the disastrous night at Ole Miss—and hours later before she finally fell into a fitful sleep. Her mood—and breath—was foul. Her eyes were swollen, her throat felt raw from crying. She may or may not have lost her best friend.

And now her dead boyfriend's obnoxious brother was smirking at her. "Do you need something?"

He held a wrapped package out to her. "Peace offering."

She eyed the package—and Jackson—suspiciously. "For?"

"Traditionally speaking, peace." He held it higher, nudging it toward her. "It's not a bomb."

She took the gift—it looked like a book—weighing it in her hand. "Uh, thanks."

"Now we're at the part where you invite me in."

Fi stepped aside. When he hesitated in the living room, Fi realized he'd never been in her house before. How odd—he'd been such a basic part of her life the past two years, but he didn't know where her kitchen was.

"Come on," she said. "I haven't eaten yet. Are you hungry?"

"Sure."

Fi pulled out apples, cheese, some crackers. She grabbed a knife, the cutting board, some glasses, and a pitcher of iced tea, and sat across from him. After pulling together a cheese-and-cracker plate that would have made her mother proud, Fi centered it between them.

Jackson took an apple. "Are you going to open it?"

"Oh. Right." Fi inspected the package, mentally preparing herself for an oh-it's-just-what-I-wanted expression. Sliding her fingers along the taped edges, she pulled the book free and turned it back and forth in her hands. "A journal?"

"It's a Moleskine. Which is just a fancy name for a note-book, I guess."

"And I need this because?"

"Read the first page."

She opened it. "'Never May the Fruit Be Plucked'?"

Underneath the title, a poem was written in the blocky handwriting she knew well. For a few moments, as she stared at the words Marcus's living hand had formed, she forgot to breathe.

"It's the poem I was telling you about," he said.

She looked up at him and he looked away, rubbing his neck. "I wasn't totally honest about how I remembered it. I've had this since he died."

Fi stared at the words a long time before, quietly, reading them. *"Never, never may the fruit be plucked from the bough / And gathered into barrels. / He that would eat of love must eat it where it hangs—"*

"Stop," he said. "Please."

She ran her fingers over the page, feeling the bumps from where Marcus had pressed too hard. "Why are you giving me this?"

"Because it was for you—or probably for you. Marcus didn't say specifically . . ."

"I don't understand."

"He had a few of these—journals where he wrote down quotes he liked. After I read that poem, he asked me to get him a fresh one. Then I had to read it, really slowly, while he copied it down. I offered to do it for him, but he wouldn't let me."

"And you've had it this whole time?"

"Yeah."

"So—why now?" she asked, too overwhelmed to be angry.

"Because he would have wanted it," he said. "Plus, I've been thinking about what you said in the park, all those questions you had. I felt bad. I didn't handle it well. Since I'm not the best moral support, I thought a journal might work instead."

She nodded. Tears splattered onto Marcus's words, so she quickly closed the book, to protect the pages. "Thank you."

He gestured between the two of them. "Hanging out with you—it's weird that it doesn't feel weird anymore. Like, we're *friends.*"

Fi remembered how Trent looked, glaring at her, saying he didn't want to be her friend anymore. And then, it felt like her heart actually *twisted* around itself—because she'd thought of Trent before she thought of Marcus. "Marcus would be happy," she said.

Jackson made a sad smile and took another apple.

"Do you think he'd want us to—" She put the Moleskine on the table, like it should be farther away when she asked the question. "Move on?"

"Move on how?"

"Dating." She hoped it came across as casual. "He'd be happy if you had a girlfriend, don't you think?"

"Not interested," he snapped.

"In dating or girls?"

Much to Fi's relief—why was he getting snippy?—he laughed. "I like girls."

"I've never seen you look twice at a girl."

He rolled his eyes. "That first day? When we first met you, in the coffee shop? I had these competing emotions—be a jerk or flirt with the cute girl." He picked up a cracker, breaking it apart with his fingers instead of eating it. "Jerk obviously won."

"I can't picture you flirting." She also couldn't imagine Jackson thinking of her as cute.

"It's not pretty." He laughed to himself. "And your cast! It was like kryptonite. I mean, I've got a serious soft spot for the fragile."

"Soft spot for the fragile?"

"Dying brother." He shrugged. "While you sat at our table looking awkward, Marcus reached a decision about what do with you before I did, thereby leaving the asshole path free and clear for me."

"And now?"

"Oh, I'm still an asshole." His voice had regained that snippy quality.

Even so, Fi pressed the conversation onward. "No, I mean, are you still resolutely anti-relationship—or dating or whatever."

"Like I said, not interested."

Fi picked up her own cracker, snapping it into bits, too. "Do you wonder what would have happened if you decided to be nice? If you talked to me first?"

"I wonder about lots of things. Why didn't I eat that piece of chicken? What if we diagnosed it earlier? What if he didn't meet you at all, and I got his last year all to myself."

"You're right," Fi said. "You are still an asshole."

They were quiet a minute or so. "What's with all the dating questions?" Jackson asked.

"It's been nine months. I've just been thinking about it."

His eyes got hard. She shuddered, remembering how he would stand in the King doorway, looking down at her with that same disapproving look.

"You're Marcus's girlfriend," he said.

She sighed, looking at the Moleskine. Then she picked it up and put in the kitchen drawer, just for now. "Marcus is dead."

"Anyone in particular?"

"Yes. No. I don't know." Why was she talking to him about this? "It's crazy. I need to forget it."

"Crazy why?" he asked slowly.

Fi closed her eyes, wondering how she and Jackson King wound up in this unlikely relationship. "I've known him forever. He's my best friend."

Jackson exhaled a loud "Oh, thank God!" and collapsed back against his chair. It almost fell backward, and he had to lunge forward to grab the table before toppling.

Fi gaped at him. "What the heck's wrong with you?"

All four legs of his chair on the ground, he placed a hand over his heart, looking like a man just rescued from drowning. "I thought you meant me."

"You?" Fi recoiled. "Oh . . . that's . . ."

"I know! Gross, right?"

Fi frowned. "Well, I wouldn't say *gross.*"

He waved her off. "*You're* not gross. But the idea of kissing you is—it's plain wrong."

"I don't want to kiss you, Jackson."

"Right. Good thing." He sat up, his mood visibly better.

Taking a happy bite of an apple he said, "So I was giving out relationship advice."

"Very badly."

"That's because I was fending off your advances. So, the guy? He's the one who always hit on you in front of Marcus? Trevor or something?"

"Trent wasn't hitting on me! Did Marcus say that?"

Jackson grimaced, shaking his head. "No, he said that y'all were best friends. Weird best friends if you ask me. Little bit dysfunctional."

"And you would be the expert in functional relationships." Fi scowled at him. "You're supposed to be making me feel better. And giving me good advice."

"Can't do both. You want to feel better, or you want the good advice?"

Fi sighed. "Good advice."

"Don't get involved. It'll totally mess up your friendship."

This was not what she wanted to hear.

Why was this not what she wanted to hear?

Fi shook her head. "I changed my mind. I want to feel better."

"Don't get involved. It'll totally mess up your friendship," he said. "The feel better part won't kick in till later."

"When?"

"When you don't lose your best friend," he said. "Because losing your best friend *sucks.*"

MARCH

FIONA

Fiona sat at the foot of the bed, tying her shoes and staring at her guitar in the corner. It wasn't tragically out of tune or anything—she'd played it plenty over the past few weeks. It was the Moleskines, or what she had left of them, that were neglected.

At least she'd met the performance requirement for music. To make up for that horrid Individual Performance grade, she'd thrown everything she had into the composition work after. She had to start from scratch, since she'd tossed her best notebooks. But at least here on out, everything in Weitz's class was on paper.

Beside her, David yawned and stretched, dragging his fingers down the cement wall at the head of the bed.

"Where are you going?" His voice was still thick from sleep. He pulled his wrist toward his face, holding the watch close since his contacts were out. "It's already ten?"

Fiona pulled on a sweatshirt. "I'm going to grab some coffee. I'll bring you some."

"'Kay," he said, stretching again.

"Don't sleep too late." She nudged his leg with her knee. "You've got to catch the 'L' by noon."

He mumbled something that sounded vaguely like "I know" and pulled the covers over his face, muttering, "God, it's so *cold*."

In the cafeteria, she lingered over her bagel and the school paper. It'd been a nice few days with David. They'd both spent too much money—eating out, going to museums, a band last night. As usual, they talked about nothing in particular. At least she hadn't needed to broach the awkward Jackson subject. She'd barely spoken to him since the beach—and the literal run-in in the dorm lobby, after her critique. The few times their paths crossed, he'd disappeared as quickly as he could.

Since fate mocked her, the one time a real conversation might have taken place was the day David arrived. Fiona had met him at the "L" platform nearest campus and walked him back to her dorm. They'd stepped into the refuge of the heated building just as Jackson was walking out. He'd held the door open—Fiona imagined he didn't realize who he was holding the door *for* until it was too late—and it was David who stopped and said, "Aren't you the guy from Memphis?"

Jackson stood there, at a loss. Finally he released the door and shook David's hand.

"Yeah. Jackson. We met at the coffee shop." Jackson nodded toward the bag. "You came to visit?"

"My spring break," David said, snaking his arm around Fiona's waist and pulling her closer.

After that rousing conversation, the three stood there awkwardly until Jackson said, "I've got class. See y'all later."

"He seemed friendlier over Christmas," David said, watching him leave through the glass doors.

Indeed, he did.

Now finished with her bagel and the paper, Fiona looked at her watch. David slept like the dead, something she hadn't known about him. Last night, two of her suitemates were partying with a bunch of friends in the suite common room—at one in the morning. David hadn't so much as flipped over.

He also took *forever* to wake up. He had time before his flight, and she didn't want it to look like she was kicking him out or anything—but still, she was ready. Her suitemates kept telling her how lucky she was to have a single—no closet space to argue over, no one else's alarm to sleep through, no quirky habits to deal with. Now she understood. Her tiny, cement-walled, perpetually cold room with poor acoustics was, at least, all hers.

Getting herself a refill and fixing a cup for David, Fiona started upstairs. She wrestled with the suite door a moment, juggling the two hot cups, before walking through the common room on the way to her own.

There on the couch sat Jackson. He leaned forward, elbows

on his knees, his hands held in a tepee in front of him. "Got a sec?"

He looked awful—bags under dulled eyes, skin more yellow than olive. His voice sounded thinned. Whatever had taken him from there to here must have been quite a journey.

She stood there a moment, not sure what to do. His eyes traveled to the two cups.

"Oh," he said, getting up. "I didn't realize he was still here."

"He's sleeping, I think," she said, looking toward her door.

Jackson looked at the door, too. "I can catch you later. It's okay."

"No," she said, too quickly. Putting the cups on a table, she pulled a chair over. She was at a weird angle to the couch, but she wasn't sure how lined up he wanted her to be. "It's fine," she said.

He looked at the door again, his expression simply *devoid*—no sarcasm, no joy, no anger. Just emptiness. He resumed his original place on the couch, looking at his knees a long while.

They sat there several silent minutes before Fiona asked, "So . . . you wanted to talk about something?"

Jackson chewed on the inside of his cheek, glancing from his hands to the backpack at his feet and back again. "I've been meaning to come by, to check on you. You seemed upset, you know, after . . ." His voice trailed away. Fiona wasn't sure to which *after* he referred.

"I've been here. You could have just talked to me." Her

voice sounded watery to Jackson's thinned. Both used only a fraction of their vocal cords.

"Yeah, well, it's pretty complicated." He dragged a hand through his hair, nodding toward the closed door. "Exhibit A." He frowned. "Or B."

She picked imaginary lint from her jeans.

Jackson's eyes were locked on his legs as well. His elbows rested on his knees. "I really fought my mom about coming up here—didn't see the rush and all that. But once I got here, I don't know, it was nice. Everything was new. Mine." He shook his head. "That sounds awful."

"No. I get it," Fiona answered quietly.

He spoke quickly, like if he didn't say it *right then* he wasn't going to say it at all. "Having a sick brother changed every part of my life. I mean, I let it. But still, it defined everything."

Fiona swallowed. She didn't know where this was going. She wasn't sure she wanted to.

Jackson leaned forward and dug through the backpack. When he sat up, he held five Moleskine notebooks. "They were sticking out of the trash downstairs. I haven't read them."

After a few seconds of gaping, Fiona carefully took the notebooks, resting them on her knees like they might break. She opened the cover of the top one, letting her fingers drag down the length of the page. As always seemed to happen in the presence of Jackson King, she struggled to speak past the lump in her throat. "Thank you."

"I know I should have given them to you earlier."

She nodded, not able to process past the shock. Maybe she should be mad. But, after everything, she figured he deserved a pass.

Jackson took a breath, looking Fiona head-on. Bloodshot veins turned the whites of his eyes near pink. "I wanted to see you. I just didn't know what to say." He gave a faint smile. "Ironic as it sounds, Marcus would have loved this little dilemma. The guy loved any and all hypotheticals. Not to mention he could talk to a post."

Fiona shook her head. She couldn't have this conversation. "Jackson—"

"Just hear me out," he said, holding up a hand. "I prepared a little speech and everything."

She gave a reluctant, terrified nod.

"Even though Marcus really believed some miracle would happen, he didn't waste a second." He gave a sad, lopsided smile. "So I learned this from my dying brother. *Don't waste it.*"

"Waste what?" she whispered.

He looked at her a long time. "Everything that makes you."

"I don't understand."

Grabbing the arms of her chair, he dragged her over until they lined up knee to knee. His eyes drifted down as he spoke. Not deliberately away—more like he gradually focused on nothing in order to stay on track in his head. "Look, in the end we're all just experiences. Some are crappy, some are great, some are just plain dumb. But the more you have, the more you are. And I think Marcus knew that, it's why he wanted to do, do, do. It made him bigger than his disease.

"Being sick was part of that experience, too. It shaped his life, but it wasn't all that defined him. Eventually, the disease killed him. But it never, ever won."

Fiona felt humbled by this boy she'd never know. Even from a sickbed, he lived bigger than she did. He had looked his fate in the eye. He had faced his fear—while she always took the cowardly route around.

Even now that she was fixed, was she really any better?

No. No, she was not.

She swallowed, shaking her head. "It's not that easy."

For the first time since they discovered the horrible May 18 coincidence, Jackson touched her. After tucking some fallen strands behind her ear, his fingertips grazed her cheek for the slightest moment. Her skin tingled beneath his touch. Then he dropped his hand, wrapping it around hers and edging himself closer. With their knees staggered between each other—Jackson-Fiona-Jackson-Fiona—he nodded to the notebooks in her lap. "We've all got baggage, Fiona."

"I'm the only one wearing it on my face."

He shrugged. "So what? Other people wear it in bruises. Or on their hearts, when they lose the people they love. Kids who grow up surrounded by hate have it all over their souls. And the rest of us? We shove it way down where it rots, poisoning us slowly. Which way's better?"

She stared at her notebooks, watching fat tears plop on them one by one. "It's too hard."

"Only because you make it that way."

Again, she shook her head. "If I get up there and sing these songs, everything I feel, I am, it's just up for grabs. It becomes *entertainment*. Everyone knows me, but no one has to give it back. I'm naked when everyone else is in fur coats."

Jackson gave a short, unamused laugh. "Fiona, no one demands you write. No one's forcing you to play that guitar. There's no grand conspiracy to know you." Using the knot of their four hands, he pointed toward the notebooks, now splattered in tears. "So the question is, if it's not *fundamentally important to you,* why have you spent a small fortune on these notebooks? Why did you come to one of the country's best writing and music schools? If this isn't who you are, why are you so tormented over it?"

"It *is* who I am," she argued, annoyed now. "That's what I'm saying."

He leaned forward, resting his forehead against hers and looking down at her. "Then be who you are."

She stared back at him, unable to come up with a reply. They stayed there, knees wedged against each other, hands knotted against the notebooks in her lap. Joined foreheads completed their breathing triangle.

When her door clicked closed, both pulled away. David stood on the edge of the common room, his bag by his feet.

He pointed to the cups on the table. "I was looking for the coffee. And you."

Jackson and Fiona stood up at the same time, the Moleskines tumbling to the floor between them. She rubbed her hands on her jeans, while he leaned over to pick up his backpack. After an awkward moment, Jackson shoved his hands in his pockets, said, "Have a good flight," and walked to the stairwell.

Fiona took a breath. "It's not what it looks like."

"What's it look like?"

"We're just . . . he's been someone to talk to. Up here."

"About?"

She pointed to the notebooks at her feet. "All this—all *my*—ridiculous stuff."

He leaned against the wall, arms crossed in front of him. His voice came out sharp, his posture seemed rigid. "We've dated two years, and you've never told me any ridiculous stuff."

"You've never asked."

"I've asked plenty."

Fiona sank to the couch. David stayed where he was, leaning against the wall. "Any particular reason you were never compelled to talk to *me*?" he asked.

"I have no idea. Maybe—I never felt the need? Like I had to?"

"And you do with him."

She shrugged.

He watched her a long time before he eventually pushed himself from the wall, shaking his head. "Guess that's all I'm getting."

"David, I—"

He slid the strap of his bag over his shoulder then stood there, waiting. Fiona willed herself to say something, to say the words that explained all of this. But the girl who could fill notebook upon notebook with her thoughts and words suddenly had nothing to offer.

David looked at his watch. "I've gotta go."

"Let me get a coat." She stood. "I'll come with you to the station."

"No. Don't." He adjusted his strap, zipped his jacket. "I know the way."

They stood there another long moment, Fiona by the couch, David a few feet from her.

"I'm not sure what to say," Fiona said.

David laughed—a bitter laugh, not like him. "That says it all."

APRIL

FI

Fi sat at her dad's desk, finishing her paper. The professor gave them the choice to write something new—or go back to one essay they'd already completed and make it better. She'd decided to redo her essay on "I should have known better than to let you go alone." She had a different view of things now.

She was working with the poem in Marcus's Moleskine: "Never May the Fruit Be Plucked" by Edna St. Vincent Millay.

It was a beautiful—and sad—poem.

Never, never may the fruit be plucked from the bough
And gathered into barrels.
He that would eat of love must eat it where it hangs.
Though the branches bend like reeds,
Though the ripe fruit splash in the grass or wrinkle on
    the tree,
He that would eat of love must bear away with him
Only what his belly can hold,

Nothing in the apron,
Nothing in the pockets.
Never, never may the fruit be gathered from the bough
And harvested in barrels.
The winter of love is a cellar of empty bins,
In an orchard soft with rot.

She was biting her nails, deciding whether the essay should be about Marcus—or about her—when Ryan's picture popped up beside the video chat icon.

"Hey," she said, accepting the call. "What's up?"

The camera angle was weird and the lighting too yellow, but Ryan looked good. Over Christmas break, their dad had remarked that Ryan's muscles were finally catching up with his bones. He filled up more space now. "Oh," Ryan said. "I thought Mom would answer."

"She's out." Fi touched the screen, surprised at how she wished it was really him and not some satellite-generated substitute. "Your hair's long."

Pulling fingers through his hair, he shrugged. "You okay?"

"Yeah. Working on a paper." She leaned back in their dad's big leather chair, swiveling it side to side. "Trent said you're playing soccer now."

He watched her a second, like he was trying to figure out where she was going with this, but with the bad video, it was hard to gauge anything. "It's fun," he said eventually. "That's actually why I was calling. There's a summer camp up here—for little kids. I think I might stay and work."

"What about Gwen?"

"She'd stay, too."

Fi smirked. "Are you going to marry her?"

"Fi, I'm nineteen." Then he shrugged. "Yeah, probably."

"High school sweethearts—the odds aren't good."

"You wouldn't have married Marcus?"

At some point in her near past, that question would have sent Fi into her turtle shell. She couldn't say when or why or even *how* she had moved forward. But she had, even if only a little. "It's one of those things we'll never know. It's not worth the energy, torturing myself over it, you know?"

Ryan nodded. "What's up with the grades?" he asked.

"So far, 3.0 for the semester. I still have finals, but I think it'll be okay."

"And then you're off probation? You can play again?"

Fi slowly nodded while biting the edge of her thumbnail.

"You're biting your nails. What's wrong?"

Fi frowned at her fingers. She hadn't realized she was so transparent. "Do you think I'd be crazy to write the NU coach? After everything?"

Ryan smiled a big, big smile—a real one. "It would be the least crazy thing you've done in years."

"There's no way she'll take me. My grades aren't great. I'm out of shape."

"Only one way to find out."

Still gnawing her cuticle, Fi nodded at his point. "I have no idea what to say."

"Do it now. I'll help you."

"Now?" Fi had planned on torturing herself over this for days—maybe weeks—before finally working up the courage to do something.

"Yeah. Pull up your email and let me see the screen."

Contacting the coach had been *her* idea. Now it felt like he was taking over. Like he was pushing too hard. "First, tell me why you want to help me."

"What do you mean why? I want you to do this."

"But *why* do you want me to so badly?"

He rolled his eyes. "Jesus, Fi—what, you think I have some sinister motive?"

"Not sinister." Fi shrugged, casually rolling a pencil back and forth while telling her brother this deep truth. "But you like to take over. Boss me around."

"*I* boss *you* around?" he repeated.

"Uh, yeah. I'm always in your shadow."

"*You* are in *my* shadow?" Even in the awkward, yellowish light, Fi detected the blood rising in her brother's cheeks. "Are you high?"

"What's that mean?"

His laugh came out a little bitter. "Fi, I was the short, mediocre brother of one of the state's best lacrosse players. The only reason I *played* the damn sport was because I got caught up in your obsession—which I didn't even realize until I came up here and did intramural soccer."

"You didn't like lacrosse?"

"You and Trent had enough fire to cover me."

Fi's head hurt a little from this sudden realization. "So . . . the offer to help, with the email, that's because—"

"You. Are. My. Sister."

"What about after Marcus died? All the comments about dating other guys and transferring schools and everything? You were about as subtle as a brick to the head."

"You were *miserable.*" He drew out the last word, like he could make each of the four syllables into its very own word.

"You were *annoying*," she said, doing her best to mimic him, but it was less impressive with only three syllables.

"Sorry," he said, though he didn't sound it. Then he softened a bit to add, "I was trying to help."

"You can trust me, you know—with my life. It's not like I want to ruin it."

"It looked like you were really trying for a while there."

Fi couldn't argue this point. "So that's it? Just because I'm your sister?" She waved her hand vaguely. "And you love me or whatever."

"Lord! Yes—that's *it!*" He dragged his fingers through his hair like he wanted to pull it out. "You're infuriating."

"I've heard."

Now he frowned. "From who?"

Fi rolled her eyes—not at her brother, more at the length of the list. "Mom and Dad. My advisor. Jackson. Trent."

"Jackson? Like, Marcus's Jackson? Why are you—"

"We've been hanging out."

"Hanging out?"

Why did he keep repeating everything back to her? "Yeah. It was hard at first, since we're not, like, *naturally inclined* to get along. Even so, it's been good. Having him around."

"Having him around in, uh, what way exactly?"

"Friends." Did these boys have to go *right there* with their assumptions?

"Oh. Okay, then." Elbow on his desk, he rested his head sideways in his hand. "I'm exhausted, Fi. I just called Mom to tell her about the camp. I wasn't expecting a heart-to-heart with my sister."

Fi idly swiveled the chair back and forth. "Think you have the energy for this email?"

He nodded, smiling slightly.

It took nearly an hour to finish. They suffered through false starts, scratched-out lines, rearranged sentences. Ryan worried she was getting too personal, she needed to stick to the facts, but Fi held firm.

She'd spent almost a year simultaneously wallowing in what she couldn't change and hiding from what she could. If she was going to start—and now was as good a time as any— she was going to do it with everything that made her.

Dear Coach Starnes,

If you don't remember me, I'm Fiona Doyle, the center from Union High School in Memphis. Even though I had to sit out my junior year because of injury, I was All-State my ninth, tenth, and twelfth grade years. I attended the Lady Wildcats summer clinics three years in a row.

You might also remember me as the girl who canceled on last summer's training camp at the very last minute, and while I can't guarantee I'm "fixed" now, I can say I'm on the way.

I've followed your season this year. I was so excited—and heartbroken—when you won the NCAA title for the eighth consecutive time this spring. The games were so amazing, I wished I could have been a part of them.

I know you don't owe me a chance, but if you have a spot open for a girl who loves lacrosse and will work hard, please consider me. I promise I won't let you down again.

Sincerely,
Fiona "Fi" Doyle

JULY

FIONA

Fiona sat on her bed, fiddling with her guitar. She had nothing else to do.

She'd been home a month—*alone*. Having landed an amazing internship at the UN, Lucy was staying in New York for the summer. Ryan was at Clemson, working at a soccer camp and sharing an apartment with Gwen, much to their parents' displeasure. Fiona imagined David was here. She'd sent some emails, a few texts; he hadn't replied.

Jackson wasn't in Memphis either. He said he was staying for summer session to bulk up some credits, but Fiona suspected he didn't want to come home. Not that this was ever confirmed. One would have thought after the heart-to-heart in her common room, things would be normal between them now.

When David had left—after finding her *forehead to forehead* with Jackson, no less—Fiona took to her room like the heroine of some melodramatic Victorian novel. *The guilt! I might faint from it!* Jackson came to check on her, but all of it just felt horribly awkward. His dead brother, her boyfriend, the music, the notebooks. May 18.

There had been nearly two full months left in the term, and still they hardly talked. Whenever she ran into him, he seemed like a jittery stray cat. If she didn't move slowly, he might spook and hide under a couch.

It wasn't until moving day that Jackson *finally* came to her dorm room, acting his normal, flirty self. Her parents had each taken a load to the car, and she was under the bed, checking for stray socks and notebooks.

"Man, I *like* this angle," Jackson had said.

She crawled out, cracking her head on the frame. Her mother came back in before she could think of what to say.

"Hi, I'm Jackson King," he'd said, reaching out a hand to her mother.

"Oh, the boy from Memphis!" Her mother sounded positively gleeful.

"Yes, ma'am." He reached over to take the bag she'd just picked up. "Here, let me."

He'd helped load the car. Like a proper southern boy, he'd endured her parents' endless questions. *Are your parents from Memphis, Jackson? Where'd they go to high school? What's your mother's maiden name? Oh, I think we might know your uncle.*

"Are you coming home for the summer?" her mom had asked him.

"I'm going to take a few summer classes, but I'll be back in July."

"When you get back, you should come for dinner. I'm sure Fiona would love to see more of you."

"I'd love to see more of her, too."

Her mother had turned to put the last bag in the car, so she missed Jackson's wink—and Fiona's full-face blush.

Her parents had probably spied through the rearview mirror as Fiona and Jackson stood by the trunk, saying awkward good-byes.

"Seriously," he'd said, all the while stroking his thumb against her hand. "When I get back, we should hang out."

Questions sat in her throat like lumps. She'd wished she could swallow them away, but ignoring uncomfortable conversations hadn't worked out well for her to date. "Why are you doing this *now*? I've been three floors away for the past two months."

"Taking my own advice," he'd said.

Her father had cleared his throat before she could ask Jackson which advice he meant. Now standing beside the driver's door, her dad had said they really needed to get going. So she'd given Jackson a clumsy hug and left him.

And now, a month later, she was ready for him to get back already so whatever this was could *start*.

When she heard the knock, Fiona eyed the door, knowing it could only be one of two people. After she called, "Come in," her mom walked in holding—of course—a stack of clothes.

"Don't bite my head off, but I found these in the attic. They're from ages ago. I'm too old to pull them off."

Fiona motioned to her desk, where her mother placed the—very bright—stack of dated clothes. She stood beside the desk, looking at Fiona and the guitar. "What are you playing? It sounds nice."

"Nothing in particular."

"Ryan called today," her mom said. "He's visiting two weekends from now. He says you're doing open mic night at the coffee shop?"

"I'm thinking about it."

More like obsessing. She hadn't been sleeping, her cuticles were a mangled mess, and she'd scratched out and written over her lyrics so many times, she could hardly read them.

Poor Lucy had to endure daily phone calls, all with the same theme: *What am I thinking? / Do you really think it's a good idea? / I should get this over with and just do it.* She could spend twenty minutes just talking around in circles while Lucy got in the occasional word, which had been, unexpectedly, encouraging. "Fiona," Lucy said, "you are a smart, talented person, and the world wants you to succeed."

"Are you in love?" she asked, stunned.

"Where the heck did that come from?" Lucy said.

"You've just never been so, uh, *kind* before."

"Are you saying I'm mean?"

"No. I'm saying you're . . ." Her dad's term of *Yankee* had come to mind, but she settled on "blunt."

"Oh." There had been a pause, and she said, "I might be in love. Just a little. I'm not fawning, like someone I know."

"I never *fawned.*"

"I will add that to *The Lying Lies of Fiona Doyle* I've compiled. Right next to: *None of them are ready.*" Lucy had said the last bit with the worst imitation twang Fiona had ever heard.

Fiona rolled her eyes—but laughed. "Go back to acting like you're in love."

"Perhaps I shall. And you—sing the damn song, already!"

Three days after that call, she forced her own hand and called Jackson.

"I'm thinking about playing open mic night at Otherlands," she told him.

"Cool," he said. "When?"

"July fifteenth."

"That's the day I get home."

"I know. I was hoping you'd come."

She figured having Jackson in the audience would be like driving on the highway with a cop right behind you. Knowing he was there would keep her from making a run for it.

There had been a long pause before he answered. Long enough for Fiona to panic that he'd forgotten about her, maybe found a new crush. But then, with a voice simply *oozing* smirk, he'd said, "Can't wait. Our second time."

Her mother was still standing by her neon eighties castoffs. "Can your father and I come?" she asked. "To hear you at the coffee shop?"

What was the polite way to say *hell, no* to your mother? "I'm not sure I'll do it."

Her mom walked to the bed, looking at the spot beside Fiona and then at Fiona, like she was waiting for an invitation. Fiona shrugged, and her mother sat. "Then we'll just have coffee. It's about time I checked out your second home, anyway."

"It's not that impressive."

"I like a good dive now and then."

Fiona snorted. "Oh, come on, Mom. I'll be trying to play, and you'll be scouring the tables."

"I hardly think I'd be *scouring*." She looked at Fiona sideways. "You know, I don't have this agenda, like you think I do. To improve everything."

"It sure feels that way," Fiona muttered back.

"I was just trying to make it better," her mom said, shaking her head.

"Make what better?"

"The accident. Your life. I wanted to make it easier."

"By dressing me in pink?"

"Well, it sounds silly if you say it like that." Her mother picked at the bedspread. "You know, I never understood how you never complained. About the scars."

She couldn't help but laugh. "You don't think I complained?"

"Not really. Not like I would have, if it were me." Looking to the wall again, her mom took a deep breath. "Your father and I, we had you two right after we got married. I was so young. I had the whole picture in front of me, how our lives would be. But then you had the accident, and it all changed. I *wanted* for you have to a certain life, but fate just . . . intervened. And I still don't think I'm over it."

She stopped talking for a moment, still staring ahead. "I hated those scars, Fiona," she said quietly. "Hated them—and the accident. You had a harder life than you should have."

"Mom, it's not that bad."

"You're right, it's not." She patted Fiona's hand and looked her in the eyes. "For all my worry about how hard it was going to be, you handled everything beautifully. So despite how much I hate that it happened, I cherish it a little, too. That accident made you, *you*. And I wouldn't have you any other way."

Her heart wanted to cry, but she was sick to death of crying. "I hate pink," Fiona said, instead. "And frills. Just so we're clear."

Her mother laughed. "Duly noted." She nodded to the guitar, still in Fiona's lap. "So, about this open mic night."

Fiona bit her thumbnail. "I'm terrified about it, actually."

"Why?"

"Singing my stuff in public—it freaks me out. Like, *really* freaks me out. I'm hoping this will get me over it."

"Sounds like a good plan."

"But baby steps might be good." Fiona fiddled with the guitar's strings, her voice now nearly a whisper. "Do you want to hear something?"

The prettiest smile crossed her mother's face. "Really?"

Fiona grabbed a Moleskine. Resting her back against the headboard, she sat cross-legged and faced her mother. She leafed through the book. "Okay, here's one. I'm still working on the lyrics—and the bridge."

Her mother smiled and got herself comfortable on the other end of the bed. She didn't seem the least bothered by how long Fiona took—didn't check her watch or ask questions, just rested between the wall and the footboard, waiting.

After Fiona tuned as much as she could, she said, "Here goes," and sang.

Father, brother, friend, and mother / Stolen words and stolen
    skin
Fear and face and guilt and place / What-ifs and coincidence
Puzzles, pieces / Nos and yeses
Bad days, scars / Notebooks, guitars
Everything that makes me

You say, Be who you are
Be the song, be the scar
Be everything that makes you
'Cause some things just are

Metaphors, heartsick brothers / Shocks straight from your
    fingertips
Cantaloupe and smirk and hope / The null and the alternative
Puzzles, pieces / Nos and yeses
Good days, scars / What's yours, what's ours
Everything that makes you

I say, Be who you are
Be the twin, fear my scar
Be everything that makes you
'Cause some things just are

FI

Her mom knocked and opened the door before Fi could say, "Come in."

She put a few shopping bags on the bed. "This is the best I could do. Finding warm clothes in July is a challenge."

Fi looked out the window at the blue-skied, 104-degree Memphis morning. She couldn't wrap her head around wearing *sleeves,* let alone fleece. "I don't think I'll need it, Mom. It's July in Chicago, too."

"It's a ten-hour drive north."

Fi wasn't sure how that negated *summer,* but she decided not to argue. Her bedroom floor was chaos—three suitcases, one gym bag, one bag for her sticks, a few crates full of supplies, a box of bedding and other stuff for her dorm room, her laptop case. "You don't think we're overdoing it?"

Her mom stood beside her, surveying the lot of it. "Well, you need it all."

"I'm just going for training camp. They haven't promised me the spot yet."

"But if they give it to you, you'll have to stay. There are only five days between summer training and new student orientation."

Fi groaned at the idea of icebreakers with eager, recent high school graduates. At least Jackson would be there to share the pain, since both would start with only one semester behind them. Jackson had taken—and easily passed—a few classes over the year. The dean at Northwestern had agreed to accept only Fi's second semester grades—which was more than she had expected, honestly.

All of it was more than she'd expected. After sending the email, she and Ryan had agreed that two weeks was a good time frame for a reply. If she hadn't heard back by then, she'd assume the bridge to NU had officially burned.

Within a half hour of pressing *send* on that email, she'd accepted the inevitability of a *no*. She was still online, searching every Division Two team she'd talked to in high school, when the reply appeared in her in-box.

Fi, so glad to hear from you. Why don't you give me a call? Candace Starnes

She stared at the email for almost two full minutes before screaming. Her father tore into the office, like he expected to find a murder victim. Fi pointed to the computer screen. He read the email over her shoulder and let out a giant whoop.

Once they'd calmed down, Fi made the call. Her father

picked up the other line and listened in on mute. At first, her voice came out shaky, but Starnes was conversational. How had Fi liked her classes? What was Milton like, she didn't know it well. How was her family? How was she holding up, was the loss getting a little easier?

As they talked, Fi's voice began to sound more like her own. She nearly forgot this polite woman—her mother would love her—was the Northwestern University women's lacrosse team coach. Nearly forgot until Candace Starnes brought it up.

"So, Fi—tell me about the Milton lacrosse team."

"Um. Well, they're club. And . . ." She bit down to keep herself from blurting *they suck*.

But Starnes already knew. "Not up to your level, are they?"

"No, ma'am."

"Have you been training?"

"I've tried—on my own. I've lost ground, though."

"It will be hard work, going from a club team to D-One."

"Yes, ma'am, I know. But I can do it."

On her end, Starnes paused. Fi and her father looked at each other nervously. Fi bit at her fingernails until her dad walked over and pulled them out of her mouth.

After a heart-pounding eternity, Starnes said, "Tell you what, Fi. We've got training camp in July. Why don't you come up and work with the team? We'll see how it goes."

"See how it goes?"

"I've got a spot for a third-string midfielder. Let me be

clear—I'm not committing that spot to you. If all goes well at camp and the school decides to admit you, you still wouldn't start, and you won't get money. That might be an option later, but lots has to happen between now and then."

Fi took a long, slow breath and looked at her father. He nodded, and she said, "Okay. That's fair."

"Good answer. So, forward me your transcripts. I'll send you the camp information, and I'll see you in July."

And here she was, packing for training camp. Her mother shoved a pink sweatshirt—*pink!*—into one of the bags. Fi sank to the bed, suddenly dejected. "What if they send me home?"

"We'll figure something out," her mom said, sitting beside her. "There are other schools you can talk to."

"I want this one."

"I know, sweetie." She placed a hand on Fi's back, lightly scratching it. "I think it'll work out. I really think you'll get to stay."

"Why?"

"Mother's intuition."

Fi shook her head, unconvinced. "I can't make any mistakes. I don't have any left."

"Well, if you figure out how to go through life without making a mistake, please pass on the wisdom. I could use it."

She couldn't help but roll her eyes. "Yeah, right."

Her mother sighed. "I know you think I pushed you too

hard. But—I just didn't want you to make the same mistake I did."

"What mistake?"

"Not thinking your life through. Not planning."

"What didn't you plan?"

"I didn't plan on having kids when I was twenty-four," she said. "I didn't plan on always being just a *mom*."

Fi's expression must have shown the surprise, because her mom quickly added, "Not that I'm not happy. Not that I'd change it."

"It kind of sounds like you would."

Her mom shook her head. "No. You know, I was working for an interior designer when we found out about Ryan. We hadn't planned on starting a family so early, but we were thrilled. Still, I wanted to get my master's degree. Your dad and I figured I could do that while he was a baby. I was six months pregnant when I started the program. But once he was born I was tired all the time, and then we found out you were coming. My plans were put on hold, just for now." She shrugged. "One thing led to another, and *now* never came."

"You could have gone back," Fi said. "You still can."

"I know," she said. "Maybe I will." Her mother nudged her with her shoulder. "See, you're not the only one who's lost her way."

Even with the explanation, Fi couldn't think of her mother as lost, at least not like she was. Her mother did *lost* so prettily.

"I'm still scared," Fi admitted. "It's going to be hard."

"*You* have never been afraid of hard."

Fi cast her a dubious look. "You've spent the last four years complaining that I am."

"I may have mentioned the times you *avoid* hard. Once or twice." Her mother gave a small sideways smile. "But you're also the fiercest person I know. The things you're passionate about, you'll bleed for."

Fi pictured herself on the ground, gripping a broken ankle and cussing with fluency. That single moment, a little more than two years ago, had changed her life. Blood had soaked through everything that day.

Given the choice, she wouldn't change it.

She'd paid for this *now* in bone and skin. In love and tears. In blood. She'd *earned* this *now*.

Leaning into her mother, Fi murmured, "You're right."

Fi curled on the bed, Panda tucked in his rightful place under her arm. Tonight would be her last night in her own bed, her own room. She was having trouble wrapping her head around the very unclear future just ahead of her. She might be back in a month—or she might not be back until Christmas.

At the knock, she glanced at her overstuffed bags and hoped her mother hadn't stumbled upon some as-yet-undiscovered insulating layer. "Come in."

The door creaked open, and Trent peeked his head through. "You're not naked, are you?"

Fi shot upright. She hadn't seen Trent since the Ole Miss debacle. She'd texted a few times; they'd had some tense conversations. When she heard from Starnes, her first call was to Trent. She'd left a voice mail, and he'd called right back. He was all polite and encouraging, without a trace of sarcasm.

It hadn't felt right—not at all.

"No, fully dressed," she said.

"Damn." He shook his head, coming in. "Long shot, I guess."

Even taking his current scruffy state into account—his long lacrosse shorts, worn gray T-shirt, and stubbly cheeks—there was no denying that college agreed with Trent McKinnon. Solid muscles held him up while sun-darkened skin held him in. But something else, a hard-to-define *Trentness*, pulled it all together.

"Big day tomorrow." Trent sat beside her on the bed, nodding his head toward the bags. "Think you've got enough?"

She looked at the bags, too, since looking at Trent was starting to feel awkward. She *hated* that it felt awkward. "I think I packed everything I own."

He reached across her, plucking Panda from her lap. "Not him."

"He goes in the morning. He'll suffocate overnight."

He laughed just a little, turning Panda in his hands. "He's kind of battered, isn't he?"

"Rough work living with me." Fi regarded Panda sadly at this revelation. Poor guy.

Trent raised a single eyebrow and handed the stuffed bear back. Gesturing at the bags again, he said, "It's like you're never planning on coming back."

She caught his eyes but couldn't figure out what they said. "I could be back after camp. *We won't know till we know.*" She did this last bit in her best Bruce Doyle voice, who'd said it over and over the past few weeks.

"Nah. You'll stay." He tapped the side of his head. "I've got a feeling."

"That's what Mom said."

"Smart lady. And scary hot for a mom."

Fiona shoved him with her foot. He caught it and shoved it back at her. "Man, you're slow. Like, turtle-in-cold-syrup slow."

She tried to kick him once more. He dodged. Shoving and pent-up laughter followed—until, slightly out of breath, they ended their spontaneous wrestling match, lying side by side on their backs. They stared at the ceiling from on top of Fi's messed-up bed.

"So you're not mad anymore?" Fi asked as Trent breathed beside her.

She could feel him shake his head. "Can't stay mad at my Fi-Fi long."

Still on her back, she moved her head sideways to get a good look at him. She didn't recall having quite this perspective before—seeing those tiny specks of green sprinkled throughout his pale blue eyes. "You're the only one who calls me that."

"Intentional." He pivoted his head, too. "A little bit of you that belongs only to me."

Fi blinked slowly. "Is there a part of you that belongs only to me?"

"Absolutely."

They stared at each other for a while. Fi didn't know how to say—explain—all the conflicts she felt. Here she was, lying beside her best friend, having distinctly inappropriate best-friend thoughts. But Jackson's words echoed in her head. *Don't get involved. It sucks to lose your best friend.* She'd hated him a little for that advice.

"Trent—" she began.

He shifted to his side, propping his head on his hand. Interrupting her, his voice came out low and husky. Uncharacteristically serious. "You remember when I said you're the reason I evolved past the fart joke?"

Fi nodded at this unexpected change of subject.

Trent closed his eyes, rubbing his forehead for a moment. Finally, he opened his eyes and focused on her. "You know, sometimes I get freaking *terrified* of the past. How the slightest thing could have changed how I got here. Like—what if Ryan got put on another team or your mom signed you up for ballet and you didn't come to the practices? What if my parents bought a different house? They were looking at another one, you know—three blocks east. I'd have gone to a different school, played on a different team.

"There are so many ways this life might not have happened."

Trent's gaze sharpened on her. He scooted down to lie fully on his side. With a quieter voice—he was just inches from her—he continued. "If you didn't pick up that stick and try to murder me with it in your backyard, if you weren't my best friend, if I was left to become *me* without *you*—God, Fi, I have no idea who I'd be. Even though it all *did* happen, even though we're right here . . . how fragile all this is? It scares the hell out of me."

Trent's hand came up to Fi's cheek. He used one finger to trace her jawline, then her cheekbone, and then her brow. Eventually, his eyes traveled to hers. "This scares me, too. Your leaving."

Under his fingers, her nerve endings felt everything—like they'd been turned all the way up. Her muscles had tightened to the point of shattering.

She wanted this from him. And then she didn't. Staying in the dark, ignoring this track they'd been on for a while—it would make the Northwestern choice easier. She could pursue the dream without second guesses or what-ifs trailing right behind her.

Trent shook his head sadly, like he could read her mind. "I'm not asking you to stay. I don't *want* you to stay. You need to do this. I can't force your life into what works for me, anyway. But at least I can tell you, make sure you understand—like, really understand. About me. And how I feel about you."

Mirroring him, Fi rolled to her side, lining up their faces. She lifted her hand and began to trace along Trent's jawline, just as he was doing to her. His eyes fluttered closed at the touch. "How do you feel about me?" she whispered.

"You know that girl I described? My type?" He opened his eyes and smiled. "I was describing you. She's you."

Fi wondered if he could hear her heart through her tank top. Not sure why she was protesting when every part of her wanted to just kiss him already, wanted to open this door that may or may not lead anywhere and walk right on through.

"You're my best friend," she said.

Trent leaned closer—and closer and closer—until his chest pushed Fi onto her back again. He propped on his elbows, hovering just above her. "I think it's time we expand my role."

Then he closed the small bit of distance left between them and kissed her.

She wrapped her arms around his neck and kissed him back.

FIONA

Fiona stood at the coffee bar, staring across the room toward her parents. They sat side by side at a small, far-off table, her dad's arm draped around her mom's shoulder. Surrounded as they were by tattoos and piercings, Bruce and Caroline Doyle looked surprisingly unflustered.

"My worlds are colliding," Fiona muttered.

Beside her, Ryan nodded and laughed. "So I want to say something—before everyone else gets here."

"Okay," she said, swallowing her coffee too fast.

"Remember when you walked home from the coffee shop, and I freaked out—before the surgery? When I told you I felt lost in your story."

Fiona fought the urge to check the date square on her watch. It was mid-July! They weren't due for this conversation for seven more months. She nodded cautiously.

"I don't think I explained it right. It's more like . . . I felt *responsible* for your story."

"Responsible?"

"That day? The zoo? Your face—that was my fault."

"What?"

"I know you don't remember. But *I* do. The snack bar was my idea. We were running around in there like crazy. And we ran into each other, and—God, this is the horrible part—I pushed you. Like away from me and *into* the popcorn cart. I fell on my butt while you fell into the oil."

"Ryan, no—"

He held up a hand. "For a long time, I felt that all the scarred parts of you—I felt like I made them."

First her mom, now Ryan—she had no idea that this much guilt ran in the family.

"But I didn't make you at all, Ona," he said. "All this time, you've made me. I'm better because of you. And whatever pieces of yourself you want to share up there—that'll make everyone here a little bit better, too."

Her instinct was to argue her way out of compliments. But she was *sick* of her instincts, frankly. "Ryan, it wasn't your fault. It wasn't *anybody's* fault. Some things just *are*."

He nodded, letting out a huge breath. He looked . . . satisfied. Lighter. How crazy that he had carried this unnecessary burden.

Gwen entered from the back door and made her way to

them. From behind him, she looped her hands around Ryan's waist and, on tiptoes, kissed his neck. Looking at Fiona, she said, "David's outside."

And then the door swung open again.

They caught eyes immediately—and so obviously that neither could pretend not to have noticed the other. Fiona watched David's shoulders rise and fall, as if he were gearing himself for some kind of battle. He walked over to Fiona, Gwen, and Ryan at the counter.

"I heard you were playing," he said.

Fiona resisted the urge to rub fiercely at her temples. Parents in the coffee shop, confessions from her brother, the ex-boyfriend, an impending public performance—it was too much at once.

Instead, she pointed to the performers' list scrawled on the blackboard, with her name at the bottom. "I'm hoping to avoid emergency laryngitis."

David smiled. "Want something?"

Fiona shook her head. Rescuing her lukewarm coffee from the counter, she drained it and handed it over for a refill. Gwen and Ryan said they'd find a table, leaving Fiona and David to this awkward semi-conversation. As they waited for drinks, they talked about finals, what they'd been doing over the summer, plans for next year. Fiona didn't know what they'd do once the coffee excuse was gone.

The guy behind the counter called her name. Claiming her mug, she turned and nearly dropped it.

Good Lord, could this evening get any more awkward?

Just inside the door stood Jackson King, scanning the crowd. It had only been a month and half since she'd seen him. Still, he looked different—straighter in his bones and more relaxed in his skin. He wore the same soft, worn jeans as always and a plain navy T-shirt. He was all olive skin, black hair, and green eyes.

Eventually his wandering eyes found Fiona. He smiled—smirked—as he made his way over. Smelling just the slightest bit of cantaloupe, he stood beside her and leaned close. "This is pretty public for our second time, don't you think?"

David pivoted around on the spot. He and Jackson shared a look that seemed equally surprised, annoyed, and uncomfortable. Fiona fought the Caroline Doyle impulse to make sure everyone knew each other—*David, you remember Jackson? You found us holding hands in the common room. And Jackson, David's the one I was dating the whole time we were inappropriately flirting.*

More than anything, Fiona wanted to hug Jackson, hold his hand, take a deeper breath of him. Anything to ground her the slightest bit for what she was about to do. But as David stood beside her, all the things they still hadn't said floated around her like a vapor—something intangible but present nonetheless. It felt so suddenly real, Fiona worried it might follow her onstage like a muggy, stifling cloud.

"Um, Jackson, could I catch up with you after?"

Jackson's eyes flitted off David to Fiona. He slowly nodded and walked away.

Fighting a primal instinct to follow him, instead Fiona turned to David, who regarded her skeptically. She had no idea what to do. But as much as she did not want this conversation, she owed it to him.

David cleared his throat. "So, you two are . . ."

Fiona shrugged, biting her lip. "I'm not sure."

"And at school?"

"Nothing happened at school." She felt a strong need to set the record straight here. It was the one bit that didn't reflect *horribly* on her. "Nothing's happened at all. It's just been, um, talk up to this point."

"Right. I got a good look at the talking bit."

Okay, maybe a little horrible. "David, I'm so sorry."

David sipped from his mug, studying her over the rim of it. "Yeah, I know."

Fiona wasn't sure where to go from here. She knew David wanted *more*, but she hadn't been able to give it to him the two years they'd dated. With open mic night starting in five minutes, she certainly wasn't going to be capable of it now.

Pointing to her guitar, he said, "Don't you need to get in tune or something?"

Letting out a grateful breath, she nodded. She gestured over her shoulder to Ryan and Gwen's table. "I should sit."

They hesitated a moment before sharing an awkward hug. David picked up his mug and headed to a table on the other end of the coffee shop. Fiona plunked herself by Ryan. "That looked painful," he said.

She groaned, letting her head loll on the table as the Otherlands guy walked up to the open mic corner, thumped the microphone a few times, reminded the audience to be polite, and told the performers they had eight minutes.

Fiona looked up when the second performer tried to clog dance while playing the harmonica. *At least the bar's being set nice and low.*

It felt too soon when the guy announced, "Okay, looks like next we've got . . . Fiona Doyle."

Taking a deep breath, Fiona stood up. Ryan held out her guitar. She took it with a stretched smile and walked to the front of the coffee shop. A few strangers gave polite applause while Ryan and Gwen whooped.

She smiled at her parents as she passed their table. Scanning the crowd she spotted Jackson leaning against the coffee bar, one elbow propped on the counter. From the distance, she couldn't gauge his expression.

Once on the stool, she retuned her guitar. She was taking too long but any change in her very deliberate pace might send her screaming for the door.

The perspective up here was different from what she expected. She didn't feel much higher than the people in chairs. The plants felt like curtains, blocking her from a full view. "Thanks," she said, adjusting the microphone. "This is a song I wrote."

She started with her eyes closed, feeling the strings against her fingers. Concentrating on her voice and her words, hearing how the amp inflated everything about them.

Turn me inside out / You'll see a heart beating.
Turn me upside down / There's my head aching.

Her voice rolled out of her, traveling away until it bounced off the concrete walls on the room's other side. The song returned a little mellower from the journey.

But turn me right side up
And you get what you see.

When she opened her eyes, it seemed like the audience had morphed from the individual to the communal—a single, organic mass held together by her song.

Unzip me / Undo me
Expose me / See through me

Fiona let her head fall, focusing on her guitar. Her left fingers moved up and down the frets while her right fingers picked out the melody and strummed in between. She smiled at how the unexpected key change she added in—*just here*—made it all come together.

You blind me / You fry me
You tempt me / You bind me

The dimmed lights made it hard to see distance. Looking to the place she assumed Jackson stood, she sang the last verse.

Now you've got me inside out / My heart barely beating.
And you got me upside down / My head truly aching.
Turn me right side up?
Please. Please, keep me right side up.

Fiona strummed the final chord, letting herself drift off with it for a second. It wasn't until the last reverberation utterly died away that she realized no one had clapped. Clearing her throat, she shifted on the stool, wondering if she should play her second song or just slink away.

Ryan was the first; she'd recognize the hoot anywhere. She laughed, not even really caring that no one else clapped. She'd done it. She'd gotten up in front of these people—not just the strangers, but, maybe more importantly, the people who *knew* her—and given herself. She had put it all out there, not for the reward, not for the praise, but because she had to.

This was who she was.

So when everyone else started to clap—when they rose from their seats, whistling—it was just gravy.

She played three more—the last one unplanned but the crowd had scolded her when she got up after the third. After a final, self-conscious bow, she said, "Seriously, y'all, that's all I've got right now."

Since she was the last performer, the lights went up and, as she walked back to Ryan and Gwen's table, she scanned the crowd for Jackson but couldn't find him. Ryan beamed at her then held up the phone. "Lucy's been on speaker."

Fiona took the phone. "Hey."

Lucy sounded quieter than normal—her edges softened. "That was really lovely."

Fiona smiled. "Thanks."

"Sorry I couldn't make it."

"It's fine. You'll have other chances."

Regular Lucy was back. "Damn straight." A pause. "Is he there?"

Fiona looked over her shoulder, checking the empty coffee bar once more with a frown. "Well, he was."

"What the heck are you talking to me for? Go track that boy down."

With that, her best friend hung up. Fiona scanned the coffee shop, squinting into corners, but couldn't see him anywhere. She slunk into her chair with a sigh. Gwen pointed toward the door to the back patio. "He's out there."

Fiona spun so fast her neck popped. "Really?"

Gwen smiled and nodded.

Fiona walked through the shop toward the door. Strangers patted her on the back and said things like "Great job" or "Awesome set," which probably would have made her cringe were she not looking for Jackson.

He sat by himself on the rickety back porch, gazing at the crappy old parking lot like it held answers to something.

When the door slammed behind her, Jackson turned his head, watching her walk across the patio. She sat beside him on the steps.

"You sounded like you'd been trapped underwater and just came up for breath—but you sang instead."

Fiona fiddled with her fingers. "Is that good or bad?"

"Good. It's good."

They sat in silence a few moments, staring at the parking lot. A few cars pulled out, temporarily highlighting them both in the unflattering glow of taillights.

"The lyrics . . ." Jackson trailed off, taking a deep breath. "They were about him?"

Fiona sucked in a surprised breath at this question. "About David?"

"Yeah."

She pivoted, tucking one leg under her so she could face him. "No. They weren't about him."

His knees still forward, he turned his head to look at her. "Who then?"

"You, dummy."

The relief in speaking this out loud surprised her. For months it felt like Fiona and Jackson had stood side by side, staring at a closed wooden door blocking their path. While both may have touched the wood at one time or another, neither had turned the knob and *pushed*. Finally speaking this truth—of her head and her heart—felt like a rush of cool air blowing from just beyond the threshold. Stepping through seemed awfully tempting.

A slow grin gradually transformed Jackson's face. His eyes looked lit from within. "I blind you?"

Fiona could feel the blush all up the right side of her face. She bit her lip and shrugged.

Undeterred by her embarrassment, he leaned a little closer. "And fry you?"

She laughed. "Definitely that one."

He brought a hand to her chin. "Tempt you?"

It felt like her heart was beating everywhere. She nodded.

Looking tall, dark, and smirky, Jackson opened his mouth again. Fiona put her fingers to his lips, to *feel* him as much as to quiet him. "No snide comments about binding."

Warmth poured out of him as he laughed against her fingers. "I think I'm done talking, anyway."

He drew both of her hands in his and gently pressed her backward. He leaned closer and closer until Fiona's back was on the wooden deck. He hovered over her, his body blocking her view of the stars.

And then they kissed under the hot, summer sky.

ACKNOWLEDGMENTS

I always read authors' acknowledgments, but not until writing my own did I realize what a challenge they are. There are so many people who have supported me and touched this book. A few, brief words doesn't seem like enough, but since I can't send everybody cookies, it'll have to do.

Firstly, I'd like to thank you, the reader. There are so many ways you can spend your time and money—I'm deeply grateful that you chose me. And while I've got your attention, let me clarify that Fiona's story is a fictional one. While I researched burns and transplants, I took poetic license with many of the details. To the best of my knowledge, no surgery can erase such significant scarring. I look forward to the day when medical science catches up with my imagination.

Jill Davis, thank you, thank you, thank you for loving this book as much as I did—and then making it better. You've held my hand all the way, and I can't imagine going through this process with anyone else. I am a better writer because of you.

Steven Chudney, you took a chance on me and have been in my corner ever since. I cannot express how much you have changed my life.

I want to thank everyone at HarperCollins and Katherine Tegen Books, especially Katherine Tegen; Laurel Symonds; my copy editors Veronica Ambrose and Alexei Esikoff; artists and designers Erin Fitzsimmons (who created the art on my beautiful cover), Barb Fitzsimmons, and Amy Ryan; marketing and publicity gurus Alana Whitman, Lauren Flower, and Rosanne Romanello; Margot Wood and Aubrey Parks-Fried at the Epic Reads team; and everyone else who's helped get *Everything That Makes You* on the shelves.

Thank you to those writers who've helped me through the rough patches. Ashley Elston, you've been a vital critique partner since the beginning. Katherine Brauer, your Crits for Water feedback was the last push I needed. Genetta Adair and Megan Basham, our weekly "Plot Walks" keep me sane.

Thanks to Class of 2k15 and the Fearless Fifteeners, who've made this debut novel experience less overwhelming, and to SCBWI Mid-South and the Memphis SCBWI group.

Thanks to the staff—and other coffee drinkers—at Otherlands, where most of this book was written. It's real and pretty much just like I described, garage sale chairs and all. If you're ever in Memphis, grab some coffee there and maybe write a book.

I'm so grateful to all the friends and family who became my consultants: Anne Andrews, my Ole Miss fact checker; Dr. David Laird, who talked me out of one disease and gave me another; and my father-in-law, Dr. Yong Hae Lee, for answering all my plastic surgery and transplant questions. And to those who read earlier stories—Melissa McStay, Anita Arbalaez, Lori McStay, and Robbie Weinberg, I'm looking at you—thank you for not laughing at me. To my face, at least.

I thank my family, especially Mom and Dad, for supporting me, always; Melissa and Jared; the GoStay clan; and all the Lees and Williamsons.

And now, for the people who need the biggest thanks of all (and who actually might get cookies, albeit the organic kind they won't want to eat): Claire, for reading everything I've written with openhearted enthusiasm; Samantha, for giving me ideas when I'm stuck; and Madeleine, for tolerating my random texts, like "Would you ever use the word *angst*?" Thank you all for being my guinea pigs, supporting this journey, and loving books as much as I do. In return, I promise a lifetime supply of fake Oreos—and even that cruise, one day.

And Sam. Every crazy, random choice I've made, you've supported me. Of everything that makes me, you are the better parts. Thank you. I love you.